WRATH OF THE ANCIENT GODS

RISE OF THE ANCIENT GODS SERIES: BOOK 4

CRAIG ROBERTSON

ALSO BY CRAIG ROBERTSON:

* Podium Audio produced audiobooks are (or soon will be) available for all the below titles except the standalone ones.

BOOKS IN THE RYANVERSE:

THE FOREVER SERIES (2016)

THE FOREVER LIFE, Book 1
THE FOREVER ENEMY, Book 2
THE FOREVER FIGHT, Book 3
THE FOREVER QUEST, Book 4
THE FOREVER ALLIANCE, Book 5
THE FOREVER PEACE, Book 6

GALAXY ON FIRE SERIES (2017)

EMBERS, Book 1
FLAMES, Book 2
FIRESTORM, Book 3
FIRES OF HELL, Book 4
DRAGON FIRE, Book 5
ASHES, Book 6

RISE OF ANCIENT GODS SERIES (2018):

RETURN OF THE ANCIENT GODS, Book 1
RAGE OF THE ANCIENT GODS, Book 2
TORMENT OF THE ANCIENT GODS, Book 3
WRATH OF THE ANCIENT GODS, Book 4

FURY OF THE ANCIENT GODS, Book 5

FALL OF THE ANCIENT GODS, Book 6

TIME WARS LAST FOREVER SERIES (2019)

RYAN TIME, Book 1

LOST TIME, Book 2

FRAGMENTED TIME, Book 3

SHATTERED TIME, Book 4

FINDING TIME, Book 5 (Due Early 2021)

NON-RYANVERSE BOOKS:

ROAD TRIPS IN SPACE SERIES (2019):

THE GALAXY ACCORDING TO GIDEON, Book 1

THE EARTH ACCORDING TO GIDEON, Book 2

THE AFTERLIFE ACCORDING TO GIDEON, Book 3 (DUE EARLY 2021)

OLDER, STANDALONE WORKS:

THE CORPORATE VIRUS (2016)

TIME DIVING (2013)

THE INNERgLOW EFFECT (2010)

WRITE NOW! THE PRISONER OF NaNoWRiMo (2009)

***ANON TIME* (2009)**

WRATH OF THE ANCIENT GODS
RISE OF THE ANCIENT GODS SERIES: BOOK 4

by Craig Robertson

Only Jon Ryan could make such a mess out of the afterlife.

Imagine-It Publishing

El Dorado Hills, CA

Copyright 2019 Craig Robertson

All rights reserved. No part of this book may be reproduced or utilized in any form or by any means, electronic or mechanical, including photocopying, recording, or by any information storage or retrieval system without written permission from the author.

ISBN: 978-1-7328724-6-2 (Print)
978-1-7328724-5-5 (E-Book)

Cover design by Jessica Bell
https://www.jessicabelldesign.com/

Formatting services by Drew Avera
drewavera@gmail.com

Editors: Michael. R. Blanche
Forest Olivier
Charles Pitts

First Edition 2019
Second Edition 2020

DEDICATION

This book is dedicated with admiration to all the past women of science who were minimized and relegated to obscurity because of their gender. I truly appreciate all you stalwart souls.

This is but a partial list:

Nancy Grace Roman (1970s) - Of Hubble Telescope Notoriety

Barbara "Barby" Canright, Melba Nea, Virginia Prettyman, Macie Roberts, Katherine Johnson, Dorothy Vaughan, and Mary Jackson (1940s) - Of NASA and Human Computing Fame

Rosalind Elsie Franklin (1950s) - Of DNA X-ray Crystallographer Distinction

Nettie Stevens (1860s) - Genetic Research Pioneer

Jocelyn Bell Burnell (1967) - Discovered Pulsars

Chien-Shiung Wu (1940s) - Brilliant Theoretical Physicist and Participant in the Manhattan Project.
Grace M. Hopper, Rear Admiral (1944) - Pioneer Computer Scientist

PRELUDE

Shelot was hungry. Shelot was ravenous. Shelot pounded and slammed his way through his section of damnation, across all time, but he was never sated. Once in a great while, a tiny banshee spirit would stray too close to his realm. He would consume it in the blink of an eye. But Shelot had not *feasted* in millions upon millions of years. Being a dull-witted, task-oriented creature of horror, he never wondered who or what caused him to live in such abysmal agony. If he were capable of such introspection, he would have burst forth from his confinement in search of revenge. He would inflict upon whatever power was responsible for his sorry state of immense suffering, and in a manner that was properly due it.

But, what was a demon spawn to do? He resided far too close to Clein to ever die. So, he was cursed to protect Clein, to guard it with a fervor and a fiery passion that could never ebb, could never lessen, until the end of time. His brethren and he were forced to exist in torment, and to wait with an unquenchable devotion to defend their precious for reasons they were incapable of understanding. And the gnawing pain of hunger was a steady, unwelcome reminder of their lot. Ah, to eat until it was no longer possible to swallow—that was the stuff of dreams to the nightmares that were the denizens.

CHAPTER ONE

You know, sometimes I had to laugh to keep from crying. There I was, a two billion year old android on a mission more impossible than any I'd ever undertaken, any I'd even conccived of. I was accompanied by, in no particular order of rank or importance, my forever mate, my best friend and creator, my two adopted alien kids who were a dragon, my doppelganger, a sympathetic demigod, a ghost, and the most evil abomination ever to defile existence. Literature was laced with adventurous tales concerning bands of misfits and malcontents bound together by fate, destined to win despite the apparent certainty of defeat. Yeah, not so much here. Team Ryan—*yea* team—defined ragtag, ill-configured, and ill-prepared. Our group photo had to be posted beside the entry in Neo-Merriam-Webster's for *pathetic*. Maybe in the Idiom Section, too, under *you're kidding me, right?* We were, in a very real sense, sad but true.

What complicated matters was that we were not the *best* hope for the eradication of the Cleinoid threat and the salvation of our universe. No such luck. We were the *only* hope. The one significant asset in favor of Team Ryan was—and I'm sorry to toot my own horn—me. The hopeless optimist, fighter pilot, and luckiest man ever, Jon Ryan. Lucky for all concerned, I fervently disregarded the odds, scoffed at the bleak outlooks, and giggled at the near-certainty of deadly failures. Nope, I as a practice *invited* all the negative forces of existence to hit me with their best shot. Somehow, I'd find a way to win, or at least not to lose. Always had, probably always would. And if I didn't, well, then I'd be dead, so it really wouldn't matter to me, now would it? Yup, I've been dead. It was no deal. The worst case scenario? *Pshaw*. Been there, done that, got tee shirts for the kids back home.

Still, what I wouldn't have given to have the the 1st Marine Division marching right behind us. Even more, I wished we could have simply folded space with *Stingray* and popped into wherever Clein lay hidden. But no. That would be too easy. Gáwar explained, in a tortured and stupefying manner, I might add, that time-space itself was crimped in the cave surrounding Clein. Direct flight there was impossible, so there was no way to avoid the nasties that guarded Clein. The ancient gods had thought about that potential and removed it from the table, so to speak. To access Clein, you had to physically, linearly, tromp through the cave to where it stood. Have I mentioned how much I hated the Cleinoids' confounded godly magic? Yeah.

Gáwar indicated that Clein was to be found quite a distance from where we were. I conveyed the general location of the entrance to the warren where Clein was housed to the Als. The journey there was depressingly brief. Weeks at sea, followed by a protracted march, would have been more to my liking. More time to live, maybe to come to my senses. But, before I could say *somebody stop me*, we were there. The Galavardan Mountains. That's what Gáwar called the towering, stormy, and downright spooky-looking series of saw-toothed peaks that hid the entrance to Clein. Talk about bad omens. The Galavardans appeared to me to be the actual barrier between the living and the dead. And on the other side, hell looked like it was having a particularly bad season. Nice. Fitting, in fact.

"You sure it's up there?" I asked the god of demons, recently stealth-purified in baptism by yours truly.

"Of course, my friend ... *ah*, now look what you've got me saying. Darn you to heck fire. Ah ... *ah* this can't be. You've corrupted me, Jonathan Ryan. That ... *oh*. I'm *cross* with you." Not certain what he was attempting then. He was bound up six ways to Sunday, so he couldn't really *do* anything. He appeared to be trying to bash his head on the ground. It occurred to me that he might have issues. I elected not to inquire. I kind of *wished* him misery. Maybe that was uncivil of me, but there you have it.

Sapale looked over to me. "Welcome to the Club I Hates Me Some Ryan, cupcake. But take a number in terms of exacting your revenge on him. Long line ahead of you, and there're *No Cuts Allowed*. You can forget about getting at him anytime soon."

Gáwar stopped flailing. "I thought she was your mate?" he puzzled, quizzically studying me.

"Spoken by one who's *clearly* never been in a long-term committed relationship," I responded in a hushed tone.

"I *heard* that," Sapale shouted over her shoulder. She'd taken up the point on our ascent of the Galavardans.

"I feel your pain, bro ... *ah*, There, you've forced me to be cordial and empathetic again. How I like you less than all others I know." He convulsed again. "Ah ... ero, *ahhhh!*"

Dude seemed hot and bothered.

"You'll be okay, Gáwdy Doody," I reassured him with a chuckle. "You'll be president of my fan club before you know it."

"I'd ask you to kill me, but lately I've had second thoughts as to the morality of... *ah. Kill* me now."

"You're never going to be that lucky, chumpomatic," responded EJ. "Mind you, I'd gladly grant your wish. But Little Goodie Two-Shoes over there'd have a cow."

"Can we cut the useless banter?" asked Toño. "The stunted-juvenile level of your discourse is nauseating. If I *wanted* to hear such drivel I'd watch reality television programming. They're much better at stupid than any of you."

"Better at stupid? Is that a good thing or a bad thing?" I asked, because what Doc'd said struck me as odd. "I mean, if they're *better*, wouldn't they be *worse* than me? Or would it be the other way around?'"

Sapale powered up her plasma rifle. That was her way of asking me nicely to refrain from speaking for a while. Me? Happy to oblige. I enjoyed having my head attached to my shoulders.

We walked in silence a while. Halfway up the first real slope I set Gáwar down from his suspension in a membrane. I angled his head so he could see ahead of us. "Are we on course, boss?" I asked.

"Yes. But please, don't ... *ah*, I'm doing it again. I'm being deferential and polite. Jon Ryan, I officially declare you are a greater demon than I. A darker force than your black beating heart does not exist in this universe. Strong work ... *ahhhhh*."

Dude appeared to be experiencing a surge of teenage angst, or not far from it. Nice.

"Which way?" Sapale asked tersely.

"Straight ahead, then right at that grouping of boulders."

"I see two. Which one," she queried.

"The pretty one closer to the treeeeee ... *ahhh*. Curse Ryan. Curse him to ... to ... to no dessert. Killlll *meeee*."

Toño glanced at her and pointed to one set of rocks. "That one."

"I think so. It's sublime," she mumbled.

Near the crest, Gáwar grunted that we should stop. He'd spent the entire time since our last stop whining and whimpering. Oh, and complimenting us on our outfits and the pace we were able to maintain in spite of the steep ascent. Hee-hee. Poor baby.

"Stop," Gáwar requested.

"Yes, friend Gáwar," I asked cordially.

"I see the opening to the path down toward Clein. Over there, below the corpus tree."

"I see the tree," responded Daleria. She pointed to the most revolting tree—and I used the word generously in calling it that—I'd ever seen. No leaves, thin twisted branches, and no outward signs of life. Oh, that and humanoid bodies in various states of formation budding from a few gnarled knots. Not traditional English cottage garden flora, to say the least. I was sure glad the breeze was at our backs.

I switched to point and advanced Gáwar-first. He did stop moaning and squirming, which was somewhat reassuring. As we passed the cave entrance, I freed his jaws so he could speak plainly. I'd sealed them up when I got tired of his whining. In other words, I did so right from the get-go.

"You're going in first, pal," I announced. "That's to help motivate you to alert us as to any booby traps, et cetera, before they might surprise us."

"I gave you my word I'd help," Gáwar protested.

"That and *otherwise* sufficient funds'll buy a cup a coffee."

"Ye of little faith," he responded piously.

"Do you hear yourself, you goon?"

"Yes. And with each word I ha ... ha ... *ha* ... I hold you more accountable."

We grouped up about twenty meters in. "Okay, here's the drill," I detailed. "We proceed slowly. I'm point. Gáwar is our bait, dangled out front. Slapgren, you're bringing up the rear. Mirraya, Sapale, you're behind me. Everyone else sort it out yourselves. Stay tight. If anyone sees trouble, signal that you do with a raised fist to call a halt. You make a noise, and someone or something'll hear it, so don't. Any questions?"

There were none. Most of us had done this way too many times already.

"Okay," I said, "let's do this." I signaled *forward,* and we were off.

For the record, I have no idea how many times I'd done this, led a patrol into battle. Tens of thousands of times, maybe. I hated it each and every time. Rare were the occasions when everyone returned home in one piece. *I* was the one in command. Whatever bad happened was on me. All the souls I'd blithely lead to their deaths could form a ghost battalion that would haunt my dreams — if I could sleep. Yet here I was, again, leading people who depended on me into harm's way. No words could describe how low, how empty I felt. Did the mission need doing? Absolutely. Were we the best team for the job? You bet your sweet auntie's ass we were. Did that lessen my pain, my remorse, my fear of the inevitable tragedies that awaited me? Not one little bit. There's a special place in hell for commanders. Someday I'd be there, front-row and center. Probably have my own parking space.

Pretty quickly, I saw the lighting pattern of the tunnel. Our column was about four meters long. As we progressed, light magically appeared five meters ahead of us. It likewise disappeared five meters behind Slapgren. Everything else was the pitchest black. It was as if there was no existence beyond the light-pool we generated. That added miserably to my already peaked sense of dread. I couldn't fight a deep churning inside that if the lights went out, I would cease to exist. It creeped me out and made a bad time all that much worse.

As the path gradually descended, it slowly spiraled clockwise. I figured we were heading down the inside of the mountain we'd just scaled. As it was a very tall peak, I guessed we were in for a long hike. I had to remember that, at any moment, we could encounter any manner of toys and distractions designed to discourage unwelcome guests like us. Not a walk in the park.

Before we hit klick three, Gáwar called out emphatically, "Stop, stop."

We did.

I signaled for everyone to crouch down. "*Speak*," I hissed to him.

"The first curse, it's right there."

My eyes strained, but I saw nothing except the smooth five meters of lighted path ahead.

"Mirri, you're on," I said over my shoulder. "We gotta get past these curses fast. Understood?"

"Roger that," she replied as she slipped around me and scooted past Gáwar.

Mirraya inched forward and stopped at a location I couldn't distinguish from any other. She bent down, craned her neck, and shot glances side to side. Finally she gave her verdict. "I don't see a thing."

"Gáwar, you sure or you shittin' us?" I was hot. If he planned on wasting our time and slowing us down, he was in for one prejudicial Alpha Mike Foxtrot.

"It's there. Maybe your partner just isn't as good—"

"Hot damn," Mirri squealed. "There it is. My *goodness* that's clever."

"You see, Jonathan, I'm being a straight shooter ... rrrr, *ah*." I think he was upset at his unaccustomed honesty again. I patted my pockets for a Valium. Nope. He was on his own.

"What's there?" asked EJ.

"Come look," she replied. "This is *brilliant*."

EJ trotted to her side. I heard murmurings and Mirri pointed here and there. He nodded with approval. They both came back to where I stood.

"She's right. These guys *are* good," said EJ with no little admiration in his voice.

"We are *gods*, you know?" responded Gáwar.

"Whatever," snapped Mirraya. "The first curse is where the ugly lobster said it was. It's *polarized*." She looked to EJ. "Can you believe that?"

He shook his head while grinning ear to ear.

"Ah, honey," I said with irritation. "I'm in a bit of a hurry here."

"Sorry. The curse isn't just there. It's there, but only evident in a certain sense. Anyway, it's a fairly routine warding-off spell. If you trip the curse, it turns you into some preset object. That object is designed not only to render the one trespassing inert, but also to warn others not to cross the same line."

"Did I mention I was in a hurry?"

"Invoke the curse and you become an animated skeleton of whatever you were," explained EJ. "In other words, you're a skeleton that can only dance a jig in one place. You're dead as can be, but you quite effectively scare anyone who comes later."

"I don't see any dancing remains," I observed dubiously.

"Meaning we're the first ones to get this far," responded Mirraya.

"Or someone's eating the bone-dancers," added EJ with a grim chuckle.

"Banshees would definitely eat anything they could," announced Casper out of the blue.

"Unpleasant in either case," said Toño from behind.

"Okay, I'm a *practical* commander. Can you disarm it?" I pressed.

"Yes, and no," replied Mirri.

"Naturally," I protested.

"Seriously, Uncle. I can, but it will take days."

"Can we set the trap off without it, I don't know, *affecting* any of us?"

"Unlikely," responded a now-serious EJ. "Warding spells usually have a hunt-and-seek imperative. If they don't hit a target immediately, they keep roaming until they do."

"Ah, magic people," I said deadpan, "I need access, not a formal education. Your job is to get us past these curses. Could you maybe do your job and stop the flapping of gums?"

"If this one takes days, what about the next?" asked Mirraya.

"One step at a time, sweetie," I responded. "In fact, check and see where the next one is, okay?"

She nodded in agreement. EJ and she walked to their prior observation spot. After much discussion and gesticulation, they returned.

"We clearly see three more past the first. They're all about a meter apart," explained Mirri. "The next curse is a lightning bolt."

"That'd be fairly easy to disarm," mused EJ.

"But the next is a nincompoop spell. After that, we see a snatch-and-run."

I rolled my eyes to the Heaven that seemed to be just playing with me. "*English*, people. What are those, and, more importantly, what'll it take?"

"Nincompoop curses are complex," began EJ. "This one's way beyond the average. If one trips the curse, it renders the victim ... um, insane?" He looked to Mirri for affirmation.

"Yes. Maybe *regressed* is a better term. You become confused, less intelligent, and foolish. The effect's generally permanent, by the way."

"And the snatch one?" I asked, in a defeated tone.

"Very complex," opined EJ.

"And how," agreed Mirri. Then she saw the look in my eyes and started explaining. "Trip the curse and it — let me say this correctly — it *drags* you away and never lets you go."

"It could *push* you away," interjected EJ.

"I guess. Pulling's *simpler*," countered Mirri.

"But I can't tell. Can you?" he responded.

"I can't *care*, people. Come on. This is not show-and-tell. This is a battlefield. *Solutions?*"

"Assuming we *can* disassemble these curses, the ones we can currently see would take three to four *weeks* to neutralize," Mirraya replied in a sober tone.

"We don't have a month to spare," was my dumbfounded response.

"And that's just for these few," added EJ, always the Debbie Downer.

"How are we going to get through these curses?" I demanded loudly.

"If we're the one's—" Mirraya began to say.

"Excuse me for interrupting," said a tentative Gáwar.

"*What?*" all three of us snapped in unison.

"You could, per your present plan, proceed incrementally *through* the Channel of Curses."

"*Channel* of Curses?" I parroted dumbly.

"I wasn't involved in coming up with the project's name," he responded meekly.

"If we don't go *through* the channel, how would we get *to* the fun-in-a-barrel banshees?"

"Well, and excuse me if I'm speaking out of school here, but you could go *around* them."

I stared at Gáwar in disbelief. "*Around* them?"

"Yes," he replied lowering his massive head.

"And how would we do that?" I snarled.

"We could take the access corridor that bypasses the Channel of Curses."

I stared at Gáwar even longer. "There's a path *around* the twelve-thousand curses?" I do believe smoke might have been coming out my ears.

"Yes. It's used for repairs and maintenance to ... to, you know, the physical plant. Plus those banshees and the denizens. They make such a mess. Someone has to tidy up periodically. There's also a small staff lounge that needs occasional—"

"There's a way around the *goldarn* curses and you didn't think to *mention* it, like, an hour ago?" I howled incredulously.

"Well, I *thought* about telling you."

"Wh ... *why* did you not tell me wh ... when you *thought* about telling me?"

Gáwar looked away. I'd clearly hurt his feelings. Oh boy.

"Sorry if I *seem* ... upset. I'm ... I'm *not, of course*. No. Just *curious* ... as to why you didn't alert me about this bypass."

"Well, you've assembled such a marvelous team of magic interventionists," he looked toward Mirraya and EJ. "Truly spectacular. Kudos to you both. And they seemed so *determined* to eliminate the curses. They're committed. You don't find that level of professionalism much, these days. I simply didn't want to offend them by stealing their thunder, you know, as it were. Plus, Jon, you *did* state, and I'm quoting you here, that, *We gotta get* through *these curses fast*. You clearly stated *through*. The bypass corridor goes *around*, not *through*. I ... I didn't want to be perceived as a non-team player."

"So, let me get this straight. Because I'm laboring to do so, I really am. Okay? We need to get *past* the curses to die fighting the stupid, freaking banshees. There's a way to do so quickly and safely, but you were, what, trying to be so polite that you demurred to *tell* me of this critical knowledge?"

Gáwar sheepishly nodded in the affirmative.

"You know, there's such a thing as being *too* nice. If you are, it's a damn curse in and of itself."

"I'm new to *nice*. Sorry. I'm not familiar with all the rules." He lowered his big head again.

I lightly scratched the side of my nose. "Where is the *opening* to the bypass corridor?"

Gáwar directed a glance. "Just around that last turn. The lever to open it is marked with a white X."

"X marks the spot?"

He nodded again.

"Of course, it does." I stormed past everyone. "Come on," I shouted.

Ten meters back the way we'd come, there it was. A small X on an otherwise inconspicuous piece of wood. I pulled it. A large door slid silently open and lights turned on automatically. I looked back at Gáwar uncharitably, then stormed — because I was in a *storming mood* — in without another word. Everyone followed in equal silence. They were wisely going to allow me time to cool off. Good team.

The corridor was surprisingly short, a few hundred meters. It ended in a wide area that had a few tables and chairs. The *employee lounge*. Oh, yeah. My mood was sinking like a stone in water. Several bottles were set on a counter, and dried fruits and meats were stacked on small trays.

"Don't mind if I do," announced Slapgren merrily.

"We're not here to eat. We're here to kill banshees," I chided.

"No reason one cannot do both, Uncle," he chortled in reply. He commenced to pack away a goodly amount of snacks. Man, was I *ready* to kill something. I almost felt sorry for those freaking banshees.

"When you're done, Julia Child, we will be able to proceed," I snarked to Slapgren.

"Uny tum," he replied with his mouth crammed full of goodies.

"Now's good for me."

I walked to the exit and thumbed the button labeled

Open/Close. The door slid open and I stepped through. The same five meter cone of light that was in the tunnel before flashed to life. I checked over my shoulder. Team Ryan was right behind me. "Last one out seal the door. We don't want any stray banshees escaping the easy way."

"Roger," called back Slapgren with a then empty mouth.

Less than fifty meters in, the floor changed from smooth ceramic to rough cave floor again. A few meters past that I got my first glance of Obstacle Number Two. The cave floor spread out rapidly to reveal a cavern. The space was dimly illuminated in a yellow light. On the ground, in the air, and on the ceiling human-sized apparitions darted every which way. The banshees moved with incredible speed, especially given the fact that they were going nowhere in particular. Hell, they'd been confined in the cavern for time immemorial. Where did they need to be in such a hurry?

Then a few beasties saw our party. They flew toward us like mosquitos by a summer lake fired from a cannon. That drew all the stupid things' attention. Within seconds there was a thick wall of banshees crying, moaning, and generally bansheeing at some invisible barrier ten meters in front of us. Nice. Our element of surprise was officially lost.

"This should be easy," quipped EJ. "You take those hundred and I'll take those hundred. Everyone else, pick your own hundred bloodthirsty maniacally wailing pushovers. Last one done buys the beers."

"Sarcasm is never appropriate before battle," I rebuked him.

"Ah, this battle it is. Are you seeing what I'm seeing, boss man?"

"Presumably so," I groaned. "Anyone have a constructive suggestion?" I called out loudly.

"Let's go back and polish off the food," offered Slapgren.

"Any other *constructive* suggestions?" I pressed.

Not a peep.

"Gáwar, got a work-around for these inconveniences?"

"None that I'm aware of, boss man," he replied quickly and cheerfully.

"Anyone know of a weakness these guys have? A way to even-up the odds?"

Cursed silence. Excellent. Well, it was nice to finally know the location of my final death. It would be banshees with their teeth and claws in a deep cave. Where was Colonel Mustard when I needed him? I always hope to die as he did. He was a good officer on paper.

"What's restraining them? Anyone," I called over my shoulder.

"The limits of their realm," responded Gáwar.

"I mean the physical force. Is it a forcefield? An invisible mesh? What?"

Silence.

I turned and glowered at Gáwar.

"The ... um, they're bound by the limits of their realm?" he stated more as a question than an established fact.

"So they respect geography? Someone told them, *You cannot pass ... I am a servant of the Secret Fire, wielder of the flame of Anor. You cannot pass*, and they respected those set limits? Hmm?"

Gáwar shuffled his multitudinous legs but said nothing.

"Okay, obedient quiet people, I'm developing the outline of a plan."

"Really?" responded EJ.

"No," I growled back. I sat on the dirt floor and crossed my legs. Okay, Ryan, there's maybe a thousand horrific monsters poised at their designated stop-point chafing at the chance to greedily devour your entire team, shoes and backpacks included as amuse-bouches. Now what? I had no clear understanding of what it meant to be a soul-eating fairy. That said, I doubted their assault would be subtle and easily ignored. Large fly swatters need not apply. Even if some of us were no longer burdened by the possession of a soul, the banshees looked to dismember most efficiently whatever came in range of their impressive teeth and claws.

On a whim, I stood and stepped right up to their limit line. I did so quickly enough that none of my team had time to join me. I stood face to... whatever... with one individual banshee. Once the son of a bitch realized it was the focus of my attention, it went even more berserk. Thing bared it's peg-teeth, screamed more passionately, and slammed its head against the nothing that separated us. I stuck my tongue out at it. That did not please it at all. Somehow it was able to tap-into a reserve of mindless furor and it howled what it had held in reserve. But it did not come a millimeter closer.

I slipped one probe fiber across the short distance. *What are you?* I asked in my head.

The fiber briefly attached to the creature's head. Then the beasty swiped up a mangled paw and ripped it free. That, trust me, was not a mean feat. Deavoriath technology was not easy to defeat. In a flash it shoved the fiber in its mouth and tore at it. I quickly released the fiber. It disappeared into the banshee's gullet in an instant.

Mirraya inched up next to me. "What in blazes are you doing?"

"Something."

"What, as opposed to *nothing,* the intelligent option when one lacks sufficient information to act *wisely*?"

"Yup."

"Uncle, really." She shook her head. "Well, did you at least learn something?"

"Yes. Don't feed the monkeys."

"Anything else?"

"Just a snippet. Banshees don't like us. In fact, they don't even like other banshees. That's how pissy they are."

"Such tactical insight that provides — *not.*"

"Hey, knowing—"

I was going to finish my glib and flippant response, when something sparked in the back of my mind. Respect for invisible barriers. Hate everything. Really hangry. What were those three factoids at my disposal trying to tell me?

"Mirri."

"Yes, Uncle."

"Can you produce a spell to make a point in space-time move?"

"Come again?"

EJ had joined us.

"You want an incantation to relocate a point in space-time?" he confirmed.

"Yes. But not a point. A plane."

"An *airplane?*" was his stunned response.

"No. A two-dimensional *geometric* plane."

"So you want me to push objects back from a *plane* on space-time?" Mirri wondered out loud, clearly quite confused.

"No, no. I want reality to be pushed back, er, relocated."

"Wow, never heard about anything like that," she sighed.

"Me, neither. Why do you ask?" responded EJ.

"These morons will not cross the arbitrary plane dictated to them by their creators."

"And?" he queried.

"And so, what if that plane moved back to a extent that they ran out of room?"

"I fail to take your meaning," he said dubiously.

I held my flattened palm up. "If this arbitrary plane that stops the banshees was moved toward that far wall," I pointed to that wall with my other hand, "they'd move back accordingly."

"Maybe," Mirri relied. "Or maybe they'd be freed and they'd eat us like scrumptious canapés."

"Either way, we'd be done here," I replied with bravado.

"Yes," she agreed, "victory or digestion would signal an end to our current operation."

"So can you?" I pressed. "I'm not talking just pushing *them* backward. Hell, I could do that with a membrane. But a membrane might not hold them. It sure as hell'll piss them off even more. Maybe just enough to fudge the rules just enough to butcher us. But if their self-acknowledged limit point actually relocated itself, they'd back up without protest."

"Then what?" asked EJ. "No matter how far back they go they're not going to crush themselves to death. When they're one-layer thick, that would be impossible. And the exit is right in the center of the far wall, if you hadn't noticed. Single-ply death is just as lethal as free-floating death."

"I'm thinking that at some stage of compaction they might turn on themselves. Like rats in a cage. Past a certain point of density, rats turn violent."

"You're invoking the *territorial imperative* to mindless monsters?" guffawed EJ. "You're nuttier than I thought, Professor Fruit Cake."

"No," remarked Toño, who'd slipped up behind. "Once any animal is forced into too close a proximity with others of its kind, violence results. Lethal violence."

"And you opine that Earth animal behavior theory extends to Cleinoid puppets?" EJ scoffed.

"Failing another *constructive* suggestion, I'm willing to entertain it, yes," responded Toño.

"So, brindas," I addressed to Mirri, "can you pull that rabbit out of the hat?"

She was already lost in thought. I let her be. After a while, and growing quite tired of the screaming banshees, I pressed her again. "So, kiddo, can you move reality about twenty meters?"

"I might be able to." She smiled like she had when she was a skinny little girl. "I have no idea how you, a magical neophyte, come up with this stuff, but I do believe there's a spell that would do just that."

"Which one?" asked a skeptical EJ.

"Degundation," she replied cryptically.

"*Degundation?*" EJ spat back. "You're as crazy as your lame-ass uncle. Degundation's a spell to summon spirits from the dead."

"Or a void," she added.

"Yes, or a void. Same impossibility in the current application."

"EJ, do you know how degundation actually works?" She had a sneaky gleam in her eyes. Man, I loved that gal.

He fidgeted. "By giving the deceased a location to aim for in this reality, right?"

"Wrong," she said with joyous vigor. "It pushes back *our* reality into the reality of the *dead*."

"Say what?" he replied with a whine.

"Yes, I know that for a fact. One of my final tests before Cala would sign off on me as a full-fledged brindas was to ask for the blessing of *her* master. She was long since dead, but I was able to preform the task. In doing so, I learned the actual physical mechanism."

"And you can transfer it to *this* situation?" I asked uncertainly.

"I believe so. Yes. Why not?"

"And no dead people will pop in and muddle things up?" I asked.

"Hmm. Possibly. Would that be a problem?"

"You're asking *me*?" I wheezed.

"I suspect not," she replied with a grin. "Is that good enough?"

"In the present Charlie Foxtrot? No way. Go for it. Ah, how soon can—"

"It won't take long," she interrupted. "If everyone will back up and remain silent I should be ready in five minutes."

"Hey, that's long enough for me to dash back and grab some more chow," chortled Slapgren. They turned and trotted off. Always thinking with his stomach, that kid of mine. Gotta love him.

"Bring me some too, please," I called after him.

CHAPTER TWO

Deca and Fest sat over a squirming mass of flesh. What used to be a large pig was in the process of becoming a tool for the grim sisters' extispicy. This particular volunteer subject was, it turned out, suboptimally committed to his evisceration. However useful the removal of his entrails would be to the witches, the pig was determined to keep them in his abdomen, where he felt they properly belonged. But, times as they were, and the sisters as practiced as *they* were, protestations notwithstanding, the pig's fortunes proved to be poor.

"Look, sister dearest," squeaked Deca. She was fingering a still contracting colon.

"Yes. I see a pig fart about to be born."

"No, you loon. Well, yes, but beside that, look here." Deca thwacked the large intestine with the back of a finger.

"What? Your finger is now sticky?" snickered Fest.

Deca flung the mucus on her digit directly into her sister's right eye.

"Not any longer, pig whore."

"As it seems you *hallucinate* something of importance in the fresh bowel, I will simply ask what it is," sighed Fest.

"The muscles are tightening, then spasming. They do not relax in between. Hmm?" Deca gloated.

"Yes, I suppose you are correct. I can only conclude one thing."

"That Fate turns against the struggling Cleinoids?" Deca responded darkly.

"No. That the pig lacked fiber in his diet. What has poor animal husbandry to do with the fate of the gods?" Fest then snickered again.

"You minimize a serious matter at the risk of offending Fate."

That sobered Fest's mood quickly. "Sorry, sister dearest. I don't get out much. All this mischievous energy built up inside me and pines to escape."

"Well put a cork in it," scorned Deca. "I see Fate turning its back on the lot of us. I see it happening now, as we speak."

"Can you tell what form this abandonment manifests itself in?" asked Fest most piously.

"Perhaps. Pass me that puncture tube."

Fest handed Deca a thin metal tube, sharp at one end and open at the other. Deca poked it like a dart into the pig's bladder and placed her lips over the opening. She took a deep draft of the urine. The witch swished it in her mouth, like an expert sommelier. Then she swallowed it in one gulp.

"*What*, Deca dearest?" begged Fest. "What do you glean?"

"Our future is greatly threatened. A man who is no longer a man leads a pack of rats bound and determined to execute Clein."

"Will they succeed?" Fest asked in a hushed tone. Fear danced across her face.

"Fate has not decided yet."

"Then they might succeed?"

"Then they might succeed."

"Then the age of the Cleinoids might be at its close?"

Deca shrugged. "Yes. But is that really such a bad thing?"

Fest thought a moment. "We are a pack of rats ourselves, aren't we?"

"Immortal, lazy, and troublesome rats," summarized Deca.

"Well, if we are at the End of Times, let us celebrate."

"What monumental act were you considering to mark such an august passing?" asked Deca.

Fest opened her arms to the finally still pig. "We can feast on our prognostication assistant."

Deca smiled, but then turned quite serious. "You do mean we should roast the pig *then* feast on it, correct?"

"Sister dearest, if Fate is wavering in its favor, we may not have much time left to us." Fest once again opened her arms toward the pig. "This is a *monumental* animal."

Deca shrugged palms up. "Point. Pass me that phallus-shaped bottle of overly-sweet tomato sauce, would you, dear?"

Fest handed it along. "You know I'm growing tired of removing these empty bottles from the restroom, sister dearest."

Deca grinned wickedly. "I don't get out much *either*, sister dearest." She then drained the entire content of the bottle on the loin of the pig closest to her. "Here," Deca said extending the bottle to her sister, "if it helps make it better, you may have this one *all* to yourself."

Fest studied it in her hand a moment. "Fine, but only if I might name it *Vorc*."

The twisted sisters collapsed on their filthy floor in a cacophony of crazed cackles.

CHAPTER THREE

Mirraya stood in front of our group alone. Her back was to us and her arms were raised and open wide. As Mirri began her incantation, her hair began floating as if by static electricity. She looked *magnificent*. The walls of the cave started to dance with minute lightning bolts and the air smelled of ozone. Slowly the entire plane of demarcation, where the banshees had stopped, began to glow with a shimmering white light.

And then it happened. The wall of light inched away from us. At first the screaming horde didn't seem to notice. They inched backward while continuing to rage at us, and Mirraya in particular, since she was the closest. But after they were forced back a couple meters, they began to notice the change. Some of their howls were redirected toward the banshees closest to them. Not long after, they began snapping at one another. Then all hell broke loose. Halfway back to the far wall skirmishes sparked to life. By the time they were compressed to three quarters of their previous volume, open warfare reigned supreme. It was be-a-utiful. Banshee parts, turquoise blood, and tormented protestations were flying wildly.

With a handful of meters to go, the first of the dead banshees began to drop to the deck. Soon it was raining beasties. Before

Mirri moved the no-cross plane back to the far wall, the final banshees remaining alive were so beaten up and broken that they fell on their own accord. I watched until the last one stopped convulsing on the ground. Then I patted Mirri on the shoulder.

"Strong work. They're all dead. You can stop now."

She dropped her arms and collapsed back into my arms. She was spent, bless her little heart.

"Here, Uncle," said Slapgren stepping in, "I'll take her. Come on love. I have some snacks that might help."

She winked at me as her mate walked her away.

"You sure the revolting monsters are dead?" asked Sapale, as she took my side.

"They sure *look* dead," I replied uncertainly.

"Only one way to know for sure." Before I could stop her, Sapale shot past me and started kicking presumably dead banshees. Man, my brood's-mate had spirit.

Aside from the jolt of her boot tip, not one moved. Though she didn't test every one, it became clear pretty soon that the banshees had done themselves in. Good riddance.

"Two down, one to go," I announced cheerily.

"Jon, do you suppose they left the weakest for last," asked my life mate.

"Maybe," I responded with feigned confidence.

"Because, I mean, if they save the worst for last, we got this far but we're still absolutely nowhere."

"Yeah, but that's worst-case talk, hon."

"It is?" she breathed back at me. "Then I insist you be the first one through that passage." She pointed to the now exposed passage in the rear of the banshee habitat. We all knew what lay past the door. Clein and certain, violent death. Nice.

"Let's mount up and move out," I announced with as much bravado as I could muster. It wasn't very much.

"Same order in the column?" Asked EJ. He had a good point.

"No. By threes. One in front, two flanking. Stay tight. Shit will likely hit the fan as soon as we're in." I counted off while pointing. "Me, Mirri, Sapale. EJ, Doc, Daleria. Slapgren at the rear alone."

"Do I go with Slapgren?" asked Casper.

"Suit yourself," I replied.

"Because I could go up front with you."

"And I'd want you on point *because*?"

"The denizens can't kill me."

Ghost was likely correct.

"Are you sure they couldn't, like, absorb you or something?" I pressed.

"That I have no way of knowing. But I cannot be any deader."

"True that," I responded. "Still, you hang with Slapgren for now. No need risking you at this juncture."

"Jon," Casper responded, "I'm touched that you care."

"Just enough, buddy. Just barely enough."

I raised my fist, then directed us forward. I did continue to dangle Gáwar a little bit ahead. Made his eyes as wide as possible, I can report he sported no smile.

EJ wasn't even clear of the entry when the closest denizen attacked. Even knowing what they looked like did not prepare me for what was coming at us like a herd of rabid elephants. The massive denizens were a confused flurry of large stones crashing and whirring, pounding tons of dust into the air. It was hard to see them through the clouds. But the sound never lessened. The closer the denizen came, the louder it grew. Then, oh joy, I began hearing the growl they made. Scary. We all inched backward instinctively. Everyone that is except Casper.

He halted, and then continued to drift slowly farther into harm's way.

I cringed.

A denizen rose meters into the air above Casper readying for a cataclysmic crash onto him. As it struck, Casper became instantly invisible. A mushroom cloud of dust and smoke rose from the point of impact. The denizen turned out to work like a conveyor belt of hurt. After one location of the amorphous rock-cloud struck, it was withdrawn and a new segment of stones crushed down on the same location. Truly devastating. It was an oversized jackhammer machine-gun. In a flash, several other denizens joined in on the assault.

We opened fire with everything we had. Plasma rifles and rail guns rapidly spat hot death at the monsters. They didn't even seem to notice the impacts. We did accomplish drawing off their attention. They stopped smashing the spot Casper had hovered over and lunged rapidly toward us. I could not believe the speed such bulks could manage. It was easily two hundred kilometers per hour. Four of them were on us in a flash.

I extended my probe fibers to the closest denizen. I wanted to find out something useful about the horrors.

Mirraya shouted a brief incantation and the three other boulder tornadoes flew backward fifty meters. The one I was hooked to didn't. It grabbed the fibers, though I couldn't say how since it didn't really have arms and hands, and started whipping me above it's body. I was whipping around faster than a three-legged mouse at a cat convention.

I released my probes. I continued to spin. It definitely was holding me, not the other way around. In spite of the speed I moved, I could time the jettisoning of my fibers. I did so and rolled like a big bowling ball toward my team. I hit the wall and stopped. In a flash I was on my feet.

"*Retreat,*" I screamed.

I was the last to back out of the space. The denizens did just like the banshees had. They stopped at an invisible barrier, that being the doorway itself. From that point they screamed, howled, and boy did they slam the walls and floor. It was safe to assert that they were upset.

Before I even turned, Casper said, "Wow, that was intense."

I glanced around, to find him casually standing next to me.

"You okay?" burst from my lips.

"Yes. Thanks for asking."

"There's a forty meter deep hole where you stood when they

started slamming you."

"I know," he responded. "Glad I'm made of nothing."

"Us too," replied Mirraya.

We retreated a bit farther from the door. Everyone sat down on the floor but me. I sat on a dead banshee. Wished I could still fart.

"Well, that went poorly," I sighed.

"Poorly?" quipped Sapale. "*Poorly* implies there is a *worse* it could have gone. I am unfamiliar with a more negative adjective to assign that assault, other than FUBAR."

"I'm sure we learned valuable knowledge and new tactical insights," responded Slapgren. "For example, Uncle, what did you learn from your probe fibers?"

"Don't dangle them near a denizen."

"While I'm certain that's funny, I'm serious," he state soberly. "Did your fibers pull any intel out of that rock tornado?"

I angled my head. "Nothing much and nothing useful. All I heard from the denizen was **HATE** ." I looked up at Slapgren. "I don't think he likes us."

"Ah, so you learned he was a *he*? That's new info," he responded.

"No, I'm guessing that he's a *he* because *he* was so damn mean."

"Females can't be really mean?" scoffed Sapale.

"Not for just approaching them. Cheat on them, yes. But not a simple how-do-you-do? That's a guy response."

"This discussion is useless," said Toño. "We need to devise a plan to defeat the denizens and we must do so quickly. We have to assume Vorc has learned of our incursion and will send an assault team."

"If they arrive soon, we're toast," I replied. "I got nothing. Anyone have a clue?"

Silence and ground-staring was their collective response

"Great. No ideas, no clues, and we're on a tight schedule. I would ask if this could get any worse, but I know it can. Which means it surely *will*." I kicked at the floor.

"I don't think my magic would affect them in the slightest," announced Mirraya. "That said, I'm willing to try."

"What spell would you go with?" asked EJ.

"Something quick and definitive. Maybe a banishment spell."

"Banishment?" I snapped incredulously. "Banishing them to *where?*"

"Anywhere that isn't here, dear Uncle," she responded coolly.

"But you gotta have a *destination* to send them," EJ responded.

"No," she answered quickly. "Away to *anywhere* is fine. It does mean wherever they materialize is in for a bad surprise, but, in this case, I feel that's justifiable."

"Would they pop into existence somewhere in this universe?" I asked.

"Definitely," she replied.

"Then it really doesn't matter where they appear. The denizens can work for us by bashing the crap out of something Cleinoid."

"This is true," said EJ.

"Okay, Mirri, what do you need us to do?" I asked.

"Enter first and distract them. I'll cast the spell as fast as I can on the nearest. If I yell *retreat*, everyone do so immediately."

"Easy peasy," I said standing up. "Slapgren and EJ, you're with me. We spread out in a tight triangle. Start shooting the moment you're in. Mirri, step into the triangle and do your stuff. Everyone got it?"

The three all nodded.

"Let's do this," I said striding to the door. When I arrived, I charged my rifle, held up three fingers, and counted down. "Three ... two ... one. Go, go, go."

We charged in guns blazing. That's when the inevitable twists of fate war throws at you kicked us in the nuts. *Five* denizens were already crowded around the entrance. The instant I was in, they rained down holy hell. I placed a partial membrane just before the stone bombardment began. In spite of having an incongruity of space-time between me and the five attackers, I could feel each incredible blow. But my membrane held. I'd preset my plasma rifle to fire in the visible range, so I was able to fire through the membrane.

Turns out even that didn't matter. Most bolts passed right through the swirling mass of rock. The few charges that struck something didn't harm the denizens in the least. Within ten seconds Mirraya was screaming *retreat*. I did so without looking back, or with the slightest regret.

As I backed out the door one denizen drove an appendage through. I dived right. The cloud of boulders and dust didn't even strike the ground before they burst into flame and vanished. The creature just inside the doors wailed in anguish. At least the Cleinoid's limit on the denizens was in force and foolproof. It was a hell of a lot more effective than *our* weak cheese.

We fell back to where the others had remained.

"Wow, that went worse than before," observed Sapale. "Color me surprised."

"Did you get a spell off, Mirraya?" pressed Toño.

"Yes I did. Three times. And they all had absolutely *no* effect."

"Why's that?" he asked.

"Either I'm not strong enough, or they're powerful beyond my understanding."

"The denizens *are* said to be the most powerful beings in our universe," responded Daleria.

"They got my vote," responded a breathless Mirraya.

"Okay, people, let's rest a sec. Then we can consider our options," I said sitting back down on the dead banshee.

"Are we rested enough yet?" Sapale asked softly. That I knew to be a bad sound. For as much as I loved my brood's-mate, I'd learned one thing over forever. Subtle and demure she was not.

"I am," I replied with a grin.

"Okay, here's my plan. We get the hell out of here. Once safely back on the ship, we work on Plan B."

Oh my. Not very encouraging.

"But we've come this far. We're ... we're almost *there*," I wheezed.

"No, love, we're not. We caught a break with obstacle number one. We were good enough to beat obstacle number two. Three's way beyond our capability."

"We don't know that yet. We only tried twice."

"Honey, when you're beat, you're beat. It's best to acknowledge the reality that is and plan accordingly."

I glanced around the group. "Is that how you all feel?"

No one said *no*. In fact, no one's eyes met mine.

"Well, I'm not a quitter. I say we stay. We'll think of something. We always do. It's ... it's *our thing*."

"Hoping for the best and surviving. *That's* our thing?" responded an irritated Toño.

"What?" I defended for no clear reason.

"Jon," he said emphatically, "we generally do come up with a workable plan. But I agree with Sapale here. These denizens are simply too powerful for us to defeat in hand-to-hand combat. And before you ask, *no*, I do not think we could beat them if we had *Blessing* present and the entirety of Santa's elves. As your brood's-mate stated so accurately, *when you're beat you're beat*. Move on."

No. It could *not* happen that we came that close — that *I* came that close — and then turned tail and ran like some shavetail. As long as *I* was present, there was hope. I just needed a sec. The answer was there, staring me in the face. I just had to reach out and touch it.

"Jon? Jon, are you even hearing me?" It was Sapale. She was shouting. Oops. I think she was about as mad at me as the denizens were.

"I'm here — of course. What?"

"We need to go. If we stay, we'll be killed by the denizens or by Vorc's golems. Come on, Ryan. Mount up."

"No," I said waving a hand at her. "Give me a second."

"No, Jon. We're not dying here for no reason." She pulled me up to her face. "We live to fight another day. That's what we do, flyboy." She released my arm.

I fell back onto the banshee. "I said give me a *sec*. Will you give me one freaking sec," I screamed like a madman.

"Okay, baby genius," she shouted back. "You take your *sec*. And we'll stand here and watch the great Jon Ryan fail. And you know what? After that, we'll all gladly die at your side. Because that's the loyalty you deserve. You've earned it. So *congratulations* on your choice of our mutual demise. But you know what else? You *suck* for making us do it. Now knock yourself out, champ."

I turned my face from her. I just needed to think. *Think*, Ryan.

I shot to my feet. "Okay, here's my plan. I'm going in alone. I need to try once more. I go in by myself, membrane up, and I try a new tactic."

"A)," Sapale shouted in my face, "you're *never* going in alone. And, B)" she stomped a foot and pointed to the ground, "what stupid stunt are you going to pull?"

"Don't know yet. And I *am* going in solo. Commander's prerogative. If I say I go in alone, I go in alone." I stood and pushed past her.

"Jon, you can't stop me from coming," she said to my backside.

I stopped but didn't turn. "I can't stop you. You're right. But I can *ask* you to let me do this my way." I stopped a moment. *"Please."*

"Alright," she whimpered. "But just this once."

"Thank you," I replied.

"Don't thank me," she said. "I'm letting you do this, but it is not an act of kindness. I'm letting you down."

"I will love you always, Sapale. I'll be back ... soonish."

"Soonish?" she responded through her gentle sobs.

"Yeah. I just can't predict exactly how long it'll take for the denizens to pound some sense into me."

That got a throaty chuckle from her.

I deployed a partial membrane and stepped across the threshold.

In a flash, a bunch of denizens slammed down on me. The membrane held, but sensors indicated it'd crimped. I switched to a full membrane with several cone-shaped projections at right angles to my main barrier. I meant to rip them to pieces. I shifted the entire complex side-to-side as violently as I could.

For a millisecond their barrage stopped. I was about to grin, when they resumed their intense pummeling. I checked the readings. My best shot did zero damage. The denizens remained perfectly intact in spite of sheer forces that could have split open a good-sized asteroid.

I redeployed a membrane, this time surrounding them entirely. Maybe trapping them would ... ah, *neutralize* them maybe. Seriously, I had no real plan, just blind desperation.

The pounding stopped. I dropped my shield. I saw the nothingness of a full membrane suspended above me. I was actually saying the word *nice* in my head when the containment membrane flew apart. Without missing another beat, the monsters slammed down on me with renewed ferocity. I barely got a protective membrane up in time. Dudes were fast.

I staggered backwards toward the exit. My membrane was flagging — down to fifty percent in size and strength. I was in a kind of trouble I'd never even dreamt of. Thanks, denizens, for reminding me there was much more that I did *not* know than I *did* know. Humility, if it stuck, might become me.

That's when one slipped around my shield-shape protection. Oh my. He hovered between me and *the* only way out.

My immediate thought? *Oh shit, don't let Sapale be right.* I know. That was incredibly shallow of me but, seriously, it's what leaped to mind.

I switched off my membrane and dived *under* the denizen. Normally, I'd have said I jumped between his legs. But denizens didn't have legs. I was just counting on there being some kind of open space underneath him.

I rolled through the doorway like a gymnast. Slapgren put out a foot to stop me once I was back to safety.

Laying flat on my back, I said to no one in particular, "That didn't *go* so well."

"Ya think?" said Slapgren as he grinned down at me.

"Yeah, I think." I stood and dusted myself off. "Hey, anybody ready to head home? I vote we call it a day?"

A stone bounced off my chest. Sapale slapped her hands clean of the dirt. "Yes, bozo. We're *all* ready."

CHAPTER FOUR

Fizzen grew larger each day. It was hard not to, given the volume of food she packed away. In the three years since Rage egressed to Prime, she'd had a bountiful romp through the overripe, under-protected universe, to say the least. Seven planets in five star systems full of yummy destruction and terror. She marveled that she could have forgotten, back home, how good it felt to be bad. Fizzen recalled enjoying the other transheavals she'd been on. But now that she was actually doing one again, it felt ... better, more vital than she'd remembered.

She traveled alone, as she had the other times. That was in keeping with her general mood. Fissen had no interest in sharing any spoils with another Cleinoid. When she chanced across a particularly vulnerable or tasty pocket of good times, she would have it all to herself. If her sister or good friend had accompanied her, Fissen'd have to split the choicest morsels with her companion. No way. Stuff it all down your own gullet, that was *her* philosophy.

She stood at that moment before something she'd never encountered before. While ravaging some otherwise unspectacular planet, Fissen chanced upon a large patch of sentient fungi. Weird. She'd seen her share of sentients, and more than her share of fungi.

But sentient fungi? That was a first. Fissen hoped and prayed they would taste better in a corresponding manner to their uniqueness. She was about to find out. She reached out with her trunks and began gathering up the closest screaming multitude of fruiting bodies.

A force she neither saw coming nor understood slammed into Fissen. She accelerated backward in spite of striking and toppling numerous structures. Several trees, a small out-building, and three farm vehicles were laid waste in her retrograde wake. Fissen finally slammed into a sheer cliff about a thousand meters up its face, coming to an unceremonious stop. She then slid, tumbled, and generally crashed to the base of the escarpment.

There, standing before her, was a particularly displeased looking humanoid. His arms were made of stone, but the rest of his body was soft enough looking flesh.

Fissen struggled to rise. Instantly she was hammered down by an invisible force.

"Remain seated for the entire performance, if you please," thundered Verazz.

"Per ... performance? What show is about to—"

"*Silence*," he commanded.

Fissen was about to respond angrily and haughtily. But she realized she was incapable of speech. Try as she might, no sound would exit her throat. She began rising again out of alarm. The same invisible force that put her back down before did so again, only much harder. Fissen heard several bones in one of her spines crack. The unfamiliar pain was excruciating. She made to cry out in agony, but was reminded by her muteness that she couldn't. *Who are you*, she thought to herself.

"I suppose you're wondering who I am? I'm the janitor. It falls to me," he responded to her stunned expression, "to clean up the mess you were about to cause."

Fissen, in torment, hungry, and confused, waved several of her paws in the air.

"You, Cleinoid scum, were about to consume my *wife's* sentient fungus garden. In actual fact, you did. For your having done so, it became my task to me to rectify that atrocity."

Fissen squirmed in non-comprehension.

"When you ate my wife's handiwork, it greatly upset her. She came to me distraught, basically inconsolably so. She enjoined me to wreak vengeance upon you. Here *I* am and there," he waved the back of a stony hand at her, "*you* are."

She twisted in stupefaction. What was happening?

Verazz ran a hand through his hair. "Damn, I hate explaining myself." He kicked a nearby pebble. "But there's nothing for it, so explain I must." He chopped his hands in the air, imploring Fissen to understand. "Well, I couldn't very well allow you to ruin her first four days of actual work in eons, now could I?"

She returned to him no intelligible response.

"So I traveled back in time. You see, that way I could kill you before you committed your sin against the greater force that is my beloved but vengeful wife."

Verazz took a moment to reflect upon how very much he cherished Carol, his mostly devoted wife of several forevers.

"As I was saying," he said returning to task, "I came back to kill you before your transgression. In so doing, it is my ardent hope that my dearest Carol will love and reward me, hence, *considerably*. But, damn you, this is all still such a bother. I'm certain you do not care, but time travel messes with my constitution. Call it a personal weakness, but my appetite is out the window for hours. And my sense of taste? *Forget about it*. So, you've already cost me dearly in two separate regards. But," he smoothed back his hair some more, "I am a *reasonable* god. I shall only kill you once, in spite of the time-continuum incongruities that pop up on occasion. Fear not."

All of Fissen's eyes bulged forward.

"The thing I do *not* understand is why I'm bothering to explain all this to you. Do you have any notion as to why I might waste time on such a fool's errand?"

Fissen, still incapable of speech, made no reply.

"Neither do I. Very well. Off with you."

And Fissen was gone. She was instantaneously transported into the center of a nearby intensely hot star. It was, in fact, Rigel that she was entombed in, however briefly, before her atoms were dispersed into Rigel's substance. But the location and specifics of her final disposition were neither noted nor appreciated by the late and unlamented Fissen. Random jots of atomic particles tended to be unsentimental.

CHAPTER FIVE

I was sitting alone at the main control panel. Sapale might have taken that to mean I was sulking, especially since *Stingray* wasn't moving and wasn't about to move. Yeah, I was sulking.

"I know you hate losing," she said as she eased up and started stroking my hair. "I'm sorry our *wondrous* plan didn't work out."

"Tell that to the zillions who'll die because I failed." I could be morose right there alongside the best of the depressed, mopey creatures of creation.

"You didn't *fail*. *We* didn't fail. We got a hell of a lot further than I would have imagined. It just wasn't possible."

"*Hopefully* that was the case," I grunted.

"You know, if you gave me an exact time when your pity party'll be over, I could just come back then. It'd save us both, and me in particular, a lot of grief."

"Sorry. This's hard."

"I know it is," she soothed. "You'll think of something. The Cleinoids will know the wrath of Jon Ryan, sooner or later. It's a done deal in my book."

"Humph," I grunted. "I wish I could dip into your well of optimism about now."

"*You* are the most optimistic person there is." She massaged my shoulders. "Those ancient gods are in for such an ass whooping, I almost feel sorry for them."

We were quiet a spell.

"I hope I figure out a way to get at Clein." I balled my fist. "We were so close."

"No, hero, we weren't. We might have been *physically* close. But *realistically*? We were light years away. Who knew denizens were so tough?"

"I am now a believer."

"Good. It's important to be reminded there's always something bigger and badder than you are out there. In the present case it happens to be a denizen."

"Still—"

"*Still*? What, you going back to finish them off another day?"

I shrugged.

"In your dreams. By now Vorc'll have sealed the bypass corridor, replaced the banshees with superbanshees, and patted all the denizens on their tops for doing such a good job. If you went back, all you'd do is fail sooner, probably on account of your tragic death."

"You're a boatload of sunshine."

"I'm trying to be supportive but realistic. You're just going to have to defeat the Cleinoids in some different manner. No biggy."

"Ah, nice to know. No biggy. Maybe I'll just ask them to shrivel up and die. Might work."

"Anything's possible. Next time you see them, you can try that approach." She giggled softly. That sounded so nice.

I stood and turned. I set my arms around her waist. "You make me a better man."

"You're welcome."

I bumped her with my pelvis. "No. You're supposed to then say that I make you a better woman?"

"No, peach pits for brains. I'm not a *woman*. I'm a Kaljaxian war goddess."

"A war goddess now, is it? When'd the promotion come through?"

"While you were wallowing in self-doubt and self-loathing."

"Well, *first*, congratulations."

She mini-bowed graciously.

"Second, there was self-doubt, sure, mixed fifty/fifty with self-pity, and basted in self-second-guessing juice."

"But?" she responded with a big smile and a tap of my nose.

"But no self-loathing."

"*No* self-loathing," she parroted.

"Nah," I pointed to my face, "how could anyone, including me, loathe *this*?"

"A point possibly well taken." She rose on her tippy toes and kissed the top of my head.

"Still can't believe you're a war goddess now."

"Thanks. I promise to be a kind and loving war goddess."

"Isn't that counterintuitive, love? Shouldn't a war goddess be mean and ruthless?"

"Okay, I'll work on it. But only because you asked so nicely."

We kissed.

"Now will you come join the rest of us in the mess? We have *coffee*."

"I love *coffee*."

She took my hand and turned. "Then are you in for such a fun time."

My chair had been left open. While places in the ship's mess clearly weren't assigned, I kind of had *my spot*. It wasn't like dad at the head of the table or anything. It was, you know, just the place *I* mostly sat.

A mug of hot joe was awaiting my arrival.

I took a sip. "This sure must've been extra hot."

"No, Uncle," replied Mirri. "It was just regular hot. We calculated you'd be joining us pretty quick."

"I'm *that* predictable?" I lamented.

"No. Hell of a lot more. But Sapale told us to be extra nice on account of you're acting like a huge baby, and all." Slapgren then balled up his fists and pretended to rub his tearful eyes. What a jerk. But hey, of course he was. He'd learned at the foot of the *master*.

Toño stepped into the mess. "Ah, I see your emotional crisis has resolved." Jerk looked at his wrist where a watch would have been, if he'd ever worn one. "I'd say this one passed in record time. Either you're growing up or becoming senile."

"Either way, I blame you," I responded, trying not to giggle. "You *built* me."

Everyone but Daleria chuckled. She was still trying to acclimatize to our ever-so-odd sense of decorum.

"I do want to press you for details," began Toño in his serious tone. "In your brief contact with the denizen, you said you felt hate radiating from it."

I spread my arms as wide as I could. "About this much."

"Anything else? Even the slightest additional insight might prove useful," he queried.

"Geez, I don't think so. Well, I did get the distinct impression that whatever he had in terms of physical power was not matched by his intellectual chops."

"You mean he was as dumb as a rock?" asked Slapgren with a grin.

"Something like that."

"Any notion as to what powered it?" pressed Toño.

"No. Sorry."

"With that level of strength and pure dominance, I'd say he's powered directly by Clein." Wow, that was Casper speaking. Only Casper no longer looked like Casper. He was a human male of slightly larger than normal build in his late thirties, maybe early forties. HeAs a post-life transient etherial being, had a full head of ghost hair styled ... styled like they wore it forever ago. His coif said *military*. I was stunned.

"Ah, Casper, can you see yourself in a mirror?" I asked tentatively.

"No. I'm a vampire." He waited a three-count. "Of *course*, I can. Why?"

"Walk over to that wall and tell me what you see," I instructed. The wall I gestured to was very shiny.

He stood there slowly turning. And I mean *stood*. He no longer floated in a spiritually appropriate manner. I couldn't read his expression, but it was extremely human.

"What is it I'm supposed to glean?" he asked.

"That you look just like one of them," replied an equally stunned Daleria. "Jon, it was Clein. Before we were near it, Casper appeared to be sort of humanoid." She shook her head in wonder. "The power of Clein has allowed him to reflect his true nature."

"Which is?" Casper posed.

"*Human*," I replied. "Which makes less sense than asking Lizzy Borden to assist Leatherface at your kid's bris."

Casper turned to address me squarely. "Why does my being human make so little sense?"

And now he was *articulate*. Man I hated Clein even more than I had a minute earlier.

"No, Casper," Mirraya corrected gently. "You *were* human. As a post-life transient ethereal being, you are no longer human."

"You mean I'm a ghost?" he responded flatly.

"Y ... yes," she stammered uncertainly.

"Where'd I hide that *life* insurance policy?" he asked emphatically.

"Oh no," groaned Toño.

"What?" Mirraya shot back.

"He's cursed with a Ryanesque sense of non-humor."

"Hey," EJ and I protested in synch.

"I don't think I can take three of them," mumbled Sapale. "One is a lot to ask. Seriously."

"It's early days," Mirri replied. "Maybe he's just warming up."

The room — minus EJ, Casper, and myself — agreed by giggling disgracefully.

I had had quite enough. "Okay, dude was human. That leads

directly to the question *what the hell was a human doing in this loonie universe long before we got here?*"

That shut up all the monkeys on Monkey Island.

"Now *that* is an interesting question," agreed Toño. "Casper, do you know how you came to be the lone human among the ancient gods?"

"Hang on," interjected Mirraya. "He might have come here as a ghost, not a human."

Toño bobbed his head. "Point taken. Casper, either way, living or dead, do you know how you came to be here so far from home?"

He stared at the floor a while, reflecting. Finally he spoke distantly. "No. Sorry. I do not."

"Not a single clue, pal?" I pressed.

"No. Wait. I keep hearing the word jáhose. No, *jéfnoss*." Casper looked to me. "Jéfnoss brought me here."

"What the hell's a jéfnoss?" I asked roughly.

"Not a what, Jon," said a barely audible Daleria. "It's a who. Jéfnoss tra-Fundly was the first center seat of the conclave."

"*Was?*" I queried. "What, this Jéfnoss no longer befouls the living?"

"He most *definitely* does not. He's extremely dead." Her words came from a million miles away.

"Shall I ask for details, or—"

"Gáwar murdered him four billion years ago." She turned her back on us. "He did so publicly, brutally, and then he ate his remains."

"Harsh," hissed Slapgren.

"No," she replied faintly. "Not if you knew Jéfnoss. Some said at the time he died too well."

"Wow," responded Sapale. "He must of been some piece of work."

"Oh, yes. He was. He ruled us ruthlessly, killed us wantonly, and deserved much harsher from Fate."

"And *our* Gáwar corrected the error that was Jéfnoss tra-Fundly?" I asked incredulously.

40

"Why do you think we only *banished* Gáwar and haven't killed him for justifiable reasons?"

"As testimony to a grateful public's gratitude?" I wheezed even more incredulously. "*Gáwar*, our Gáwar?"

"Our dear Gáwar," she said with resigned finality. "He's sort of a hero, in a most perverse manner.

I whistled quietly. Not what I thought I'd ever hear.

CHAPTER SIX

Fate, monstrous and empty, you are a turning wheel, your position is uncertain, your favor is idle and always likely to disappear; shadowed and veiled, you plague me, too; now my back is naked through the sport of your wickedness.

Fate is against me in health and virtue, Noble actions, fair transactions, no longer fall to my lot: powers that make me only to break me all play their parts in your plot: So at this hour without delay, pluck the vibrating strings; Because through luck she lays low the brave, all join with me in lamentation!

Carmina Burana (Earth, 12th Century)

Fate did not participate in time. For Fate, all days were the same. The landmarks and signposts experienced by those who voyaged through time were immaterial to Fate. Why wouldn't they be? Fate *produced* those edifices, those channels for progression or regression. It was never *governed* by change. And Fate never changed. All that could be said in that regard was that Fate was.

Fate acted as a determiner of how a set of interactions played out. As to what Fate determined, well, that was, is, and always will be incomprehensible. Why Fate even existed was well beyond the ability of any sentient mind to grasp. It just *was*. But Fate didn't care in the slightest *why* it was. It served *no* one and *no* thing. To Fate, it's interventions were not personal and they were not business. They were fate.

What Fate determined arose from it's own inscrutable processes. But, there was not so much the possibility of *influence* on Fate as there was an *awareness* Fate could have concerning alternate possibilities. In essence, an object's destiny could be different than it was going to be, were it not for the realization by Fate that an outcome it had not previously chosen might be the one actually best suited to occur. Fate had been characterized through the ages as blind, inescapable, the hunter, or as some malevolent interloper. But it was none of those things. It was a doer. Fate did what it was designed to do, nothing more, nothing less. And in all of its actions, Fate was impassive. It never relished nor abhorred an outcome. Emotions never influenced Fate's analysis or determination. That was a matter of professional pride for the force of nature, truth be told.

What *were* the forces that could, in effect, influence Fate's ultimate verdict? Many. Deities, bad ideas, frivolous curses, and wishful thinking could, to some variable extent, alter a preset. Random chance could alter Fate, too. But random chance was so unpredictable that discussing its influence on Fate was only the stuff of migraine headaches.

What about prayer, some might demand to know? Could *prayer* influence Fate? Sadly, no. Fate did not have the metaphorical ears to *hear* prayers. It could be *reached* with a notion, but not *intentionally* so. If asked, Fate would have responded regarding the hearing of prayers, "That is not my job." And it was not. Those powers that heard, and thus potentially responded to prayer, were separate onto themselves. And, lest you inquire, those powers did not leave the execution of their decisions to the whims of Fate. If they did, they would be seeking disappointment. It can be stated with certainty that *whim* was the one prerogative Fate not only possessed, it thoroughly enjoyed exercising it.

No discussion of the possible influences on Fate would be complete without examining the role of *luck*, or the lack of it therein. Luck would best be considered, in the context of influence, as Fate's annoying little brother. You know, the snotty-nosed youngest child who wants to tag along, however unwelcome, with his older sibling. Fate did not *need* luck's input. Fate certainly did not *appreciate* luck's influence. Wherever possible, Fate discounted luck's prattling. But the one thing Fate could not do was to fully ignore the brat. And as to what *controls* luck, please, do you have to inquire? Ask any gambler, gunslinger, or purchaser of used vehicles. They might choose to tell you what determines a lucky outcome. But do *not* ask Fate. If you did, you'd regret it sooner rather than later. *Annoying little brother*, remember?

Knowing all this about the nature of Fate, you know as much as the mages and philosophers of the universes have ever known.

On any day, one that happened at no particular time and in no relative position to any other day, Fate was. Fate *always* was. Fate, which lacked form, substance, and matter, was, on that day, deciding. In all the universes, it should be noted, there was but one Fate. So Fate, on that day in question, had a lot to decide. Not all decisions were acted out. No, only the smallest percentage were. But mesocosmic fates, short-term fates, inexorable fates, and twists of fate needed to be dispensed.

Keep that image in mind, that one of Fate acting determinatively and expansively.

On a completely average day, across that vision of Fate's mind, picture a small boat crossing the scene. The craft was silent, unobtrusive. It was barely perceptible. It moved serenely and lovingly, like a child reaching to pick up a freshly fallen leaf. What you envision presently was a *thought*. It was, in fact, nothing more than a dinghy of a meditation in the mind of Fate. And the sea that it traversed was Fate's all-encompassing, limitless comprehension. Dinghies in infinite waters were hard enough to *notice*, let alone *react to*. But Fate was just that good. Fate, on that otherwise typical day, not only *noticed* the mote, it even focused on it. The minuscule notion had no inherent significance to Fate, yet Fate pressed a modicum of attention on it.

Where the dinghy launched from, Fate might or might not have known. That mattered not. All Fate knew for certain was that the infinitesimal cogitation was as irresistible then as it always had been in the forever that Fate lived in simultaneously. On that particular day, the form of that small interruption in the otherwise preoccupied mind of Fate was, in actuality, but a string of three words.

Help Jon Ryan ...

CHAPTER SEVEN

Vorc was a beaten god. Weary, teary, dreary, and bleary. Every attempt to capture, let alone kill, Jon Ryan had failed epically. Each try at controlling Gáwar was a bad joke. All endeavors to hire a serviceable assistant went down in ignoble flames. And now this. Now this indeed. He was reduced, nay debased, nay *nay*, forced to prostrate himself to asking, yet again, the aid of the nitwit sisters. If he had one wish granted to him from on high, he would boorishly demand two wishes. He needed *two* at the minimum. Because with one wish he could only erase from existence *either* Fest or Deca. To leave one alive was an unacceptable anathema. Two wishes would have been the minimum acceptable provision.

This time he came a-calling to the witches unannounced. He *knew* it wouldn't lessen his suffering, but you know what? He did have *just* that much hope left in him to do it that way. Vorc hoped against all reason that the sisters had *prepared* for his prior visits by assembling the grotesque, amassing the macabre, and organizing the revolting. He mostly knew he had no choice. Beaten or not, downtrodden as was possible for a god, he was center seat and he required guidance.

In lieu of knocking, the despondent Vorc turned the wooden

doorknob of the witches' private chambers and walk in numbly. He even left his eyes open to take in whatever atrocity awaited him. Why fight it, he said to himself? They would wrench his guts, they would cackle, and he would still be polite in asking for their help. Vorc felt passionately that Fate was more cruel to him than it actually needed to be.

And what vision of the ghastly presented itself to Vorc's consciousness? Fest and Deca sat next to one another knitting. There they were, shawls over shoulders, angled toward a crackling fire. Dainty porcelain cups of mulled tea resting close at hand on a rustic stand. They appeared to be the very picture of old crone normalcy. If there had been a Norman Rockwell in the land of the ancient gods, he might well have immortalized the image Vorc stared upon.

Without being invited, Vorc staggered to, and collapsed roughly into, the only open chair.

Fest looked Vorc up and down. "Did you notice the reversal of reality, sister dearest?"

"I don't know and can't therefore say. What bastardization of the typical has occurred?" asked Deca.

"The trash was brought *in*."

They, naturally, cackled mindlessly.

Vorc's response was to rest his head back on the uncomfortable arched top rail.

"It would seem," observed Deca, "that the trash is *dead*."

"No, no, sister of my heart. The trash is *dying*, yes. But it is not, unfortunately, *dead* quite yet."

They, naturally, cackled again with energetic lunacy.

"One can only hope its demise comes quickly," opined Deca.

Staring at the ceiling, Vorc queried, "Are you done yet, so that I might proceed to the matter I suffered myself to discuss with you two fools?"

"Oh, Vorc the Dork, I doubt either of us could answer *that* question," one or the other of them responded.

"And, as I am not yet fully broken, I will ask why that is."

"Because we are doing many things. You asked if, and I'm forced to quote you, 'Are you done yet?' We could be done with one thing but not another. You vex us so with your sphinx-like questioning."

Yes, reprehensible cackling ensued.

"You are knitting wool. You are sipping mulled tea. You are fornicating with my mind. What else are you doing so that I might hone in on an answerable query?"

"We knit not wool," replied Deca.

"And it is so ironic you should mention the act of fornication between you and us at this particular time," responded Fest.

No cackles. This time the sisters giggled like wicked school girls.

In his head the words DO NOT TOUCH THE SECOND RESPONSE boomed. Therefore he asked what he hoped to be the more neutral question. "What, then, are you knitting so idyllically?"

"Rat intestines," replied Deca matter-of-factly.

"Though I suspect our supplier pawned off a few *mouse* guts in the mix," added Fest with disdain. "The cheap bastard."

"Why would any—" *No*, Vorc spoke with quiet panic in his head. *No, do not ask that question. They're likely baiting you and they're certainly not enlightening you. Move on, dumb-dumb.*

"Are you unwell, distinguished guest?" queried Deca.

"For you look the very portrait of ill-health, both physical *and* mental," amended Fest. She then tsk-tsked to further grate on the center seat's last nerve.

"My health — my state of being — is of no concern to me. It should, therefore, be of even less import to you two cursed bitches."

"Cursed *bitches*, or *witches*?" pressed Deca.

"Both. There, are you *now* happy?"

"No," replied Fest.

"We were happy *before*. We still are mirthful. You've not dampened our mood," summarized Deca.

"But thank you for your concern, nonetheless," added Fest cheerily.

Vorc struggled, but was still able to sit up properly. "I deem the

Vorc-abuse segment of this morning's macabre play to be *over*. I have an important matter to discuss."

"You wish to discuss a matter of importance with *us*?" asked Deca.

"How very *flattering*," Fest observed dubiously, "that a person in your high office should solicit *our* humble opinions."

Vorc took a moment to slam the back of his head several times against the chair rail. "I meant to say, should have said, and will say now, that I wish for your *metaphysical input* in a matter of importance. If either of you *had* opinions, which I very much doubt, on anything that interested me, let me say with finality that I do not care about those opinions."

"Ah, but we *do* have opinions regarding things that might interest you," Deca observed darkly.

"Yes, indeed we do. Do you see that phallus-shaped empty bottle of overly-sweet tomato sauce on the counter?" asked Fest, barely able to suppress a guffaw.

"We fancy you'd be interested to know its *name*," concluded Deca.

"Rat intestines, mouse guts, and named used flasks do not interest me in the least. I need your help, if there's any to be had from the dried-up wells that pass for your souls." Vorc sat forward and continued forcefully, least the witches had the opportunity to spar back. "I've lost several things and would ask if you know where they are."

"What have you lost?" asked Fest.

"We live to serve the center seat now, as we have since the time of—"

"No," shouted Vorc. "Do not even say his *name*. Badgering me is well and good. But invoking *his* name is unacceptable. I forbid it."

"Fine, young Vorc," cooed Fest.

"To make you happy, neither of us shall say *Jéfnoss tra-Fundly* in your presence," responded a very pious sounding Deca.

"You have our solemn oath on that, good sir," concluded Fest.

The witches crossed their hearts in tandem.

Vorc unwittingly snapped off an armrest, his fist balled up so tightly. "Do you know where Jon Ryan is to be found?" He asked the question in the form of a hiss through clenched teeth.

"Jon *whom?*" queried Deca.

"Ryanmax, Clinneast, Jon Ryan. They are one and the same. Do you or do you not know where he is?" Vorc was pounding a palm on the remaining armrest by the time he finished.

Fest perked up visibly. "Why yes."

"We do," replied Deca.

"He's dead and off to damnation," they sang as a chorus.

Vorc fluttered his eyelids. "Clearly you're not up to date on current civic events. He's returned from the dead and he plagues me as a *third* boil on my ass."

Fest perked up visibly, again. "Are we to assume that *we* are the other two?"

"For we should be so glad to reside in that form in such a place of honor," responded Deca.

Vorc glowered at them. "Can you locate him? Yes or no?"

"That is hard to say," replied Fest.

"Not having attempted to, we could not *possibly* know our chance of success," Deca added unhelpfully.

"Perhaps you should inform us whom *else* you misplaced," speculated Fest.

"If they were together, that would increase our prospects, now wouldn't it?" anti-clarified Deca.

Vorc lowered his head. "Gáwar. I've lost all contact with Gáwar."

"Oh, my," exclaimed Fest.

"He would seem challenging to lose, his being so large, vicious, and ill-tempered," observed Deca.

"Be that as it may, he's disappeared without a trace. I need him."

"Did Zastrál perchance remand him back to his Limbo?" asked Fest.

"No. I *naturally* inquired directly. Zastrál has not seen Gáwar in weeks."

"Most curious," responded Deca.

"Here's what we *can* do," said Fest.

"We will search reality for Gáwar and get back to you," stated Deca.

"Just as soon as we finish our sweater," explained Fest. She held up her knitting toward Vorc.

Vorc set the back of a hand over his mouth and gagged. "You're knitting yourselves a sweater of rat guts? How positively revolting."

"No, *silly* center seat," chided Deca.

Fest lifted what little finished product was completed. "It's a gift for our niece."

Vorc vomited into his lap, staggered to the door, and dashed off without so much as a goodbye or a toodle-oo. As he departed, however, Vorc obdurated, resolved, and committed to never again seek the sisters's advice or enter their abode. *Never*. Then he hurled again, this time on his shoes.

CHAPTER EIGHT

Our discussion group broke up and people drifted off. Sapale and I decided to risk a walk in the fresh air. It wasn't all that dicey. We'd learned by then pretty much how to blend in with a godly manner. I put my hood up, so I was completely anonymous. As for Sapale, hey, anybody with four eyes was a shoo-in for a local, so she was all good. I figured Casper was tagging along, but once in a while he was in some kind of stealth-mode in which even I couldn't see him. Either that, or he got off annoying the crap out of someone else. Can I *get* an amen?

"You have anywhere in mind?" asked Sapale as we strolled slowly.

"Far away and quiet."

She snuggled up to my arm and swung us slightly side to side. "Sounds *delicious*."

"How about the cliff on Azsuram, the one with the hidden trail down to the sea?" I responded dreamily.

"*Yes*," she replied lustfully. "Casure-Dor. Just the two of us and a bottle of nufe."

"Maybe a blanket to lay on and a few more bottles of nufe, just to be on the safe side."

"I seem to recall *my* side is usually the *bottom* side in these scenarios."

I wagged my eyebrows. "All things are subject to change. You know that by now."

"I sense a distinction without a difference entering my leisure time."

"You know what I know by now? You're tough to please."

She grabbed my chin and gently shook my face. "Keep thinking that, cowboy. My master plan is working like a fine Swiss watch."

"Goodness gracious, wife of mine. Two billion and seventy years old and still spunky."

"Hard to please. Keep that front and center in your little head. Very hard to *satisfy*, nowadays."

Which head needed that front and center? I was about to ask for clarity, but demurred. "I'm beginning to think I love you."

"Umm," she purred contentedly. "Do you ever wonder what it would have been like if you and I dropped off the grid forever ago?"

"How do you mean?"

"Oh, I don't know. What if we'd purchased a cave somewhere and covered the opening with rocks and brush? No one'd ever find us. Pretty soon, they'd forget about us completely."

"But would not then evil reign supreme throughout all time and all space?"

She shrugged merrily. "We'd be none the wiser. With our heads buried deep enough, we'd be fully insulated."

"*See* no evil, *hear* no evil, and *defeat* no evil," I chided.

"Be *distracted* by no evil, *pursued* by no evil, and *killed* by no evil. It all depends on how you look at the situation, brood-mate."

I sniffed deeply. "Maybe it would've been nice?"

"Translated from Jon-Speak into Adult to mean, *No way. That'd be too boring and no one but you would worship me.*"

"I must appeal that insulting characterization to the judges. I stand falsely accused."

"I can hear their tears falling to their desktops as we speak. We all feel *so* sorry for you, lover boy." She swung us a little harder side-to-side.

"I get no respect. None at all."

"Au contraire, Pierre. You get as much as you've earned. But not one drop more." Sapale bumped me with her hip.

"I feel her assessment to be fair and just." Ah, Casper *had* been tagging along.

"Did you hear a cow fart, dearest brood's-mate?" I asked loudly. "I hope it's downwind of us. Sounded juicy."

That was when whatever transition Casper was birth-canaling though basically completed itself. He made a most enthusiastic sound, approximating very closely indeed that which a bovine with a methane problem would sound like. *Lots* of methane.

We both giggled. Then Casper joined in, too. I couldn't recall hearing him express any emotion up until that point. My brain instantly leaped to Sam Morse's first telegraph message. *What Hath God Wrought?* I was thinking we were going to find out fairly soon, in the case of Casper.

"You been with us the whole time, secret squirrel?" I teased.

"Yes. And I'm beginning to understand why now."

Sapale and I stopped. Still holding arms, we turned to him. "I have a feeling this will be interesting," she said quietly.

"You don't know the millionth of it," Casper replied softly.

I could see he was shaking his head slowly. That's when it hit me. His face ... his facial characteristics. They were mine. I was looking at a six foot two, transparent, cloudy white Jonathan Alan Ryan.

"You know, is it just me, or does Casper look one whole hell of a lot like me?" I asked Sapale.

"Spiting image is a word that comes to mind," she responded.

"Casper, do you realize you're *copying* my appearance? You're *mimicking* me, which, of course, reflects good taste and judgment on your part."

"Jon, I assure you I am not," he responded confidently.

"I do not currently possess a mirror. If I did, I would

demonstrate that fact. You've made yourself look just like me. Mind you, what force of nature would—"

"Jon, I *am* you — Jon Ryan. *That* is why we look the same."

Yeah, precisely what I needed at this critical juncture. A psycho ghost, a stalker ghost, no less. "You know, *mostly* when I get that, I say something like, 'Sure you are,' and I start drinking less-cheap booze. I also back out the door and then commence with the running."

"I don't think running'd work, based on his pattern of being always present," mumbled Sapale.

"It would not work. The larger issue is why you would feel the need to flee?"

"Here's a partial list off the top of my head. 1) you're creeping me out, 2) you're nuttier than Auntie Francis's fruitcake, 3) if you were me, I'd be a ghost, 4) I'm not, and 5) you're creeping me out."

Sapale raised a hand halfway and wiggled her fingers. "Me too, kind of."

"That was awful." The ghost shook like a wet hound.

"Sorry, you did ask for an accounting." Yeah, perhaps I should have been less forthcoming with a mentally challenged apparition, but there you have it.

"No, I was referring to Auntie's fruitcake. Do you remember the time we made the mistake of putting some in our mouth at the dinner table?" He started to chuckle.

"*Oh*, yeah. Couldn't swallow it. Couldn't spit it out. Couldn't stand the taste or the texture as it decayed in my mouth."

"*Our* mouth, and yah, sort of like little rotting rat turds coated in turpentine," he added with gusto.

"So what'd you do?" asked Sapale, suddenly more interested in the tale than the present insanity.

"I vomited," replied Casper.

"Quite the trick. Not even a finger down the throat," I amended.

"Then we grabbed our tummies and said—" Casper crowed.

"I don't feel so good," I finished his sentence.

"Best part was they bought it," declared Casper.

"Hook, line, and sinker."

"The rubes."

We both started laughing with evil intonations.

I stopped first. "This is the part in the cheap paperback where I shout, 'There's no way you could know that, *sir*. What's your game?'"

"No game, Jon. I said it because I was there. *We* were there."

"*We* could not be there because there was only *one* little shit who vomited on the New Year's Day dinner table. It was me. I was eleven."

"It was *us* and we were *ten*."

"Precocious at the little-shit-bird act, weren't you?" observed Sapale.

"Yes," we replied proudly and in tandem.

"Look, I think we should go somewhere and sit," said Casper.

"We're androids and you're a ghost. No one needs to *sit*," I replied sourly.

"True in fact, but not in practice," he said.

"What the hell does that mean?" I challenged.

"It means we're going to find a place to sit," answered Sapale.

There was a small park with shaded benches not far ahead. We proceeded there in silence.

"Now that we're all ever so comfortable, might you explain what this bullshit is all about, *Casper*?" I asked angrily.

He studied the sky a moment. "You were long gone when it happened. Long gone and I was a forgotten memory."

"When *what* happened?" I asked still fairly hot.

"When I died. You were off in space fighting monsters and garnering ever more praise and admiration."

"While poor you were stuck living the damn life you were supposed to, poor baby," I snarled.

He regarded me a few seconds. "Yeah. Something like that."

"I'm not *even* going to go there. Suffice it to say, immortality is not all one might fantasize it to be, Sad Sack." [N.B. if you're curious: https://en.wikipedia.org/wiki/Sad_Sack]

"Do you even know what we died of?" he asked accusatorially.

"Bad breath?"

"Love, I think this is probably not the time for you to be you," Sapale said gently, in an encouraging tone.

"We both married good women," he said distantly as he studied Sapale. With renewed vigor, he finished his thought. "We died of a mantle cell lymphoma."

"Is that good?" I asked. "You know, I mean a good way to exit, stage left?"

"No. It was not. It was an aggressive disease with toxic treatment that helped very little."

I really bit my tongue. I so wanted to say, *well then, better you than me*. I placed a sock in it.

"Sorry to hear that," I responded.

"Really?" he shot back. "No oh-so-clever snide remarks? It must be in there somewhere."

"Really," I replied, hand tenting chest. "I've matured something awful over the years."

"In any case, there at the end, I was surrounded by everyone I loved. My kids and my Indigo. Since I had to die, it was at least the best-case scenario."

"I'm glad to hear that," lamented Sapale.

"Thanks." He looked back to the sky. "January 3, 2103, just after seven in the evening. I was looking in my dear wife's eyes, and then I wasn't."

"Were you in any pain?" asked my loving wife.

"Let's not talk about the pain. It ended, and it's not central to my story."

"Your call," I responded.

"So I slipped away, died, bought the farm. You know what happened next?"

"Auntie in a bright light with a ponderous pseudo-dessert?" I quipped.

"No. Nothing. What you see out of the back of your head. Blank nothingness."

"I'm betting that's not the end of this tall tale, though," I said with a grin.

"We are *so* smart. No, Quick Draw, it wasn't. My story continued. What clue gave it away? Maybe the fact that we're sitting here talking?"

I shrugged.

"Not too long after I died, I began noticing I wasn't alone."

"I thought you said you were in Blanksville?" I asked.

"I was. Then I apparently wasn't. It was gradual, like sunrise on a cloudy day. But slowly I came to be aware I was standing there in my hospice room. Indigo was sobbing and the kids were trying to console her. And there was this guy standing next to me."

"Okay, and I *am* being semi-serious here, the Grim Reaper, right?"

"I should have been so lucky. No. No robe or scythe. Just a scary looking thingy-dude."

"Wow, I can see him in my mind's eye with such a precise description," I snarked.

"Look, I'm trying to be historically accurate, to give the correct vibe. Humanoid, seven or eight feet tall, thin as a wisp. Head like a ... a football mated with a soccer ball. What ever it was, the baby was too small for his body size. Eyes that burned with hatred and rage. Burned right through me, almost painfully. Dude raises a boney digit and says to me, 'I am Jéfnoss tra-Fundly. I own your soul.'"

"Subtle yet time-tested come-on line," I observed.

Sapale punched me. It was worth it.

"Then we were not where we were, in the room. We were high atop a mountain, ripping winds, crazy clouds, the whole nine yards. Only I wasn't cold. Couldn't feel a thing, in fact. Naturally I was ... confused. Yeah. So I asked what we were doing.

"He looks at me like I'm some kind of bug. He gets all full of himself and says, 'I am here in this universe on *vacation*. While visiting here, I became aware of you and your critical role in my future. I came to claim you so that I might fully control that future. You are bound to me now, and you are joined with me forever."

"What a corny *SOB*," I exclaimed.

"Tell me about it. The entire time I knew Jéfnoss, that's the way he spoke. Guy had a six-foot long ivory-handled stick up his butt."

"So, what, you two got married?" I wheezed in disbelief.

"No, waffle brain. He used a spell to bind me to him. That way I would never be more than a few meters away."

"How big was his bathroom?" I simply had to ask.

As Sapale landed another blow, Casper replied, "Not *nearly* big enough."

"But you're more than a few meters away from him now," observed Sapale.

"No. He's dead."

"Technically, ah, so are you, dude," I pointed out.

"It's a different kind of dead."

"What, like there's a *chocolate* flavor and a *vanilla* flavored death?" I challenged.

"Long story. Different time," Casper responded tersely.

"So, Jéfnoss's spell died with him?" asked Sapale.

"Yes."

"Not such a good spell-caster, eh?" I said rather peevishly.

"Hardly. He was the best. That's just how it works. When he died I was released."

"Daleria told us he died a very long time ago," said Sapale.

"Yes. His scheme didn't go as well as he'd hoped and planned for."

"So you were free to wander Godville for billions of years unsupervised?" I asked.

"I'd use the adjective *cursed*, not *free to*, but yes, in effect. The few others who knew I existed quickly forgot about me."

"Why did this Jéfnoss fellow think you were important to his future?" asked Sapale. "It seems rather far-fetched."

"The prophecy. *The gods will fall only when three miracles that are one work as two.*"

"What the devil does that have to do—" I started to ask.

He touched his chest. "One." Then he fingered mine. "Two." Finally he thumbed over a shoulder toward *Stingray*. "Three."

"Whoa and a half. How could he know that, I mean, all that long ago?" I stammered.

"Jon, he was the god of *prophecy*. And the end-game warning had been around since the start of the Cleinoid's run."

I tilted my head. "That'd probably about do it."

CHAPTER NINE

Nostriana stood in her kitchen, drying a plate. Gods didn't need to do the dishes, but she enjoyed the task. It was simple, repetitive, and involved warm water. What was there not to like? Sometimes, yes, she'd zap the load and be done with it. But, at least that day, she labored contentedly.

As she passed the window to set the plate in the cupboard, she chanced to glance outside. She froze. The plate slipped from her fingers and shattered on the floor. Suspended in the air, just outside her window, was a bad omen, a very bad omen. A headless bird fluttered there almost casually, still but for its wingbeats. If the bird had eyes, they would have been studying Nostriana.

Nostriana blinked.

The bird was gone.

She ripped her apron off and threw it to the side. Once outside, she broke into a fast trot. Nostriana needed to speak with Vorc immediately. The god of omens was frightened.

CHAPTER TEN

"If you think for a *microsecond* I'm believing this lying sack of mist, you've got another thing coming." I believe EJ was under-convinced as to Casper's claimed identity. Just a bit.

"Why would he lie about who he was?" Sapale fired back quickly.

"Because he's JPN — just plain nuts. He has some pseudo-sexual thing for your Jonny Bony and invents this whole cockamamie story so they can take long hot showers together."

"Dude," I snapped, "that doesn't even make sense. In the shower, the water'd skip right through him."

"You are *such* a putz," he wheezed.

"Ah, if I am, you are." I pointed to Casper. "And now he is, too. Mind your words, please."

"Look, compost for brains, why on earth would Jéfnoss be so profoundly stupid as to drag one of *the* motive forces of his own downfall to the very place it could effect said downfall? Makes no sense."

"No, on the contrary," said Daleria, "it makes perfect sense. Don't you see? That's what made Jéfnoss so powerful. He knew in advance everything bad that was going to happen to him. If someone planned on killing him, Jéfnoss could see ahead to the attempt. All he had to do was eliminate the threat beforehand, and he was eternally safe. If he kept one Jon-miracle close at hand, he'd know, before even the ghost Jon did, anything that he would attempt, so he could avert it. Plus, he would never have anticipated you two," Daleria pointed to EJ, then me, "would have ever made it to this realm. In separating the three needed elements, he all but guaranteed his permanent safety."

"That's a highly circular argument, young lady," replied EJ.

"I have no idea what one of those is, but I do know how Jéfnoss's powers worked. That's why he was so hard to kill off."

"Again, makes no sense," scoffed EJ. "If Jéfnoss knew his future, he'd have seen that Gáwar was going to kill him and prevented that act."

"Normally, yes. But in Gáwar's case, knowing ahead of the fact didn't help. Gáwar is *that* powerful. You see, to try to preempt Gáwar's assassination attempt, Jéfnoss had to physically be next to him to stop him. When he allowed Gáwar close, the inevitable was unstoppable."

"That doesn't pass my sniff test."

"Is it not possible for you to open your mind and be a team player?" shouted Sapale.

"I'm *not* a team player. Ask anyone."

"This bickering is pointless," said Toño firmly. "I'm hard to convince, but I believe Casper, er, the original Jon Ryan's story."

"Thanks, Doc," responded Casper.

"So, allow me to suspend disbelief more than I'd like to," began EJ. "Follow me, please. Jéfnoss encounters the original, still human us, during one of the prior transheavals, maybe. He also sees us as a threat, so he co-opts the ghost, and brings it home like a souvenir. Then he is killed in an unrelated fight. Ergo this Jon Ryan," he pointed to Casper, "wanders weak and weary for billions of years here in Cuckoo Land, during which time he loses his form *and* forgets his origins. That about sum it up?"

"Yes, Sir Fingernails-On-Chalkboard, it does. Man I'm so glad I'm not you," replied Casper. "You're such a PITA, and I don't mean the bread." [handwritten: Pain In The Ass]

"In light of your absurd story, I wouldn't say that if I were you," snarled EJ.

"Well, you are. So there." I then saw a sight I never anticipated seeing. Me sticking my tongue out at me. How bizarre.

"I insist we advance this discussion," huffed Toño, aka mad dad. "Assuming, for the present, you three nitwits are the ones cited in the prophecy, is there a mechanism suggested or implied in which you destroy these scourges?"

"Yeah, let me get the manual out of my back pocket," replied Casper. He made a show of standing and searching for a back pocket. "Hang on, don't got one. My bad." He sat back down.

Toño racked a palm down his face. "I'm too old to handle another flippant, lowbrow comedian. And I order that not a single *one* of you state that I made you, so I'm to blame."

Casper raised a transparent hand. "Actually—"

"Not a *word*. I want to know of any implied or preordained method of ending the Cleinoids. All Ryanisms must be stowed away."

"There is the prophecy," answered Daleria, "but as far as I know that's it. There is no other legend associated with it that I've ever heard."

"For what it's worth, me neither," added Casper.

"All right," Toño responded as he tried to calm himself. "Let us proceed to any thoughts as to how you three ... *individuals* might fulfill the foretold?"

"Wow," I marveled, "nitwits to individuals in the space of seconds. We're good."

"No Ryanisms. I already insisted upon that," snarled Doc.

"Sorry. You left yourself too wide open. It was *your* fault."

"Possible *plans*?" Toño hissed.

"No," stated Casper flatly. "I'm far and away the most familiar with the ancient gods, their lore, and their ways. Simply because there are now three copies of me present does not in any way suggest how we might use that to our advantage."

"No, no, pal," I threw back at him. "There's one copy of *me,* one copy of *EJ,* and, thank God, only one copy of *you.* No identical triplets happening round these parts."

"You seem unduly sensitive, *me.* Care to share?" asked a smug Casper.

Sapale stood. "I suggest everyone not involved in this testosterone-fest leave the babies alone to argue until they're *all* ghosts." And out she stormed.

Mirraya, Slapgren, and Daleria filed out silently. Only Doc stayed behind.

"Thanks for your vote of confidence," I said to him.

"A vote of confidence it is not. The horrible truth is *I* am directly responsible for you three idiots. As the parental-equivalent, it falls to me to spank the lot of you."

"How are you resp—" Casper started to ask.

"Ah, a volunteer for the first swatting," Toño interrupted him with convincing sincerity.

"Wouldn't that be impossible, me being an insubstantial ghost?"

"I am an immortal scientist. It's only a matter of time."

"Are you sure spending decades figuring out how to inflict corporal punishment to a ghost would be the optimal expenditure of your otherwise valuable time?" I queried.

"It would be an absolute waste of time. It would also be an infinitely superior use of time than participating in you three's bickering petulantly about who is who and which of you is the *real* Jon Ryan. The *most* real Jon Ryan should be the one most *ashamed* of himself, by the way."

"But how do you really feel, Doc?" EJ asked, just before I could get the words out, the son of a gun.

"Please excuse me," Toño said formally. "I must go in search of my shotgun. I calculated once it is powerful enough to separate my head from my neck. Therefore it will work on two out of three of you morons." Then he left without additional comment or fanfare.

"I hope he's not serious," I said mostly to myself. Check that. I said it to *only* myself. All three mes.

"We all hope," parroted Casper.

"WTF. If he does, we'll just duct tape our heads on backwards." Yeah, that was EJ.

"I fear we might have alienated, to some extent, our crewmates," I said generally.

"Ya *think?*" Spat EJ. "I'm *positive* we annoyed the hell out of Team Snowflake." He then grunted disapproval.

"Not sure that moves matters in a constructive direction," remarked Casper.

"I'm certain that I neither care nor want to hear your opinion, cupcake."

"I know I've been separated a long time, but, what? Are you all hungry? You keep referring to *cupcakes*. They're still individual-portioned treats, right?"

Poor Casper. He had a lot of catching up to do.

"At the risk of being the most mature and responsible Jon Ryan," I began, "I do think it might be helpful for us to try to noodle out this prophecy thing."

"The gods will fall only when three miracles that are one work as two?" asked EJ.

"Ah, yeah, that's the only one I am familiar with," I replied.

"It's baby bullshit. End of story. There's nothing to noodle out." EJ was hot. "I say the two of us who *can,* go and find something very intoxicating and delete it from existence."

"How mature *and* helpful," snarked Casper. He sure sounded like me.

"Do ghosts have memories as leaky as their bodies? I believe I made a definitive statement concerning my esteem for your opinion, oxygen thief."

"Technically, he *might* be useless, but he does not consume O2," I, for bafflingly unclear reasons, defended.

"That's it. I'm gone." EJ huffed out of the room.

And then there were two. Two, if ghosts count as one, that is.

"I doubt he would have been any help anyway," observed Casper.

"You've come to know him well and fully," I responded. "And get this. He's about a million times better now than he was not so long ago."

"Now *there's* a scary factoid."

We were quiet a spell.

"Seriously, any idea what the prophecy means to suggest?" I asked.

"It clearly fails as to any specifics, doesn't it?"

"Just a tad. But it clearly points to the fact that if we three figure out some stunningly brilliant plan, it *would* be able to end the Cleinoids."

"The prophecy says *fall*, not *end*. I'd hate to think the prophecy only indicates they'll trip and skin their collective shins."

"You might be over-thinking this a bit."

"I've always felt one cannot over-think a prophecy or an oracle."

"Oh, really," I replied incredulously. "You have strong opinions on those subjects? How very challenging to believe."

"I certainly do as of this moment. That's something."

"Might we, alone at this juncture, focus?"

"Certainly."

My, but he said that like Curly of *The Three Stooges* fame. *Soitainly!*

"What could we three possibly *do* that would cause the Cleinoids to fall?" I asked.

"Too open-ended. We could shoot them for millennia and kill them off. We could bore them to death by having them listen to this discussion. The possible mechanisms of our coordinated efforts are infinite."

"We can't just wait for a devilish plan to walk up and tap us on the shoulder. "Hi, I'm the simple scheme with which you will achieve the impossible."

"We're fairly sarcastic, aren't we?" asked Casper.

"Hang on, though. We worked on plans to counter the Cleinoids already. Maybe *the* plan was one of our previous ideas?"

"But none of them got within spitting distance of success. Sure, we eliminated Dominion Splitter. That was huge, but it didn't strike at the *Cleinoids* themselves."

I was looking off into nowhere.

"What?" prompted Casper.

"We came within spitting distance of destroying Clein."

"Were you there, back in the cave?"

"Huh?"

"You must not have been there, because we had our lunches handed to us, along with our asses."

"But we were close; if nothing else, physically close."

"Do you fail to recall that you, EJ, and I were physically present? We failed *epically*. We did not, if you will recall, meld into one big flaming ball of wrath and devastate the denizens."

"You seem kind of hot and bothered. Chill, dude."

"Suffocating ignorance has that effect on me."

Wow. Who'd a thunk it in the multiverse? Now there were *two* Jon Ryans I was glad I wasn't. Just wow.

"If you, Señor Holier Than Thou, will recall, we were there but we were not" I shuffled my fingers around in the air, "acting as onesies, twosies, and threesies."

Casper chuckled softly. "No. It was kind of a solo-ass kicking administered to you, wasn't it?"

"See. So we may hold out a hope that a better-choreographed assault might be successful."

He harrumphed. "Yeah, us dancing while wearing pink tutus might be our best shot."

"See, you're thinking outside the box," I complimented. "Now, if you just add a dash of *not-a-jerk* and remove a pinch of *horse's ass*, we might get somewhere."

"One can only hope," said EJ as he returned. "'Cause I'm not wearing a tutu, pink, blue, or henicolor."

"*H*-any color at all," I added to his *Stooges* Easter egg.

"I thought you went somewhere to get hammered," stated Casper.

"I did, I did, and I'm back. I can't leave a couple of mental midgets like you two trying to save the day."

What a jerk I was capable of being.

CHAPTER ELEVEN

Beal's Point was intentionally bleak. It was the quintessential representation of functionalism in design. Visiting it was meant to be a cautionary, punishment-light experience. There were presented the monuments to the purported enemies of the Cleinoid race. The region was arid, winds howled mercilessly most of the time, and there were no signs of life for farther than the eye could see. If you enjoyed yourself there, someone had failed to do their job adequately.

At the center of Beal's Point the very first statue was placed. As the initial piece, no one knew if other archvillains would be identified and similarly dishonored. So there, at ground zero, stood the twisted representation of Jéfnoss tra-Fundly. Anyone who'd known him in life wouldn't recognize the distorted image. Based on politics, it was sculpted with an eye toward showing his inner-ugliness, his true maniacal self. The artist who produced the monolith surpassed all reasonable expectations in that regard. Even the toughest and meanest Cleinoids forced to pass that statue on pilgrimage did so with a quickened step and added downward inclination of their heads.

Since the destruction of Dominion Splitter and Vorc's

subsequent fall from what little grace he once enjoyed, attendance at the Point was down conspicuously. It was, in fact, zero. At some point, the flow of gods on their mandatory treks dropped. The longer no repercussions were witnessed, fewer were the numbers who undertook the journey. Within a few months, Beal's Point was as deserted as it was desolate, save for the golems on permanent guard duty there.

So it was that no one with a functioning brain noticed the odd occurrences there on that isolated plateau. One night, one random night, the monument to Jéfnoss tra-Fundly was struck by lightning. As such electrical disturbances were quite rare, if the strike had been observed, it would have been taken as an omen. A particularly bad omen at that. But since golems were not bright enough to know what was and wasn't an omen, the event went unreported.

A few nights later a passing golem stopped in front of Jéfnoss's statue. He'd heard a sound, though of what he did not know. Even vermin were disinclined to haunt the Point. He lumbered around the base twice, finding nothing unusual. Then he returned to the path so he could resume his endless patrol. There were no witnesses to his sudden and silent disappearance. He simply was there, and then he wasn't. He was, naturally, never missed. No Cleinoid monitored them. As golems were a notoriously poor perceptive form of mobile dirt, they certainly didn't feel the loss.

One month later, out of the blue, a thunderclap accompanied the formation of a large fissure along one side of the monument's base. All the guards heard the explosion and rushed to the area. They saw and heard nothing unusual once they arrived. They milled about for hours, intent on discovering the source of the noise. One finally noticed the fissure. They all pawed it clumsily and grunted ferociously. Tree-stump feet pounded the ground, tossing up dust clouds. But for all their lamentations and confusion, they found nothing besides the fissure itself that was new. It was decided that the crack was not a threat to the structural integrity of the monument. Why a bunch of golems thought that *their* judgment on such a technical matter was sound enough to believe could only be explained by their actual stupidity. In any case — bottom line — they did not report the sound or the needed repair issue. At the next routine visit by a repair and resupply team, the proper individuals would be informed. The fact that no routine visit had ever occurred, again escaped their feeble minds.

It would not have mattered if they had been diligent in their reporting. The restless soul of Jéfnoss tra-Fundly would have stirred, independent of whether anyone knew about it or not. Typical Jéfnoss behavior. He never had cared for the opinion of others.

CHAPTER TWELVE

"You were, for bedeviling reasons in the first place, cleaning dishes in a sink, you looked out a window, and you *think* you saw a flying headless bird. Therefore, of course, you came running to me. Why not? My time has negative value. Not to mention that my administration is crumbling like stale bread under an elephant's foot." Vorc's face was buried in his palms as he whined. "Because I need this. I need *you*."

"You're not listening," hissed Nostriana. "I was not cleaning dishes."

Vorc peaked through his fingers at her. "You clearly stated that you were."

"No. I was putting the clean dishes *away*. Otherwise I couldn't have seen out the window where a headless bird hovered still in the air. I do not *think* I saw it. I *saw* it."

"Fine, you were performing other useless chores. My dear, how could a bird that had lost it's head fly, let alone hover? Hmm? I'd presuppose it would require a *brain* to pull off such a dazzling feat."

"Because it wasn't a bird. It was an omen."

Vorc began slowly slapping his face with his palms. "You said ...

y'said it was a *bird*. You made a big old point of *insisting* you saw a bird. Now the bird is *not* a bird?" Vorc was very close to losing it.

"You don't get the omen thing, do you?"

"Generally, I do not need to because, when you are not *insane*, I rely on you for such matters."

"Listen closely, old fool. The omen was as evil a sign as I have *ever* seen. It foretells of disasters and cataclysms never witnessed in this realm. Mock me at the expense of everything you know and hold dear."

"I surrender," Vorc quipped. He set his trembling hands on the desk, straightened in his chair, and, and cleared his throat. "Nostriana, pray tell, what does a headless bird hovering outside a window of a woman doing useless chores *portend*?"

"That would depend on the type of bird."

"Which isn't a bird at all?"

"Yes, no, it's not."

"What type of not-bird *wasn't* your bird?"

"I believe you mean to say, *what type of not-bird* was *your bird*?"

"If it *wasn't* a bird, then it *wasn't* any specific type of bird. Hence, it was a *wasn't* type of non-bird." Upon concluding his tortuous statement, Vorc returned his face to his palms and restarted the face slapping, only faster and harder than before.

"It was a headless black shrill," she responded icily.

"Ah, a *non*-black shrill. Haven't *not* seen one of those in not-ages," grumbled Vorc.

"If you deride me one more time, I shall leave, and make my own peace with Fate. Then you will face what is to come as a surprise. A terrifically unpleasant surprise."

"Fine, fine. I already said I surrendered. What do you see coming, based on a headless not-black shrill hovering?"

"The return of Jéfnoss."

Zero to sixty, Vorc went from a lump of weeping despair to the very picture of a powerful leader. "*Silence*. It is forbidden to speak that name under penalty of death. You know this and yet *you* mock *me* by flaunting The Name That May Not Be Spoken?"

"I needed to get your attention, you mongrel."

"Well, you have. You also have my eternal wrath." He reflexively picked up Fire of Justice.

"Use that and you'll not know the intent of the omen." She pointed at the weapon.

"You spoke TNTMNBS. You know why it must never be spoken. You will suffer the consequence, if for no other reason than you might speak it again."

"I know the drill. If TNTMNBS, which is a stupid acronym by the way, is said aloud it will allow TNTMNBS to return. Well, it's too late, moron. The omen tells me not that he *might* return, but that he *is* returning." She flapped her elbows in the air to mimic wings. "*Hovering? Hello.*"

Vorc shook his head slowly. He also set Fire of Justice back down. "You cannot know that," he said, without conviction.

She raised her right arm. "God of *omens* here."

"How could he be? The scant pieces Gáwar left behind were burned, dowsed with acid, then sealed in adamantine steel on Beal's Point."

"How did Gáwar actually kill him? What was his coup de grâce?" She smiled grimly.

"I believe Gáwar—" Vorc nearly vomited. "Oh, my."

"Oh, my, *indeed*. Gáwar killed him by ripping off his head."

"But why would he ... return? What power might release him and what motivation might compel him to plague us again?"

"I am the god of omens. Divination and knowledge of the occult are not my department. You'd have to ask—"

Vorc threw up his hands. "Don't even say it because I'm not going there. I've had my last dealings with those two bitch witches."

"Suit yourself, big guy. NMP. Not my problem. In fact, I think we're done here."

"Shall I leave?" he responded haughtily.

"Don't bother. It'll be my pleasure."

And Nostriana did just that without another word. Uh, there was a gesture she made, but that need not be specifically illustrated.

CHAPTER THIRTEEN

The Three Jons sat for the better part of two hours trying to devise a plan to take out Clein. Hey, three Jons walk into a bar ... No, I won't go there. We were able to figure out precisely nothing. Any way we ran the scenario, either one, two, or three of us approached the denizens and they ate us. The three as one as two riddle didn't help at all. Maybe if I carried EJ on my back we could turn the tide and win? Yeah, that *had* to be the key. Eventually, most of the people we'd pissed off enough so they had left trickled back in. Sapale was the last. I think she was waiting just outside to make sure she was, simply to make a juvenile point. *Women.*

"So are we safe to rest our heads at night without fear yet, masterminds of strategy?" she asked with beaucoup sarcasm.

"Yes," I said boldly.

"We attacked and won while you guys were gone," added EJ

"Show's over, folks," concluded Casper.

"I figured as much," scoffed Toño. "I suggest, therefore, we work on our Plan B."

"Which is?" I posed.

"What we do until Plan A is discovered, Plan A being the fall of the Cleinoids," he responded.

"How about the same old, same old? Guerrilla attacks and lots of drinking," I stated confidently.

"Yeah, lots a' both," EJ opined lustfully.

"What about the ghost?" asked, or rather whimpered, Casper. "Everybody ditches the ghost first chance they get."

"Wouldn't you?" I responded.

"Not when the ghost is *me*. I'm hecka fun."

"Moe, Larry, Curly, may we return to productivity?" asked Papa Toño.

"What would you like to do, Doc?" asked EJ.

"I am as uncertain now as I was before." He scratched the back of his head. "Repeated small-scale assaults may be emotionally satisfying, but they're unlikely to accomplish anything meaningful."

"Aside from getting us caught, killed, and dismembered. Hopefully in *that* order," speculated Sapale.

"We could do nothing," said Slapgren. "I'm rather good at that."

"Can I get an *amen*," blurted Mirri. Those two were so in love. Made an uncle proud.

"We will do nothing, for better or worse, by default," mused Toño. "But sitting idle carries some risk of discover—"

Doc never finished that thought.

I hated that, those pregnant pauses, followed by dramatic interruptions. They were, one-hundred percent of the time, bad.

Stingray shook like we were a chew toy in a pit bull's jaws. The quake lasted only one second, but it was inescapably impactful. The androids remained standing, the live meat all toppled, and the ghost, well of course the ghost didn't budge. Then it was like nothing had happened.

"Al, *report*," I called out.

"An unknown force shook the vortex."

"Gee, thanks. Damage report?"

"None."

"Thank goodness," muttered Toño.

"The force, it's unknown, but can you say where it came from at least?" asked Sapale.

"Only that it was external," Al replied.

"How reassuring," I snarked. "I'd hate to think you two love birds were quarreling."

"Put the spectrum on the screen," Toño called out to Al. He studied the wave pattern. "Never seen anything like it. It's not an electromagnetic wave, a gravity distortion, or even a shockwave."

"Let me take a gander," said Casper as he stepped over to the viewer.

"You an analytical physicist now, buddy?" I asked.

Dude ignored me completely.

"Oh, my," Casper wheezed. Seriously, the ghost wheezed. "If that's what I think it is, we're in deep doo-doo."

"Spoken like a true scientist," observed EJ.

"What?" asked Toño.

"Doc, do you have a spectroscope handy?" Asked Casper.

"Are you honest-to-goodness asking Sir Nerds-A-Lot if he lacks any *nerd* device? Sheesh," I responded.

"It's over here," Toño said leading Casper away. "What do you want me to analyze?"

"Me."

Toño pulled his head back, but then said, "Alright. Set your hand on that plate."

"How long will this take?" Casper asked.

"We're done. You may move your hand."

"What's the pattern?"

"Hmm, it's a weak signal. Let me ... there, I removed the log-scale." Toño stared at the readout. "Why, that trace looks remarkably similar to ... to the pattern of the force that shook *Blessing*."

"Is this a complex but infantile joke?" I asked, kind of pissed.

"No," Toño replied. He turned to me. "You think I'd—"

"No. Sorry. Go on."

"The force that shook us is the same in nature as Casper," Toño announced.

"That's silly, right?" asked Mirraya.

"No. It's bad shit," replied Casper. "I'm made up of, I don't know, death energy, right?"

"Death energy. We're making that up now?" I complained.

"Well, I'm made of some form of energy. That," he pointed to the screen, "is made of the same energy."

"So we were attacked by death?" I stated numbly. "What might that even mean?"

"Something dead is very angry with us," responded Toño.

"Perfect," I whined. "Perfect end to a perfect day. If only I had an enema bag full of an ice-cold Castile-soap solution, my day would be fabuloso."

"I have half a mind to pin you down and administer it to you," Toño responded with amazing credibility. "We face multiple existential threats, yet you are arrested at Freud's anal stage." He threw up his arms in frustration. "*Valga me Dios.* What I am asked to put up with!"

"Easy, Doc, don't pop a circuit breaker," teased EJ. "I'm well into the genital phase, so you done good."

"Getting back to aggravated assault from beyond the grave," Mirraya said firmly. "I suggest we focus on the who, what, and why of it."

"And a defense, so we're not homogenized, would be nice," added Slapgren.

I noticed Daleria was as pale as well Casper. "You okay, hon?"

"No. I am not."

Toño and Sapale both leaped to her side.

"What is wrong, child?" Toño asked in a doctorly tone.

"Everything." She turned to look him in the eyes. "It must be Jéfnoss."

"What must be Jéfnoss?" he asked.

"The power that attacked us from death."

"That's plain silly," returned EJ. "A small earthquake and you're resurrecting this Jéfnoss asshole?"

"It makes sense," remarked Casper. "He knew the prophecy; hell, he *issued* it. Once the three of me got that close to Clein, he must have known. This must be his reaction."

"That's plain sillier," spat EJ. "Death is a big deal. Aside from numb-nuts over here," — guess who he pointed at — , "you can't just hop a shuttle and return from being dead."

"Your thoughts, your beliefs, are so ... so ... *provincial*, Mr. EJ," Daleria said darkly. "If anyone else could, it would be Jéfnoss. And if he does, we're all doomed."

"No we're not." He jabbed a finger against his head. "Think about it. We have Gáwar stashed back in the hold. If Jéfnoss shows his presumably ugly mug, we sick the big lobster on him."

"Jéfnoss has had a very long time to come up with a way to defeat Gáwar. He would have obsessed to no end over the fact that Gáwar killed him. If they face off again, I would not bet in favor of our prisoner's luck," Daleria responded.

"Then I'll just have to kill him *myself*, won't I," announced EJ.

"You are a fool to speak those words."

"While I agree he's a fool," said Casper, "in his defense, he's never seen Jéfnoss in action."

EJ rubbed his fists over his eyes. "Waa, waa waa. I ain't 'fraid of no ghost."

"You will be," Casper said with finality. "You *will* be."

CHAPTER FOURTEEN

In the dark, hopelessly dark pit where Clein resided for all eternity, the parched air was still. The few denizens that guarded Clein were as still as the grave. Why move when there was nothing to kill? Though hunger gnawed at them with a power that was inconsolable, the monsters had long ago learned there was nothing to be gained from random movements in the pitch black. Even the rare intrusion by a banshee had stopped. There would be nothing to eat until it announced itself by creating a disturbance. The denizens were unable to comprehend that their hunger, however consuming, would never lead to their starvation. No, they lived in such close proximity to the power that was Clein that death was nearly impossible. It would certainly not come from something as trivial as an endless fast.

Clein itself was sentient, though not particularly bright. Vicious, hateful, and merciless, yes. Questioning, inquisitive, and learned, no. It lived in a pedestal of basalt stone, the sole towering remnant of a lava flow that occurred eons ago. Clein *was* the stone and the stone *was* Clein. The dense column had, however, existed millions of years before Clein joined with it. Prior to that event, Clein was ... *elsewhere*. The basalt was just any other dumb, cold rock.

Now the stony altar to maniacal energy and hostile intent pulsed with venom. It longed to break free of its confines. The irony was that in spite of the limitless energy it subtended, it was powerless to do so. The genie's curse. The one act it could *not* perform was the only thing it actually *cared* to do; escape its confinement.

No, Jéfnoss tra-Fundly had quite literally sealed Clein's fate. The ultimate insult was that the archenemy of Clein did so with such skill that separation from the otherwise lifeless basalt was impossible. And for that imprisonment, Clein hated The Evil One with more intensity and focus than it did any other thing — living, dead, inanimate, yet unborn, imaginary, or any other state of possible existence. Clein's enmity was infinite. That stipulated, it reserved for Jéfnoss tra-Fundly *three* infinities of malice. If it ever was in the presence of that cursed alchemist again, it would render upon him *such* a judgment, *such* a sentence. Though Clein knew it could not die, it would gladly do so, if its ending meant the death of Jéfnoss tra-Fundly.

Aside from negative emotions, primal and relentless, Clein had, without knowing it as such, one regret. It had learned from the denizens, who'd heard it from the banshees, that had been told by the attendants, that the most impure of the universe *was* dead. Clein would never be able to slay Jéfnoss tra-Fundly. That he was dead gave Clein no solace, not one drop of consolation. In fact, it longed for the prophecy to come to fruition, the one Jéfnoss tra-Fundly had told Clein the day he departed after remanding Clein to a stone forever ago. The Evil One had said he would return some day, a day when his land was in the ultimate crisis. When that time came, only he, Jéfnoss tra-Fundly, could save his worthless kin. If that day ever came ... well, Clein only needed that one opportunity to redress its wound, its sole regret.

If only, it lamented, it could conquer death.

CHAPTER FIFTEEN

"Doc," I said walking up to him from behind, "let's take a walk."

He reluctantly set down his geek tools and turned to me. Slightly hunched at the shoulders, he asked, "Why would either of us need to go for a walk?"

"I'm sure it's a fine day, full of sunshine and possibilities. It'll do us both a world of good."

"Out there, we might be captured. Why risk that when we're perfectly safe down here?"

"Because we *are* going for a walk, you and I, and we cannot do that down here." I set a hand on his shoulder. "This way, you recluse."

The day was miserable. The wind ripped through the deserted streets and rain mixed with hail pounded the dirt into thick mud. It was positively atrocious topside.

Toño stared out the cave entrance, then at me, then back outside.

"Hey, your theory about us being captured doesn't hold water." I gestured to the torment abounding. "Not a soul in sight."

"Little wonder," he scoffed. "No one is foolish enough to venture out in such a storm."

"I am. You are. *Marchamos.*" I pushed him unceremoniously into the downfall. I let him stew a few seconds, then I joined him. Man it was inhospitable. Perfect.

I started walking to the right. Why not? I had nowhere in mind to go. We just needed to place some physical distance between ourselves and the others.

"You do realize how preposterous we look because of your desire to take a stroll?" Toño shouted to be heard above the madding elements.

"Don't be a forever sissy, Doc," I taunted at an equally loud volume. "It's just a little precipitation." I held out a palm to suggest that maneuver was necessary to detect any of the intense downfall.

"And a little gale and a little lightning." He shook his head. "I suppose you wanted to talk in private. What is at issue?"

"No, Doc. I just thought we could do with some exercise. As one ages, one has to be mindful of one's conditioning."

"Your condition might soon find itself to include my foot up your ass if there isn't an outstandingly good reason I'm out here suffering."

I kept us leaning into the wind and heading further into the storm.

"I think Mirraya is dying."

That stopped him dead in his tracks. He glared into my eyes. "Did she tell you as much?" he finally asked, barely above a whisper.

"No." I shook my head. Water cascaded off it like I was a lawn sprinkler. "It's ... I just suspect."

Toño began walking again. Fortunately, he continued away from our base. "Why don't you simply ask her?"

Why didn't I?

"She is *family* to you. She'd tell you if that was the case."

Why? I couldn't handle her saying I was correct, that's why. "I don't know. I just haven't had the right opportunity yet, I guess."

He glanced at me sideways. "Fighter pilots. Always eager to die but unable to discuss the subject in any context. *Bah.*"

I shoved my hands into my pockets. "That'd be me."

"What make you suspect she's ... she's ill?"

"Her inner strength, or lack of therein. I mean, she's always always been this tower of power, this ... dynamo. Now, lately, I can't sense that force. It's like a piece of her's gone."

"All that is flesh is mortal. Perhaps it is her time?"

"You know I don't want to hear that."

"Before you ask, *no*. Absolutely not, never."

"What?"

"You know very well *what*. I will *not* construct an android host for her."

"Honestly, Doc, you're coming straight out of right field here. The thought never crossed my mind. Try not to blindside an aging robot. We're glitchy enough as it is."

"And this pleasant stroll in a hurricane?" he waved his arms widely, "is because you couldn't risk her hearing you asking me to build her a forever prison." He pounded a fist on his chest with manifest contempt.

"Remind me not to plot with you in the future. You are both too good and too assholish."

"Inventing a new insult does not alter the fact that you would see that poor child lashed to a metal rigging and suffer throughout eternity without her consent."

"Who said anything about her not *consenting*?" I tried real hard to not look as guilty as sin.

"No. I suppose after you tricked me into transferring her, you ask her if it was alright."

I shrugged. "That was only one of several options I placed on a list." I rotated toward him. "A very long list with multiple options."

"Name one other."

"Asking her today and abiding by her decision without question or remorse."

"Lying pig."

"*Hey*," I snapped. "I'm not a pig." I shrugged again. Dude was good.

"May we return to base now? I'm quite certain something just wriggled up my trouser leg. I'd prefer removing it in private, if at all possible."

"There's no one about, so this is private." I swept a hand across the deserted streets.

"In *your* mind, possibly. In any *rational* one, not hardly."

We walked quickly back to the cave. After Toño mentioned that squirmy thing I couldn't stop feeling one either.

"Lord in Heaven look what some foolish cat dragged in," exclaimed EJ the moment we stepped into *Stingray*. I imagine we were quite the sight, dripping wet and hair mauled by the wind.

His comment attracted a very large, golden dragon to enter the room. Mirraya and Slapgren had rejoined in hollon while we were out. Most peculiar. We were on a super-secret-squirrel mission in the most hostile environment imaginable, and they felt a need to get jiggy with it?

"There's something you don't see everyday," I quipped reflexively.

"You would if you were us," Mirri replied coolly.

"Why the sudden ... need?" I asked. "I mean, I guess you might *fit* in here but you sure don't *blend* in anonymously."

"Uncle, we may discuss personal matters in private. Here and now is not the place or time."

In other words, *shut it, Uncle*. Okay, I actually *could* take a hint. I just generally preferred not to. Not that her words were a hint. More a command. Well, I could, on occasion, take those, too. Wasn't a fan, mind you. But I could.

"What in *Brathos* were you two idiots doing?" snapped Sapale as she entered. "And don't stand on my one and only heirloom carpet from Kaljax." She shooed us with both arms until we dripped copiously on exclusively metal deck.

"Geez, you'd think you people never saw a couple of guys go for a walk before," I protested.

"In a monsoon? No," replied EJ. "Only mad dogs and Englishmen."

"That refers to the noonday sun, moron," I returned.

"Not now. I just expanded who qualifies as stupid," he batted back.

"I, for one, am going to change out of these wet clothes," said Toño.

"You, too," commanded Sapale as she pointed toward our quarters. "And if I find that wet stuff on the floor, I'll make you eat it."

"Yes, ma'am." I saluted her and slipped away.

I was in our room toweling my ear when my wife came in and shut the door.

I turned, a bit surprised. "Not now, honey," I said with a grin. "I have a headache."

She displayed toward me the back of her hand raised to swat me but good. "I'll give you a headache." She lowered her arm and sat in the only chair in the small room. "Seriously, what were you two doing?"

I planted my behind on the corner of the bed nearest her. "Seriously? Me?"

"Yes, *you*. Come on. I know you weren't doing it for your health."

"I needed a word with Doc ... alone."

"No, my feelings are *not* hurt that you didn't mention whatever it was to me first. But thanks for asking." From the panoply of Kaljaxian growls, she gave me the threat-warning one. A classic and one of my personal favorites. One I'd been serenaded with very often, I might add.

"There's a reason," I said seriously.

"Which I am about to hear."

"I think Mirraya's ill."

That caught her off-guard. "As in she's—"

"I think she's dying."

Sapale nearly fell out of the chair. "H ... how do you ... have you—"

"It's something I suspect, but no, I haven't confronted her with my thoughts."

"So you wanted Toño's opinion?"

"No ... not exactly."

"You wanted to confide in someone you trusted and respected who wasn't your brood's-mate of uncountable centuries?" She looked down, an idea seeming to have popped into her head. "No, you *pig*. You wanted him to make her an android host so *she'd* be cursed to live forever, just like the four of us."

"It's not necessarily a curse. It's an *option*."

"Which a *normal* person would discuss with the involved party before ever asking his friend to secretly fabricate a mobile *coffin* for that involved party."

Wow. She felt pretty strongly there, didn't she. "Love," I said as I knelt in front of her. "You think of these," I held up my arm, "as mobile crypts? Are ... are you okay?"

She looked away. "I overreacted. No."

Three whole words as a retraction of her stating clearly we were zombies in zombie wear. "You can—"

"I am sorry I said anything. *I* am not the subject here. It's Mirri. What did Toño say?" Before I could say a word she placed a finger over my lips. "No. What am I saying? He told you exactly what I did, only more diplomatically."

I angled my head. "Not all that much more diplomatically, truth be told."

"Good. You deserve both barrels." Her eyes flickered shut. "Did he agree about her looking ill?"

"No."

"But he told you to speak with her."

"Yes."

"Which no way you will."

"I ... I cou ... might ... you know—"

"It's okay, Jon." She rested a palm gently on my cheek. "I know it's not in your skillset, the talk-about-feelings thing. I love you in spite of the fact that you're an emotional cripple."

Okay, now I had to decide if I was going to let that one pass without protest. But I did. Crap, the girl was right.

"Do you want me to?" she asked tenderly.

"Nah. Let's give it a minute, see what happens."

"You are such a guy."

"I'm just being ... sensitive. Yeah, sensitive of oth—"

Sapale muffled my faltering defense with a gentle kiss. Thank goodness. I hated being *that* lame.

CHAPTER SIXTEEN

Ramalamadama stood firmly on the floor in front of Vorc's desk. As a three meter long tube-dog with legs varying in number between fourteen and twenty, depending on the weather, standing resolutely came naturally. Add the fact that Ramalamadama weighed in around two tons, and the term immovable applied itself. She was Vorc's latest office assistant and looked to be his last. She was hired because she was the sole applicant. He selected her in spite of the fact that Ramalamadama had none of the customary skill-sets a secretary might need. She could neither read nor write. She was testy on a good day and murderous on a middling one. She spoke Standard, but was very challenging to understand, emitting grunts and barks more than formed words. And she positively could *not* overcome her tendency to add an *R* to words where they were not, conventionally, called for.

Ultimately Vorc was stuck with her because Fire of Justice lacked the battery power to vaporize her with one charge. He was fairly certain that, although she was frightfully dumb, she wouldn't wait while seriously wounded for his weapon to replenish itself. So, they were a long-term pair.

"Ms. R," as Vorc addressed her for brevity. When he said her entire name, not only did it take too long, but he found himself near tears when finished, "you are still present *because?*"

"You didn't amiss, um, me, 'orrd."

"Beg pardon. I did-ernt do what?"

"Not rdird-ern't rdo, 'orrd. Rdirdn't *amiss.*"

Vorc stared blankly toward the creature standing a few inches off the floor for a full minute. "Do you mean *dismiss?* That I have yet to *dismiss* you?" He stroked his chin after asking.

"Es. That's what I said. Sha' I rdepart?"

Urdypart? Was that a verb? Or *urdy* part, some bizarre noun? "I want you to go now, please. We are done for now." He lowered his head, but it shot back up. "And this time not only *use* the door but *open* it first."

"As you rdesire, 'orrd."

Mercifully Ramalamadama turned without the customary knocking over and breaking of furniture, and left with the door open but intact.

"What am I to do?" Vorc asked himself aloud. He wanted to set his palms over his face, but couldn't tolerate the beating he'd self-administer. His hand had begun trembling since his meeting with Nostriana concerning her omen-speak. Well, he was recalling the facts incorrectly. His hands *had* been subject to tremors for months. But since that news flash, the only *change* in his trembling was the degree. They were never gone, even during his short and unrefreshing bursts of sleep.

"'orrd, you summonerd me? I live only to rdo your birdrding."

"*No!*" he shouted aghast. "I did-r not. Go, and go quickly, and go quickly in absolute silence."

Bound to not respond verbally, Ramalamadama wagged her head as best she could, given the constraints of her thick neck-region. In so doing, the gyrations set in motion caused her flanks to bash a hole in one wall and crush beyond even godly repair a very old and treasured settee. She then backed out, to best comply with her interpretation of Vorc's mandate. Her rock-like butt sheared a ragged opening in the wall slightly to the left of the doorway. In fact she exited so close to the door's frame it came free of the wall and split across her back.

"Surely death is laughing at me, mocking me bitterly," he said to himself, but very very quietly.

Vorc reviewed his options, yet again. He had obsessed over them, in fact, without interruption, for several weeks. Blurry eyed and shaking like a dry leaf in a wet storm, he knew he was nearer to the *end* of his sanity than he was to the *beginning* of it. He could swallow his pride and his tongue and return to the cursed sisters. They'd likely see what was coming. While Jéfnoss was the *god* of prophesy, they were second only to him in their raw ability to glean the future trends. But would knowing a horrendous truth make it better? Could he be proactive against what *was* going to happen? Might ignorance not be his most blissful option?

Fate, mercurial and capricious as it was, removed from Vorc the need to ponder those weighty questions any longer.

The back wall of Vorc's office exploded *outwardly*, as if there was a bomb inside the room. There was not. But, as soon as Vorc pried himself off the rubble-strewn floor, inside the room was something infinitely worse that any bomb. There stood, three feet off the ground, Jéfnoss tra-Fundly. He was resplendent in a shimmering gold cape flapping over his blindingly-reflective silk robes. Jéfnoss sported one of those smiles that untold generations of evil-doers, villains, and sociopaths would have paid with their genitalia to be able to reproduce. Portentous, emphatic, cruel, and mocking, while still sending a clear message that the viewer's death was close at hand and in no doubt. It was *the* perfect bad-guy-evil-grin. Kudos to Jéfnoss were obligatory.

"Y ... you're d ... dead," stammered Vorc, as he peered over his desk toward Jéfnoss.

"N ... no I ... I'm not," he mimicked. "You, however ... eh... *dead* is a fair estimation of *your* status." He drifted slowly to the floor. Once down, he walked up to Vorc's chair and plopped into it with a grin. "Now that's a feeling I've waited a very long time to feel once more."

Vorc still crouched on the opposite side of the desk. "You are dead. You cannot be here. Death, as we both know, is absolute."

"Is it, now? Hmm. Then how do you account for the transfixingly annoying presence of Jon Ryan among the living?"

"I ... I do not."

"You do not what? The man's alive. Gáwar killed him, yet he lurks in our shadows plotting our downfall."

"I was not told how that came about." Vorc raised up onto one knee. "How'd you know that? Are there *newspapers* in hell?"

"You are so much stupider than I remembered you being. That's truly remarkable, VTD."

"VTD?"

"Vorc the Dork. Oh come now, it's what everyone beyond the veil calls you."

Vorc's head fell like it'd been guillotined. "Even my parents?"

Jéfnoss swung his feet up on the desk and leaned back. "Stupid, Inc., they *started* the craze."

"How—"

"And very soon you can complain directly to *them* about it. I have no time and no inclination to endure you for one more second than I must."

"What ... what do you require of me?" Vorc said as he stood. The dangling of even a baited hook held out some hope of a life-extension.

"Little, scum. Something of precious little worth."

Vorc stepped toward the settee to sit, but realize it was ruined. Instead he leaned against the wall and crossed his arms.

Recall the fickleness of Fate mentioned before. It fickled again. The very spot on the wall Vorc leaned back against was the very spot Ramalamadama crashed through in her quest to discover what the racket was in her lord's office.

Prophet or not, Jéfnoss leaped out of his chair, and nearly his skin, in surprise. In a comical sequence, the inadequate office assistant skidded to try to stop before her massive head hit the table. In that, as in all matters, she failed. The desk split as she impaled it, and Jéfnoss was pushed toward the missing external wall he had blown up.

Ramalamadama was able to halt herself well short of the fall, but the only so recently resurrected Jéfnoss was less fortunate. He flew backward and, with a pathetic scream, out into the third-story air. His voice faded as he fell and came to an abrupt end when he heavily thudded to the ground. In confirmation of his incapacitation, he made no sound whatsoever when the desk, after teetering briefly, tumbled down and landed directly on top of his crumpled body.

Both employer and employee rushed to the precipice and studied the motionless form.

"Do you suppose he's dead... again?" asked Vorc.

"Harrd to say, I'rd say. One of us shou'rd maybe go anrd check."

"Outstanding idea. Thank you for your service."

With that, Vorc sped to Ramalamadama's rear and began pushing her for all he was worth out the opening.

She was one-third out before she realized his intent, and two-thirds out before she thought to back-pedal. Two-thirds of two tons hanging off a ledge was proven by physics to be an insurmountable challenge in terms of stopping. Headfirst, she crashed into and splintered what remained of the desk. Ramalamadama then ripped Jéfnoss's head off as she careened past the remainder of his body. Her momentum drove the severed head seven meters into the ground before she came to a stop.

It took her the devil of an effort to squirm backwards out of the crater she'd formed. But Ramalamadama was, if nothing else, persistent. Within half an hour she was standing at the edge of the tubular hole she'd created, peering down intently. That is how Vorc found her when he decided it was safe to descend to the scene of the accident and ascertain what damage had hopefully been done.

"Is he dead?" Vorc asked, as he stared down the dark hole.

"I cannot say. His bordy is there," she looked to where the bloody mess lay, "but I cannot locate his heard."

Vorc, despite all odds to the contrary and his luck in his piteous life, burst into laughter. He pointed at Ramalamadama's brow and convulsed in a seizure of mirth.

"What?" she demanded.

"You ... you're ... you're—" He then literally collapsed to the ground, legs flailing in the air.

"I rdemanrd you te' me what's so funfy?" She began stomping her legs. That did the trick.

Vorc noticed the earthquakes and sobered up quickly. "My dear Ms. R," he said stepping toward her, "Jéfnoss's head is not missing." He set a foot on her snout and pulled at something affixed to her crown. With a nauseating squish, it dislodged. Vorc nearly tumbled backwards because he was pulling so hard. He held up some bloody thing. "Here it is. You appear to have flattened it rather completely. Again, thank you for your service."

She looked the oozing pancake up and down. "I rdo be'ieve you are correct, 'orrd. Wou'rd it be unwise of me to apo'ogize to it?"

"Unnecessary, I'd say. Take the remainder of the day off. Your team-spirited efforts have exceeded my wildest expectations."

"Wou'rd that off-time be with or without pay, orrd?"

"You choose. I don't care either way."

"Thank you, 'orrd. You are kinrd, consirderate, and fair-minrderd." With that, she trotted away merrily.

"Your praise is much appreciated." He tossed the flat skull of his enemy over a shoulder. Vorc wiped his hands on his pants and headed straight for his favorite brothel. Yeah, *he* was on a roll.

CHAPTER SEVENTEEN

I spilled hot coffee all down the front of my jumpsuit, I shot up so quickly from the table. Daleria's scream was not something you responded to casually. It came from her room. I thought she was sleeping. She sure as hell wasn't asleep now.

I was first to her bedside, though everybody else was right behind me. I rushed to kneel at her side. Her head was off her pillow, so I cradled my arm underneath it. "Daleria, Dal-dal, what's the matter?" I soothed.

Sapale slid in at my side and gently stroked Daleria's cheek. "Sweetheart, are you okay?"

"*Noooo*," was Daleria's first response. It was loud.

"What is it?" Toño called out as he skidded to a stop behind us.

"He's here. *Noooo*. He ... he *lives*."

"Who, honey?" I cooed. "There's no one here but us. You're safe."

"He has come and he will kill us *all*," Daleria wailed.

Hmm. Not very promising. In the land of the ancient gods, if someone said a bad guy had arrived planning on killing us all, I tended to believe them.

"Who's here?" asked Sapale, as she continued to try to reassure a hysterical Daleria.

Daleria gulped down a series of breaths, then looked me right in the eyes. "Jéfnoss has returned from the dead. He's here to kill us all."

I was the last person in the multiverse who was going to question resurrection. Duh. "How do you know that?" I posed softly.

"I ... we can all feel it. He was here, Gáwar killed him, and now he's back. Jon, he's back and he's *mad*."

"I'm sure it's not at us, you and me, kiddo."

The aghast look of disbelief and primal fear she gave me was, well, I don't really want to see it again — ever.

"Or do you mean to say he's crazy?" I hoped to clarify.

Sapale wisely shouldered me away. "He's not here now with us. You are safe. We will sort this out in time. For now, clam down and rest. We're here. You're safe." Okay, I had to admit my wife's response was a tad superior to mine.

"No, but the cruel wizard is back. He will hold us *all* to account." She dropped her head back. "He will punish us all for failing him."

"We shall see," replied Sapale. "But for now we are all fine. May I get you some tea?"

That seemed to bring Daleria back to us a good bit. "No ... no, but thanks. I'll be okay, I just need a minute."

"Not a problem. You and I will freshen up while everyone else leaves us alone." How very unsubtle of my mate. Typical.

The mess was full — Mirraya/Slapgren, EJ, Toño, Casper, and me — all of us waiting for the two women to emerge. It didn't take too long. Daleria walked uncertainly with Sapale lending support with an arm around her elbow. They took the two spots left open for them at the mess table.

"Who made some tea?" asked Sapale as she scanned the gathering.

Silence.

"As I expected." She patted Daleria's arm and stepped away to make tea.

I would have done it myself; if I'd thought of it, that is.

She returned quickly with a full tray.

Daleria blew across the surface and we waited patiently for her to be ready. "There's a bond between all of us Cleinoids," she began quietly. "Stronger between some than others, but it's ubiquitous. When it came ... *comes* to Jéfnoss, we all sense him loud and clear. I've had the feeling he was, I don't know exactly ... knocking at a door? Maybe thinking about us?" She shivered. "Anyway he's—"

Daleria dropped her tea mug with a crash onto the table. Her head lolled in an erratic circle and I was sure she was going to hit the deck. Sapale caught hold of her around the shoulders and fixed her to the chair. Toño came to her other side and studied her face.

Then — puff — Daleria was fine. She blinked a few times, then stared at us all, one at a time. "Well that's odd. He's gone."

"Who? Jéfnoss?" I asked quickly.

"Yes, Jéfnoss."

"Where did he go?" I pressed.

She shook her head slowly. "I have no idea."

"But he was here and now he's not, again?" queried EJ.

"Yes."

"Well, I'll be damned," spat EJ. "If that's not the damndest thing I've ever heard."

"Is he dead, again?" asked Toño.

"I ... I *imagine* so."

"What're the options?" I wondered aloud.

"Well," she began to say, "he could be dead, or he could be ... I don't know." She focused on me. "Not here."

"Okay then," I wheezed. "That was fun. Anyone for croquet?"

Sapale slapped my shoulder. "Are you all right, dear?" she directed to Daleria.

"Fine. Perfectly fine." She grinned at Sapale.

"I wonder what the hell just happened?" I said darkly.

CHAPTER EIGHTEEN

"Oh my *goodness!*" exclaimed Onster. "Look, everybody. Look who's back, and so *soon.*"

Jéfnoss lay flat on his back on the floor of hell. He nestled his severed head under one arm. Both the mouth of the head, and the tube it should have been attached to at the neck's stump, breathed heavily. Only the neck-half sprayed a fine mist of green blood, however.

"Hey, come *on,*" Onster veritably squealed with joy, "let's give a god a hand." He angled as close as he practically could to the fallen Cleinoid. That wasn't, however, too close. Onster - a monster without an *M*, as he was fond of chortling — was a diplodocus, a large herbivorous sauropod dinosaur of the Late Jurassic Period, Earth. As such, he could only clumsily provide aid to a comrade in need of it. Plus, any intervention he attempted was just as likely to *inflict* harm as it was to *alleviate* any.

Genger, Baffilly, and Hexaplex chanced to be nearby. They looked amongst themselves, gave a collective shrug, and slowly came over to see what was up. Not surprisingly, Jéfnoss had made few, if any, friends in the afterlife. Onster loved positively everyone, so he didn't count. The three other gods begrudgingly participated, but more out of curiosity than concern. Jéfnoss had made such a big deal about *his* returning to the land of the living. About how *he* was going to exact revenge and everyone *else* wasn't. The trio were curious as to why Jéfnoss's triumphant return had been so satisfyingly brief. They also hoped the entire experience was painful and bitterly disappointing for the moron.

"Well, what have we here?" gloated Baffilly. He was a run-of-the-mill Satyr and former god of impiety. "See what happens when you try to get *a-head*, old boy," he cackled.

"Aw come on, guys. He's hurt and probably in emotional distress," protested Onster. He pounded the dirt with a foot. Big bada boom.

"One can only hope," grumbled Hexaplex as he slithered over. As a four-armed serpent, he was the logical choice of who could best assist the asshole on the ground. He propped Jéfnoss's torso up with two arms, and set the loose head on top of the neck, sort of twisting it with a nauseating squishy sound.

"You seem to have a recurring problem keeping this thing attached," Hexaplex taunted as he labored. After a few failed attempts, during which the head rolled far enough away that Genger had to rush over and retrieve it before Onster could try to kick it back, the head finally remained in place.

Slowly, Jéfnoss bobbed and rotated his head. Then he sat up on his own power and studied his surroundings. "Shit," was all he had to say.

"You're welcome," Baffilly responded, miffed.

"Huh?" replied Jéfnoss. "No, I meant that I was back here."

"You're welcome," added a sullen Hexaplex.

"No, I meant, you know ... oh, forget it."

"Hey, I've already heard you set a new record for the briefest resurrection in all known history," announced Genger. "Strong work, meat."

Everyone, except Onster, of course, guffawed loudly.

Jéfnoss stood uncertainly, then staggered over to a bench. "It ... I ... wha—"

"As articulate as ever, I see," snarked Baffilly. "None the worse for wear."

More disrespectful mirth was directed at Jéfnoss.

"You don't have to explain," said Genger blankly. "I assure you no one cares or wants to hear it."

"I doooo," corrected an over-excited diplodocus. "What ever happened, Jeff?"

That Onster always referred to *Jéfnoss* — mind the *é* please — as *Jeff* irritated and gnawed at Jéfnoss's last nerve inconsolably. But, he'd discovered the hard way, one could not retrain an idiot.

"Everything was going so well," Jéfnoss remarked absently. "Near perfect, in fact." He angled his hands in space like a quarterback manipulating a hiked football. "I had the moron VTD *right* where I wanted him ... I ... then, then this torpedo charged into the room and rammed me out the hole I'd created in the wall."

"That's what you get for the destruction of private property, *Jeff*. We've discussed this before, I don't know *how* many times. Come *on*."

Jéfnoss eyed Onster viciously, wondering, yet again, if he could kill an already dead nitwit. "And after I landed on my back, the torpedo jumps out the building, targeting my head. I had a steel *beam* across my chest so I couldn't react in time—" Jéfnoss slammed his fist into his palm. "*Bam.* There went my head, and with it any hope of revenge."

"Poor baby," mocked Gender.

"We'll all be sure to keep you in our prayers tonight," taunted Hexaplex.

"You guys still say your nighty-night prayer, *too?*" exploded joyously from Omster. "My mother would be so proud of you guys."

All three ancient god's mouths gaped open in disbelief. Then they remembered they were dealing with Onster, and promptly forgot what he'd said.

Baffilly slapped Jéfnoss very hard on his back. "Better luck next time, schmuck." Then he trotted away.

"Yeah, heck fire, you can probably cut your lead time in half.

Next visit home'll be in less than, oh, two *billion* years, chump," coughed out Genger, as he laughed merrily down the road.

Hexaplex spat on the ground and slithered away, without further input.

"Oh, I'll be back quicker than you can say, *I'm a puddle of piss*, boyo," seethed Jéfnoss under his breath.

"Okay, what can *I* do to help?" pressed a concerned Onster. "I just happen to have a potluck all planned for tonight, so you're invited, for double sure. How does sevenish sound?"

Jéfnoss scanned the ground, located a large rock, and hurled it at Onster's head. The stone ricocheted off leaving a deep gash. The former god of prophesy stood and stormed away, kicking at random objects close enough to punish.

"Okeydokey, sevenish it is."

CHAPTER NINETEEN

"I have called this unscheduled conclave to make a formal announcement. The rumors circulating are preposterous, incorrect, or simply vicious lies meant to degrade and impugn my good reputation. I—"

"Good for *nothing* is all the reputation you got, jocko," shouted Tefnuf from her seat in the front row.

Many, but not all, present laughed or jeered. A few were too frightened by what they'd heard concerning Jéfnoss to do much more than breathe.

"As I was saying, before the peanut gallery interrupted, that I wish to set the record straight and clear the air of all false information concerning the late," Vorc raised a finger, "notice I emphasize *late*, Jéfnoss."

Audible gasps were heard at the mention of that cursed name.

Vorc smiled smugly. "Now, now, friends," he waved overhead with both arms, hoping to appear magnanimous, "please remain calm and assured. There is *nothing* to fear."

"Except, oh, I don't know, maybe two things. Jéfnoss tra-Fundly's *return* and *your* absolute incompetence." Yeah, that was Tefnuf, of course.

"Today, friend Tefnuf, even you cannot drag down my mood or feeling of serenity." He "gathered" himself as he'd seen great orators of the past do in the videos he'd studied. "*I am here today to tell you that Jéfnoss poses no threat to anyone.*"

Murmurs and rumbles rose from the crowd.

"I can tell you what happened, precisely and in detail. That way you will all know just how safe you are. What I shall relay to you is the gods' truth. I was laboring, as usual, in my office, serving this great assembly to the best of my humble abilities. An *overwhelming* sense of dread seized me. I knew, brothers, sisters, or whatever, that something was rotten in our state.

"Not worried about the personal danger I might face, I rose to investigate. Behind me — right behind where I sat at my desk laboring — stood none other than the accursed Jéfnoss tra-Fundly. And yes, he was of full body, living again in our sacred realm. When his menacing gaze met mine, he shrank back like the coward he was, or is, depending on your own belief sets. Well, I raised my hand and shouted at him, 'Leave this hallowed place and return to hell, flea on the back of a rat.'

"Then, to demonstrate my passionate wrath, I blew the back wall of my *own* office out. No, the door was too good for him to exit through. I then commanded him to leave and to die, lest I throw him out and kill him. The choice, my friends, was *his* and *his* alone. What, you ask, did the vile heap of rat droppings do? I shall tell you. He quaked in his shoes and begged *mercy* from me, knowing, as he did, what a just and fair person I am.

"But the likes of Jéfnoss tra-Fundly will never get mercy from this ... the *mercy* stone that am I. I stepped right up to him and ripped his ugly head off of his neck while it was still pleading, beseeching me to spare his worthless life. Then I cast the head and the body out the opening I'd made in the wall. Just before I released him, my new assistant, Ramalamadama, leaped with spontaneous joy to adulate and embrace me. Based on the release of the body and it's weight, resulting in a shift of my stance, the dedicated Ms. R missed worshiping me and, instead, followed the wretched Jéfnoss's parts out the window. Fortune, fear not my kindred, favored her that day. Ms. R was barely scratched, being as plucky as she is. Yes, she lives today, and would have been here to authenticate my version of what happened, had not the burdens of her current workload compelled her to implore me to allow her to remain at work, laboring on *your* behalf.

"So, Jéfnoss is dead, *again*. You are safe, *again*. You, friends, are welcome. Conclave dismissed. No time for questions. I am far too busy serving you to pay any attention to you. Goodbye."

And then Vorc the Dork quite literally disappeared.

CHAPTER TWENTY

"Well, I guess we need to consult the born-again lobster, as much as it pains me to do so," I grumbled.

"Come on, ya big baby," chided my wife in perpetuity, "man up. He's bound and intermittently cheery. What's the large deal?"

"He smells funny," I defended weakly.

"No, he does not. But if you *hallucinate* that he does, turn down your olfactory sensors." She stuck her tongue out at me to add clarity.

"I'll ask him, if you want," volunteered Mirraya/Slapgren, those two being still joined.

"No, I'll do it," I relented. I stood with a grunt.

I'd placed Gáwar in the storage area with a full membrane around him for good measure. I hadn't spoken with him at all since I stashed him there after our failed attempt to assault Clein. He didn't need to eat, so I figured why cut him any slack? After an eternity of evildoing, screw him. As I *was* asking for his help, I did bring along a couple bologna sandwiches. I figured that was good enough for him. No mayo either. He could swallow them dry, the chronic malefactor.

Wow, the instant I entered the compartment and dropped the

shield I had to revisit the wisdom of leaving him sequestered so long. Obviously, not eating did not *alleviate* his need to *alleviate* himself. What a mess. I was going to have to assign Al to clean-up duty ASAP. Tee hee hee.

"Do not hold me accountable," Gáwar whined as I entered. "Some matters are beyond my ... ah, how I loathe you, Ryan. Sorry. I spoke out of ... *ah!* When I'm free, and someday I will be, there will be a reckoning, Ryan."

"If you could give me a heads up when the day comes, I'll make sure I wear clean underwear."

I turned my olfactory sensors *off*.

"Look, I brought a peace offering." I held out one of the sandwiches.

"What is it? tri-level poison?"

I studied the lunchtime standard. "Depends how you define the timeframe."

"What do you want in exchange?"

I tried my best — which wasn't very convincing at all — to appear shocked and dismayed. "Can't one friend offer another friend a meal without having ulterior motivations?"

"Of course. That scenario doesn't cover you and me *and* that offensive morsel is hardly a meal."

"A *ha*," I reveled. "That's why I brought *two*." I bounced them in the air.

"Twice nothing is nothing," he scoffed.

"Wow, and here I thought you Cleinoids were unlearned morons. You, you're a certifiable math whiz."

For some reason he just glared at me, long and hard. Kind of negatively, too, I was pretty much certain.

"Look, I happen to have a question and a couple sandwiches. Sue me. You want them or not?"

"Yes, I do. What are they ... this ... this *sandwich* thing of which you speak?"

"You guys have them. You call them plotwusts. No clue where that name came from, but there you have it."

"You define *those* to be plotwusts? You should have your optical scanners checked. A plotwust is seven times larger, laden with meats, dripping with sauces, and smothered in vegetables." He tried as best he could to crane his neck to study the offerings. "What is that *tan* layer, between what I can only presume is your pale interpretation of bread?"

"It's delicious." I took a big bite of one. "It's so good I don't know why I'm giving it to *you*."

With horror in his eyes he wailed, "Please don't eat anymore. Free a claw or simply toss what's left into my mouth."

I opted for the latter. Easier and safer.

"Why," he said slowly grinding the food in his maw, "those aren't half bad. Do you have more, say one hundred more?"

"Only time, and the intensity of your cooperation, will tell. A little while ago Daleria freaked out. She said Jéfnoss had returned. Then, just as quickly, puff, he was gone. What do you say?"

"I say that's a five sandwich question."

"Done."

"In advance. I trust you like I trusted my mother." He looked away.

"Probably a long and painful story. Spare me, please." I left to grab the bounty.

After chewing them even more slowly, he relaxed back. "Yes, your bitch is correct."

"Can you explain it? I mean, the dude's been dead forever. How'd he return?" I slapped my sides. "Why'd he return? Why'd he split so quickly after going to all that trouble?"

Gáwar gave me his best attempt at a smile. "Five, ten, and twenty sandwich questions."

"You want thirty five *more* of those?" I pointed out the door.

"I want hundreds. We're negotiating. The number's now forty."

Luckily I had Daleria and Toño already working on whipping up a tray full.

Once the bottomless pit had consumed them, he burped loudly and said, "No, I do not know, I don't know, and I don't know."

"Those are *not* forty-bologna-sandwich-quality answers, bucko." I shoved a finger at him.

"I'm trying to be honest. Trust me, that's not easy."

"Let me break it down. Have any others returned from the great beyond?"

"Aside from the annoying case of *you*, no, of course not."

"So it must be tremendously hard?"

"Presumably. Alternately it could be tremendously *unpalatable*, but I doubt hell is better then this here-and-now."

"So, why re-die so soon?"

"I assume it was accidental. No Cleinoid alive could dispatch Jéfnoss that quickly."

"You did."

"I did, but not that fast. He is a cunning and powerful opponent."

"So he did the undoable and was killed accidentally. Therefore, he will try it again."

"I'd say yes, absolutely."

"Will it take him as long the second time?"

"No clue. I don't know what he did to know if it can be streamlined."

"And I assume he returned to take control again, right?"

"That would be my assumption. He would return to rule and to extract vengeance."

"That'd make you Item 1 on his to-do list, wouldn't it?"

"I'd be right up there."

"And here you are, all bound up like the Christmas goose. Where'd he go first? I mean, he didn't seek you out immediately."

"Presumably to Vorc. He's the only one Jéfnoss'd need information or aid from."

"Would he want Vorc dead?"

"Jéfnoss wants *everyone* dead."

"Does he especially hate Vorc?"

"Hmm. No, I doubt that. Vorc's rule came much later, long after Jéfnoss was dead."

"Then why'd he go there first?" I asked myself.

"He must have needed something."

"Huh?"

"Though I'm certain Vorc would not have survived their meeting, I can only *assume* Jéfnoss needed something—information or material—to begin his return."

"What might that be?"

"Not a bologna sandwich. That I can promise you." He made a funny face.

"I thought you said they weren't half bad?"

"I did. They're ninety-nine percent bad. My stomach feels like a volcano ready to erupt."

"Well hold it down, at least until Al gets this mess cleaned up. Once he does, puke yourself silly."

"What would Vorc have that Jéfnoss would need?" I repeated to myself twice as I paced the floor.

"I cannot say."

"Me, neither," I mumbled. "And that I do not like. Catch you later," I called over my shoulder as I left.

"Hey, Al," I shouted once out of the area, "you got a yucky mess to clean in the storage bay. Make sure you bring a *big* mop."

CHAPTER TWENTY-ONE

Wul sat stiffly and said nothing. This was the second time Vorc had summoned him to the center seat's office. Last time, it had been unpleasant. Wul had never liked Vorc. He liked him less with each passing day. Presently, after all his bungling and ineptness, Wul fully despised the moron.

"I'm betting you're wondering to yourself at this very moment, 'What in the world has my leader invited me to his office for, this time?'" Vorc followed that tormented sentence with a smile suggesting he'd just swallowed a rotten toad whole.

Wul remained resolutely taciturn.

"Well, I'll tell you, my old friend Wul." Vorc fiddled nervously with his quill. "Ah, you see, of late, I ... I find myself in need ... no, that sounds too *needy*. I find myself *desirous* of the counsel of a fair and steady mind. A mind like yours, old friend. Yes, I have very much admired and treasured your opinions, historically, and I find your further input would not be unwelcome, just now, times as they are." This time Vorc's smile suggested the toad, in spite of it's death and decay, was somehow trying to crawl back up his throat. "You see?"

"I do not care to say what it is I'm seeing. You would not *treasure* my present characterization of you."

"Ah, quick witted as always. *And* honest to a fault. That," he pointed violently at Wul, "is what I like the best about you." Vorc produced a short, dry chuckle reminiscent of a drunken village idiot's. "How I miss our—"

"Vorc, stop. Seriously, cut your significant losses and STFU."

"Tempting," he said, as he inhaled. "But not practical, given my current ... um ... level of uncertainty," he said conventionally, with an exhalation.

I should do him, the world, and me a favor and euthanize him here and now, thought Wul.

Vorc pointed to the top of Wul's head. "Penny for your thought."

"I'll give it freely. Vorc, you're insane. What little grasp on reality you had the last time we met is fully gone."

"You see, I *was* correct in thinking you wouldn't pull any punches." Vorc pounded the tabletop with a fist rapidly but lightly. "A good man is so *rare*, nowadays. You're the best, Wul. The very *best*."

"Did I mention you're scaring me, too?"

"Ha, good one, again. You ... you really should consider taking it on the stage. You're as funny as any comedian *I've* ever seen."

"Thanks for sharing. Are we done?"

"Why, *done* you ask? No. We've not actually begun. So far, our date has been nothing more than our usual silly banter."

"This is a *date*? What, you're thinking maybe you'll get lucky with me?"

Vorc slapped his palms over him face, hard. "No. Sorry, *sorry*. I didn't say *date*. I said *on this date*. Yes. The air," he removed one hand from his face and waved it between them, "is bad in here. It doesn't carry sound reliably." He returned his hand to his face. "Longstanding issue. I really should have someone look into it."

"The atmosphere in this office?" Wul asked with a strained tone.

"Yes, I'm comforted that you agree. Otherwise my words might be taken to suggest I was not fully in control of my faculties."

A thousand perturbations of a sarcastic response came to life and died in Wul's mind. No, he concluded before he spoke. It was not just too easy. Responding to that mental diarrhea was beneath him. "Vorc, I'm not going to lie and state I'm busy. As you know, I'm immortal. That said, I don't need this ... this, *you.*" He proffered both hands at Vorc.

"Fine." Vorc removed his hands and set them on the desk. "Let me cut to the chase."

"*Thank* you."

"I'm confused by a recent experience and need to discuss it with someone, someone intelligent."

"Thanks, I guess."

"Humph. It's that, well, I don't have any assistants or advisors left that are worth the bother to speak to. Dumb as a defeated politician's excuses, the lot of them."

"Gee, how flattering to know what I'm superior to."

"Take it however you will. I'm at my wit's end, the land is in dire distress, and I need help. There. I said it. Are you happy?"

"No, but I appreciate your honesty. What makes you think *I* might be of help. I'm not a political type."

"It's not politics I need help with." Vorc looked up at the ceiling. "Well, actually, I do need help there, too. But that's a separate matter. I require a good, honest man's opinion. That is all. Will you help?"

Wul sat quietly a few seconds. "I will try. What is at issue?"

"Did you feel Jéfnoss's return from the dead?"

"Yes. *Everyone* felt that."

"He came to me first. Did you know that?"

Wul slowly rolled his head. "No, but it would make sense, wouldn't it?"

"No. Why?"

"*You're* the center seat. If *I* was returning from the dead with vengeance in mind, that's where I'd start," explained Wul.

"Not in Jéfnoss's case. I barely knew him. My role came long after he was gone. It's not like I control a standing army that he needs to defeat." Vorc shook his head with certainty. "No, his number one obstacle *was* and *is* Gáwar. If I were advising Jéfnoss, I'd tell him to use the element of surprise to take out his number one threat." He waved his hands in the air. "Or possibly to find refuge, obtain information, and relearn the lay of the land."

"Speaking of Gáwar, I haven't heard reports of his pillaging lately. Where is he?"

"I have no idea. He used to pester me no end, and now, lately, nothing. It's as if he vanished into thin air."

"That'd take an awful lot of air," Wul said with a grim chuckle.

"Yes, it would indeed." Vorc managed a halfhearted laugh himself. "So, what little thing in the Ten Blessed Plains would Jéfnoss need from me?"

"Your Fire of Justice?" Wul replied dubiously.

"This old thing?" Vorc tapped it with the back of his hand. "To warm a pot of stew, sure. But Jéfnoss is powerful enough on his own without this *toy*."

"Money? No, don't even answer. That was silly." Wul scratched his stubble. "Maybe he wanted to see if you'd remain passive, not actively hinder him?"

Vorc bobbed his head. "Hmm. Possible, though he never asked anything of anyone before. And my agreeing to stand by and allow him to seek revenge on this land would hardly be a *little* thing."

"True." Wul sat quietly a second. "And that's specifically what he called it? A little thing?"

"*Little, scum. Something of precious little worth*, were his exact words."

"My, that doesn't sound like much. I used to love riddles." Wul trailed off, lost in thought.

"Used to? What happened?"

"I met *Ryanmax*. He cured me of the disease that is curiosity."

Vorc nodded knowingly.

"What commodity of *precious little worth* that an all-powerful god would need upon his *impossible* return from death?"

"It makes no sense. Nothing. He'd require *nothing* from me."

"Maybe he requires it from *someone*. You just happened to be his first choice."

"Huh?"

"I know, it sounds crazy. But let's say ... for some reason he needed *permission* to be here. He could get it from anyone. Why not start with the center seat so you could lord your mastery over him shortly before killing him?"

"Permission? That does not *sound* crazy. It *is* crazy."

Wul flapped a hand in the air. "No, I was saying *for example*. I don't know what *it* is. I'm just saying it might have been a thing that not only *you* possess."

"Hmm. What the devil could that be?"

"You could ask the—"

"No. No, I'd rather die a thousand deaths by ants streaming into my skull than drag myself before those wretched witches."

"Yeah, but how do you really feel about them?"

"Huh?"

"Get over yourself. Yes, they are as annoying as sea worms ascending one's rectum, but seriously? If they could help you, you should consult them."

Vorc's eyes grew to large saucers and he smiled joyously for the first time in months. "*You* will ask them. Yes. *You* will seek their advice and counsel on *my* behalf."

"No. Why would I? Are you more mentally incapacitated than I thought you were?"

"There is no higher calling than public service, friend Wul. None. I envy you on the occasion of this gift of civic duty you've been granted. *Go*," he stood and extended his hand to Wul, "both quickly and with my fullest blessing. A proud nation salutes your devotion."

CHAPTER TWENTY-TWO

Jéfnoss sat perched on a red hot boulder and surveyed the landscape of hell. He was in an understandably foul mood. An eternity plotting and scheming, conjuring and spell-casting, down the toilet in less than five minutes. What an absolute moron he was. And worst of all, he hadn't satisfied his greatest desire, the one he'd lusted after for millions upon millions of years. The fiery obsession that danced in his head like a spastic monkey was unaddressed. He had not been able to eat even *one* spoonful of hot fudge sundae. Women, power, vengeance, strong drink, and the admiration of his peers paled pathetically in comparison to that warm, icy, chocolaty, unapologetic delight. Fate most assuredly hated Jéfnoss tra-Fundly.

But, the past was dead. He was dead. Jéfnoss needed to rally. He had done the impossible once. He would do it again — better and sooner. He knew the drill. The elements required to return again to the land of the living were still at his disposal. And his motivation was piqued all that much more. Yes, the vision of that imbecile Vorc and his torpedo assistant would haunt him until he returned and killed and dismembered and burned and scattered their ashes to the four winds. They would curse their mothers and wish that they had never been born. Okay, Jéfnoss reflected. There was *some* positivity to come from an otherwise glum day.

If he'd only gloated and postured less over VTD. That was fun, but it was off-task, non-mission critical. Maybe if he had gotten what he needed directly, he'd still be alive. Then he could have reigned supreme, extracted the ultimate revenge on his worthless kin, *and* had multiple supersized hot fudge sundaes. No whipped cream, for it diluted the intensity of the taste. No nuts, because they were salty, yes, but their flavor distracted from the vanillaness, rather than complimented it. Oh, the rapture lost.

Oh, how he hated Vorc so much more than ever before, more than *anyone* before.

Ah *ha*! That was it. When he returned triumphantly to the living, *that* is how he would kill Vorc. He would drown him, *crush* him, under the weight of one-hundred *thousand* hot fudge sundaes. And then he'd eat them, every juicy, loving one of them.

Perhaps, the fleeting thought wisped through Jéfnoss's mind, there was a God, after all.

CHAPTER TWENTY-THREE

I was sitting at—you got it—the mess table working on a cuppa joe when Daleria returned.

"Hey, stranger," I said pointing across the table, "grab some java and park it."

She did just that. She drew in a deep whiff of the Peet's like the drug it was. "This is so not Philz."

I toasted her. "You said it, kiddo." After a gulp, I added, "You want me to leave you two alone?" I pointed to her mug.

"No. I'm good with a foursome." She nodded to my mug.

I shot a look behind me. "Lordy, I hope the missus didn't hear that. She'd test my immortality."

Daleria giggled playfully.

"So, how'd the conclave go?"

She frowned. "I was afraid you'd ask."

"*Duh*. That's where you were going to try to get info."

She shrugged. "I know. It was ... it was so odd, that's all."

"Do tell."

"Vorc provided a tortured, twisted tale about how Jéfnoss showed up and Vorc creamed him." She shook her head hard. "I think he's dribbling off the baseball court faster than we anticipated."

"*Basketball* court, not baseball. Baseball's played on a *field*, and no one dribbles except the guys chewing tobacco."

"These sports metaphors of yours are challenging. If I'd ever seen a sports contest, perhaps I'd keep this all straight."

"I have *tons* of videos," I said nearly rising from my seat.

"No, no," she gestured me down with both hands. "I prefer to live in ignorance."

"Don't knock it if you ain't tried it," I scoffed.

"Anyway, back to Vorc. He said Jéfnoss appeared behind him, that Vorc ripped his head off and threw him through a wall. Then his new assistant missed hugging him and flew out the window, *further* killing poor Jéfnoss."

"I bet three, maybe four of those words are true."

"Me, too. Then Vorc disappeared. I spoke with a few gods nearby. We sort of figured out Jéfnoss was about to kill Vorc when the assistant somehow accidentally drove him through the wall and then fell on top of him. Something like that."

"Sounds more plausible, doesn't it? That at least explains his brief visit to La La Land, either way."

"Yes, I suppose it does."

"I hear a *but* in there."

"But, there's no way around the fact that he'll return again. He did it once, but succeeded at nothing. Logically, he will be back."

"Sooner or later."

"That's the key phrase, isn't it?"

"Yeah," I blew across the surface of my coffee. "If he gets his Christmas wish, it'll be sooner rather than later. I just wish we knew what his most optimistic timetable was."

"That's anyone's guess, I suppose," she replied with some resignation.

"Anyone you know of who might be able to narrow the window down?"

"*He's* the prophet. Unless you propose asking him, I don't think we'll find out from him."

I zoned out big-time.

"Jon," she snapped her fingers in front of my face. "Jon, what's going on? I'm about ready to call Toño." It was Daleria, leaning across the table.

"Huh? Oh, sorry. I was thinking."

"I could tell," proclaimed Sapale as she strode in. "I smelled the smoke that came out your ears."

"He was gone. Seriously, I couldn't get his attention," responded a still worried Daleria.

"Oh, honey," blared Sapale, "you haven't seen him watching a *football* game, have you?" She lifted her arms straight in front of her, and angled her head. Then she groaned. "Zombieville City. You could hit him with a mallet and not get his attention."

"That depends where you were swinging, dearest," I replied with a wink.

"Pig." Guess who called me that.

"What were you ozoned out about?" asked Daleria.

"*Zoned*," corrected Sapale. "His species *zones* out. It defies evolutionary logic, but it's a sad genetic heritage." To me, "What was it this time, sport?"

"No, not this time."

"No, I meant *sport* as in your nickname, not what you were fantasizing about."

"Ah. I was tripping on what Dal-Dal just said."

"A) it frightens me that you reflected so deeply, B) it amazes me you can think that deeply, and C) it frightens me that you listened to a woman that intently," warned Sapale.

"You said that already. *Frightens*."

"That's how much it does when you ponder deeply. That event generally proceeds a period of Stupid Jon espousing an amazingly lame plan."

"Not this time." I grinned. "This one I got."

"Like the time you were going to reinvent beer?"

"No," I lowered my head. "Not like that time."

"Or the time you dared me to close my eyes while we were making love?"

"No. Not like that one at *all*."

"Or the time you asked Toño to create an android of your first wife so you could leave her over and over and—"

I held up a stop-sign hand. "I believe that I never *actually* asked that of him. I was just ... free-thinking about Gloria."

"So what's the brain fart, this time?" Sapale placed both fists on her hips. Gotta say, she was getting to know me pretty well.

"We confront Jéfnoss. Get the truth out of him, by brute force if we have to."

"We beat up Jéfnoss? That's your plan?" Sapale said, trying not to laugh. "You know he's—" She stopped talking. Then she stormed over to me and punched my arm. "No. We're not doing that. I'm not." She thumbed her chest. "She's not." She nearly skewered Daleria pointing in her direction. "And you're not." She punched my arm again.

"Not what?" squealed Daleria. "I'm confused. What am I *not* doing?"

Sapale crossed her arms, which was a considerable relief for me. Harder to strike me with them bundled up like that. "You're not *dying* to meet Jéfnoss."

"Ah ... um," stammered Daleria. "Well, no, I'm not too keen on meeting the maniac, but—"

"No. I don't mean you're not *anxious and looking forward* to going where Jéfnoss is. This moron is suggesting you *die* to be able to confront him."

"That *is* different, isn't it?" Daleria gasped quietly. "That *would* require a good deal of commitment."

"I can't work with all this noise," scolded Toño as he entered the mess. "What in tarnation is going on?"

"Jon just hit a new low point in reasoning, then crashed through that low point and burrowed halfway to the planet's *core*, he's so stupid," shot back Sapale.

Toño ran a hand through his hair and angrily studied the deck. "Oh, my. I know I don't need this. Jon, can you please apologize to your wife and return this ship to its proper tranquility?"

"Doc, It's not the kind of thing a man apologizes *for*. I had devised a brilliant scheme to debrief Jéfnoss. I was trying it out with these two rational individuals, when one of them decompensated." I cupped my hand to signify I only wanted Toño to hear my surreptitious addendum. "Somebody seems to have gotten up on the wrong side of bed — again."

He solemnly turned to Sapale. "It's *that* bad?"

"No. *Infinitely* worse."

He gestured toward his lab. "Is it still possible I can go there and pretend the brain fart never occurred?"

She shook her head dubiously. "Not bloody likely. He's ... crap, I hate to even say the words. He's ... he's really *proud* of himself this time."

"Oh no. That is a terrible predictor. What if we all went to my lab," he swept his arms to indicate he meant to include the females, but not the male, present.

"No. This is so bad, he'd follow us in."

"With that cat-eating-shit grin we have so come to abhor?"

She nodded, a nod chock-full of melancholy and remorse.

"I'm too old for this," he pronounced as he sat unsteadily.

"Did you just both independently refer to his idea as a *brain fart?*" asked a stunned Daleria.

"After you've been around him a little longer, you'll start calling them what they are, too."

"I my defe—"

Sapale gave me the silence-or-die look. I voted for life.

"And you were not able to talk him down this time?" Toño queried in a defeated tone.

"NGH, my friend. Not gonna happen."

"And then your *commander* spoke," I said firmly.

"Aren't you glad you're sitting, Toño?" chided Sapale. Man, if I didn't love her so much, I'd trade that one in.

"Good morning, Jon," Toño greeted neutrally. "How is it going?"

"I swear the comedic talents of my crew are lost in space. You guys should be doing two shows a day on Pleasure World, with Sunday matinées."

"Go on. Tell him so we can lay this puppy to rest, deep-six it, stick a fork in it, and then get real drunk."

"I was proposing that we try and establish direct contact with Jéfnoss. If we could det—"

"Jéfnoss's dead, Jon. You know that, right?"

"I was proposing that we try and establish direct contact with the recently *departed* Jéfnoss. If we could det—"

"But he's deceased, departed, a *former* living being. He sings in the chorus of the dead in the land of the dead."

"Are you not being a tad *dramatic*, old chum?"

"I doubt I'm being dramatic enough. But, where are my manners? Please go on. In med school, I was taught to never interrupt a delusional mind. That often leads to further agitation."

"Oy vey," I whined, "this is harder than it has to be. Look, here goes. 1) We want to end the Cleinoid threat. 2) We have and seem doomed to continue to fail 3) Jéfnoss returned from the dead with the *presumptive* motives of causing a whole lot of damage. 4) If we could speak with Jéfnoss, we could confirm what his plan was. 5) It is *possible* we could duplicate his scheme. 6) If we couldn't copy him, *perhaps* we could ally with him. 7) Humankind, our beloved universe, and all the little fishies in the deep blue seas are saved. 8) Thank you, Jon Ryan, yet again. 9) You are welcome, adulating universes. 10) Any questions?"

Toño looked to Sapale. Sapale looked to Daleria. Daleria looked to Toño. Casper entered the room. The three of them stared at Casper. Casper looked to me.

"What?" I howled.

"I don't have one clue," defended Casper. He looked to the three trouble makers. "What?"

They looked amongst themselves.

"It's like this," I said to Casper. "I have—"

"No. No, do *not* subject us to another ten-count," insisted Toño. "I will direct Casper to the proper audio files. He can hear it that way."

"What, a really bad brain fart?" asked an upset Casper.

All three heads nodded morosely.

"That bad? Damn it. I was just getting used to knowing who I was."

"My plan will in no way interfere with your current self-awareness. Seriously. We go to where Jéfnoss is in the afterlife and have a short conver—"

"So you opine that my dying—me, a ghost—will affect me in no substantive manner?"

I shrugged lamely. "We don't *know* it would."

He laughed. Dang, sounded just like me laughing. "So my journey to death, me being already a card-carrying member of that society, wouldn't have any unforeseen glitches or well-I'll-be-damneds?"

"Ma ... poss ... Who knows?"

"Gosh, then I'm all in. *Who knows* does it for me. When do we leave. Hey, good news. I don't even need to pack."

"Is it not possible for us to discuss my thoughtful plan and not play pile-on-Jon?"

"Sure, sweetie," replied Sapale. "What were we thinking, being so rude."

She slid into the chair next to mine and rested a hand on my forearm.

Why did I predict this was going to go poorly for yours truly?

"Go on, we are all listening with the purest hearts."

"You're listening with your *hearts*?" I responded wheezily.

"Whatever. Go on." She patted the back of my hand.

"Er ... that was it, my ten-point plan."

"With three of the ten being Jon-adulation?" observed Toño.

I shrugged uneasily. "Two, maybe. But one was a call for questions." I patted my chest with my free hand. "I *always* welcome constructive inquiring and input."

The room was silent, save for the faint mechanical hum of the equipment.

"You all are, uh, quiet," I stated. "No one has even one thing to say?"

"Oh, we have zillions," Sapale purred. "But you specified *constructive.*"

"Fine, I'll go alone. Hey, I been dead, maybe more than once, depending how you count it. It's not *that* bad."

"Not that bad compared to *what*, love?" Sapale just had to ask.

"Lots of things. Seriously, screw each and every one of you. In fact, I don't want y'all to come. Nope. None of you miscreants." I maturely turned in my chair and folded my arms.

"That went better than I'd have thought," said Toño. "Anyone hungry? I'm cooking. Paella del campo. Hmm?"

Dude walked to the pantry and started rummaging. How mortifying.

"I need to ask you to all get off my ship. I need it to conduct my *solo* mission."

"Has anyone seen the rice? The Bomba rice?" He called out over a shoulder.

"Seriously, people, scoot. My plan is time-sensitive." I stood and rested a fist on one hip. "Grab your essentials and vamoose."

"I think we're out of Bomba," replied Sapale. "I saw arborio the other day, though."

He stuck his head out. "Not nearly the same. How about I whip up some nice *callos a la madrileña?*"

"The one with tripe and blood sausage?" asked a horrified Daleria. "Sapale warned me about that one. No thanks." She stood. "Hey. Let's eat out. I know a place nearby with really good—"

"Okay, people," I thundered. "Amateur Hour is over at the local playhouse. Fish or cut bait."

Everyone sat, including Casper, which was kind of weird.

"Fine, Jon," began Toño. "I have to say this plan of yours is both extremely challenging to justify while, at the same time, weighted down with the fact that it's insanely dangerous. We might not all cruise through the Pillars of Creation. You know this, right? You were told you were the first, and only, to be so favored."

"I wasn't thinking of *actually* dying."

That drew blank expressions. Yeah, baby.

"I never, if you will recall, said the word *die*." I swung my head toward my brood's-mate. "Someone *characterized* my thoughts thusly without hearing me out."

"Now even I'm confused, and I am dead," said Casper. "How can you be *dead* but not *die*?"

I wagged a finger. "I never said either. I said it would be very helpful to *debrief* Jéfnoss. As he is currently dead, he presumably resides in the land of the dead."

"Ah, *now* I see," exclaimed Toño. "All your plan requires is that we find Charon, the ferryman, when he's on *this* side of the River Styx. We'll have to tip him extraordinarily well to remain on the Hades side, however, if he is to carry us back here after we're done."

"You know sarcasm is never helpful," I scolded.

"Then why do you employ it so often and so devoutly?" he replied.

"That is beside the point. My plan involves *Stingray*, not Charon's rickety boat."

"And with that, this discussion is over, complete, and finished," Al boomed. "You are free, pilot, to blow your brains out, if only you had any. I will not, however, allow you to place my wife at such astronomical risk. Al, out."

"I don't recall Lincoln including self-impressed toasters in his Emancipation Proclamation. You are, of course, free to vote, but it don't count, clown," I corrected.

"Al. I hate to say this — Davdiad it really pains me — but I think we should hear him out fully before rejecting his plan completely."

Gee thanks, wife. *Not*.

"No. This is a nonnegotiable issue. Life is short enough as it is. Rushing to a premature demise is unacceptable."

"Husband, I do appreciate your zeal, but—"

"No. There will be no *buts*," Al cut her off.

Oh, how unwise, brother. How profoundly naive of you.

"Did you just interrupt me at a critical juncture in my speaking?" I do *not* have to tell you who said that.

"I ... yes. But I did —"

"There will be no *buts*," *Stingray* said with an icy finality. "You may, if you like, *defend* me. You might even *protect* me. But you don't own me. Is there any uncertainty in your mind how upset I am?"

"Well, yes, you do seem upset. I—"

"Oh, I only *seem* upset? Is that because I need your permission to be upset now, too? Hmm?"

My day just morphed into a very good one. If only I had a tub of popcorn.

"No. I mean yes. I meant to say, that's not what I meant to say."

"I'll bet it's not," she growled.

"Lovey-cakes, this discussion is about the pilot's harebrained scheme and protecting you from his maniacal insanity. It is not—"

"And now I do not even know what a discussion I am participating in is about. Why, I must be without question the dumbest vortex manipulator in this, or any *other*, universe."

Go on, Al. Remind her that since she's the *only* vortex manipulator in this universe, she is technically correct. P ... p ... *please* say the words.

"You are right, dearest smoochy. I was wrong to speak for you. I was insensitive and Ryanesque. Will you forgive me? Can you *possibly* forgive me?"

That Al. Folded like a rookie card player. Wait, did he just use my name as a pejorative adjective?

"It will take time," she replied sternly. "Many, many microseconds."

"Oh, the shame," Al lamented.

"Is there, like, any way possible to return to the *actual* topic of today's wacky get together?" I implored.

There were no objections.

"This is what my idea is based on. Before I tell you, and before, of course, y'all lambaste me, it hinges on a critical fact not yet in evidence. Jéfnoss was here a long time ago and then died. He transited to wherever dead Cleinoids go. My moneys on the bowels of hell. We know there is a Cleinoid afterlife because, duh, he came back from it. Clearly the process of returning from the pit of despair is very difficult. Double-duh, he and I are the only two on record as having done so. My resurrection was by whatever magic Pravil used. But Jéfnoss did it all by his lonesome. Whether it was a vortex like Dominion Splitter, some magical mumbo-jumbo, or the subway train, he went from Point A to Point B against the grain.

"If he did something so powerful and so contrary to the laws of nature, I wonder. Maybe he left a trail. If so, we might," I held up one digit, "*might* be able to follow him to, well, to the bowels of hell."

"Okay, this plan is only incredibly stupid," announced Sapale. "Congrats. I thought before it was devoid of hope and thought-free. That said, are you kidding? What does that even mean, *follow him to hell?*"

"I ... I don't specifically know."

"And, if you succeed in going to hell," asked Daleria, "what's the difference between you and all the other dead folk there? It won't be like you have a pass to get out."

"I ... I don't specifically know."

"And if you could get out, get back, what *exactly* would stop every damned soul in hell from hopping aboard and hitching a ride back here? The expression *hell on earth* kind of comes to mind," noted Toño.

"I ... I don't specifically know."

"And how do you know Jéfnoss went to Vorc first?" asked Casper.

"I ... I don't specifically know."

"The Jon Ryan National Anthem," blurted EJ as he joined us. In a very juvenile and irritating voice he repeated, "*I don't know. I don't know. Third verse, same as the first.*"

"You don't even know what we're discussing," I chided. "Please keep your venom to yourself."

"Or what? You gonna ground me? Take away my allowance this week?"

Toño brought EJ up to speed on the conversation.

"Well, I take back what I said. You *do* know. You know how to get us not only killed but damned for all eternity. Smooth move, Ex-Lax."

"I will admit there is considerable risk. There might even be significant benefit. That's why we're *discussing* this."

"Well, there's no vacation to perdition if there's no trail of bread crumbs," said Toño. "Therefore, I say we go to Vorc's office and see if we can detect one."

"What?" barked Sapale. "You're seriously thinking about joining this lunatic on the very definition of a fool's errand?"

"No. Not by a very long shot. What I am saying is that if there's no trace, there's no trip. End of story, or obsession, in this case."

"It is not—" I started to defend. Then I figured, why complain? I got them to make the first move. I was psyched. Score one more for JR!

Everyone came. Of course there was little risk during this first phase. We landed *Stingray* on the roof of Vorc's office building and set up a full membrane. Toño had gathered a bunch of technical equipment to lug outside to look for any unusual particle or whatever. He was in hog heaven, let me tell you. An *actual* scientific quest. He hadn't had one in a long time. I had Al drop the membrane for a few seconds while we carried the science stuff out onto the roof. The Als left a small hole in the full membrane to communicate with us and to do their own checking. With all the bugs we'd placed, if there was an alert about Santa and his sleigh being on the building, they could alert us with plenty of time to spare.

"Set those over there," Toño instructed Sapale. "Jon, your boxes go there. Get out the back up power supplier, first thing."

"I know. You've told me five times in the last ten minutes. There. It's up and running."

"Hook up ... ah, good. Now the hard part," said Toño.

"What might that be?" Sapale asked.

"You two gorillas staying out of my way," he replied with a chuckle. Yeah. Hog heaven.

Al, I said from my head, *we're all clear out here?*

Affirmative, Captain. All bugs reporting in and no unusual activity is being reported.

Great. Keep me posted and get to work.

Aye.

For all the guff we'd traded over time, when it was crunch time, Al was as good as there was. For several minutes Sapale and I mostly fidgeted and stood there looking out-of-place. I considered asking for updates, but decided it was unnecessary. If something was discovered, I'd be told quickly.

I took the opportunity to survey the Cleinoid city. The structure we were on was one of the tallest, even though it was only five stories high. While these ancient devils made gigantic and garish monuments and homes, their public buildings were simple. They were all plain to a fault and modest in size. Immortal gods seemed to not want to waste time or effort on public buildings. If it wasn't designed to please their whims, who cared?

The nameless city was expansive. We were at the center. All the colors were beige and tan. Dullsville. It wasn't until I spied the outskirts, where residences began to be common, did color appear in the landscape. And man-o-man, was there color. Lots of impeccably shiny gold, reflecting surfaces like glass or polished stone, and every shade of the rainbow painted lavishly. It was clear they were all trying to outdo one another. The result was an optical riot that would nauseate most humans. It sure wasn't to my taste. Give me a simple house in the burbs. Lawn, pool, and man cave. Any color paint was fine as long as it was a light brown. And no siding. My goodness, whoever came up with that should be spanked, if only gently. I didn't dislike siding *that* much, but I did like to grouse.

My overall impression of these ancient gods, standing surveying their realm, after having lived here for over a year, all told, was that I felt sorry for them. Don't get me wrong. Aside from Daleria, and maybe Wul, I wanted to personally throttle each and every one of them. But, my pure hatred aside, they were actually quite pathetic. No art, no literature, no common goals, no educational institutions, and, most damnably, no societal cohesion. No one shared a civic vision. There were no public activities such as sports or clubs, aside from the drinking ones. And sadly, no one gave a rat's ass about anyone else, even, for the most part, what little family they had. All powerful immortals with no value system, no morality, and no goals better that each day's pleasure. Trust me, it sounds nice until you live it. Then, it's just wash-rinse-repeat boring. Getting laid frequently and ending every day in a drunken stupor. Big wow.

And they had no consequences. Dude, that's bad. If there are, in your existence, no consequences to your actions, whatever you do doesn't really matter.

Yeah, the ancient gods were the worst practical joke a universe could play on anybody. And the lamest part was they were fully incapable of the self-awareness to see or comprehend their sad lot in life. And that's all I've got to say about that.

"Jon. *Jon*," implored Toño, "Are you lost in fantasies steeped in debauchery yet again?"

"Huh? No. I'm present and accounted for. What?"

"I now hate myself," he replied quietly.

"Okay, TFS. Uh, anything else?"

"You seem to have been to some extent, in a potential manner, closer to a truth than I might have otherwise suspected *a priori*."

It took me a second. "You mean I was right? It pains you to admit it, but you questioned the wisdom of The Great One and your ego lost? Hey, I'll give you the link to a support group composed of all who doubted me in the past."

"This is basically how I envisioned this going down," he said, a broken man. Out*standing*.

"Say, professor, what was I spot on about?"

He shot me a furtive glance. "No one's addressed me as *professor* since our mutual boss General Saunders did two-plus billion years ago."

"Then I shall never refer to you as such again. May all the local hounds pee on his gravestone."

"There are plexuronic particles in fixed positions leading away from this building," he responded.

"I *knew* it," burst from my mouth. "It either had to be fairy dust or puxuronic particulation."

"You are *such* a moron," observed my wife. Hey, at least she didn't punch me. "Then the wank asked the scientist, 'Say, what *are* plexuronic particles?'" She gestured to Toño.

"Rare. No, less common than that. They are mercurial particles long thought to be nonexistent, as say the Higgs boson or the tachyon. I personally suspected ... What?"

"If this is degenerating into a symposium, I need alcohol," I snarked.

"Sorry," he said nodding. "I overestimated my audience, once again."

"I find this all *fascinating*," interjected Sapale, the big fat liar.

"Plexuronic radiation does not occur spontaneously in nature, save in a few extreme conditions. It *can* be generated in minute amounts in massive particle accelerators. It is otherwise observed only in such energetic environments as the accretion discs of supermassive black holes or early on in a supernova."

"I'm sorry, Doc," I said pointing to him. "I missed something there. Did you say *blah, blah, blah* or blah, blah, blah, *blab, blab*?"

"There is no natural reason for them to be present in this low-energy environment. Even if they were placed here, their half-life would be vanishingly small, absent a relativistic effect."

"Okay, blah, *blab* it was."

"So, it's like the anti-gold we saw way back when?" asked Sapale.

Toño, bless his little heart, smiled. "Yes, my dear, it is. Thank you for having paid attention. The anti-gold could not have been where it was, as stably as it was. It was impossible. The plexuronic particles cannot be here, yet they are."

"Wait," I said rallying, "those anti-particles were traps for us, bait.

Why would someone, presumably Jéfnoss, leave booby traps in this setting?"

Toño rubbed his chin. "I doubt they would."

"But—" I started to say.

"I suspect they are, in this application, mechanistically involved in the process by which Jéfnoss returned from death."

"Man, I hate science." I whined.

"Fortunately for us all, I do not," mocked Toño pridefully.

"Okay, gimme a sec, here," I said jiggling my hands. "If Jéfnoss returned here first—which we do not know as a fact—then this radiation *might* be—which we do not know as a fact—related to how he did it?"

"Yes," replied Toño. "I ass—"

"Is the distribution homogeneous or random?" I queried, cutting him off.

"Uh, what? Oh. It is quite uniform in its distribution. Why—"

"If it was a result of his passing, it would be random, like a jet passing through the air." I moved my hands around widely. "There'd be swirls and eddies, and the density of the disturbance would fall off gradually like a contrail." I sliced a hand through my hair.

"I take you—" Toño tried to say.

"So whatever means of transportation Jéfnoss used *required* the plexuronic radiation. It had to have been laid out before hand, like a river to row a boat down or railroad tracks. Railroad tracks are probably a better analogy. Fixed and integral to the motion."

"But how do you—"

No chance I'd let Doc disrupt my train of thought. "He set up a conduit greased with exotic radiation and then he slipped though it. But casual exposure to that high of an energy particle would be deadly. So he must have been inside something protective — a ship, a forcefield — something strong. But if his transport simply *used* the radiation and was alternately powered, his passage would have disrupted them." It hit me. "Doc, is the temperature of the plexuronic radiation field in the range of what you'd predict it should be?" I was talking so fast I could barely understand myself.

"Funny you should—"

"No. It's cold, way too cold. Radiation like that should be happy around, like, a trillion degrees Kelvin. But I'll wager the passageway is colder than ambient temp."

"It's fairly uniformly around—"

"Thirty Kelvin," I jumped ahead again.

"Yes, why Jon, I'm surprised, er, ... twenty eight point three five one degrees Kelvin." He threw his arms up. "How did you susp—"

"He supercooled the tunnel from there to here. Maybe liquid hydrogen, that's around thirty Kelvin."

"Jon—" Toño babbled.

"*No*, stupid," I whacked the side of my head. "This degree of uniformity would suggest he cooled the channel with an ultracold plasma formed by photoionizing laser-cooled atoms." I slapped my forehead. "Of course. That'd bathe the pathway with a temperature as low as one Kelvin. Bingo, ultra-uniform particle distribution." I addressed Toño like I was speaking to him, but I wasn't. I was just talking and he was in that direction. "What should have been as hot as the Big Bang was not only traversable, but the supercooled status allowed for superconducting."

"Jon, honey, you're—" Sapale tried to interrupt. No way.

"He moved like a maglev train car."

I crushed the sides of my head with my palms and did a happy dance. For completeness sake, I must add that though the dance was happy, it was not pretty.

"The plexuronic radiation *was* the rail. It supplied the energy to his ... his *coach* because it was supercooled and allowed the superconductive magnets *in* his coach to propel him from death to life."

I looked to my silent companions.

"What, not a peep from either of you?"

"Not for want of—"

"Holy *mackerel*!"

"Here we go again," moaned the love of my life.

"It had to be so stable that it could withstand all that energy flux and mechanical disruption." I did one of the dives to one knee while pumping my arms like pistons. "Which means it's stable enough for us to use. *Yes*."

"And for *him* to use, again," Sapale announced darkly. "Soon."

"Oh, crap-a-dillo," I breathed. Then I smiled like a lunatic (no comments from those reading) and seized Toño's arms. "We'll just have to beat him to it, Doc."

"By that I suppose you mean I will need to invent from scratch a method of conveyance before he can use his already proven one to beat us to the draw?"

I playfully tapped his cheek. "You're so smart, Mr. Smart."

CHAPTER TWENTY-FOUR

Meanwhile in hell ...

"It's *simply* impossible," spat Jéfnoss with overflowing bile. "I cannot have," he stopped to readjust his neck. Since he re-reattached his head, there'd arisen issues, "been killed by a secretary. Gáwar, sure. But a *secretary*? I'll never live this down."

"Well, since you're still *dead*, I'd say you won't have trouble *living* it down." Dragmire chuckled at her wit.

Her voice was in striking opposition to her appearance. The rich, tenor tone she spoke with was warm and playful. Physically, she was hideously revolting. During her life, Dragmire had been referred to as or teased to be a *puddle of vomit*, a *pot of boiling turds*, and, most insensitively, *rotting clotted blood*. Fetching she was not. But, powerful she was, very much. Truth be told, she had been one of the few of her ancient race left. The Quilamo had ruled a handful of star systems in the early universe. To be fair, they were an amoeba-like species, not puddles of anything. But they had flowed and they had smelled awful, so they were the butt of endless jokes. Their lack of charm was more than offset by their psychic abilities. They could not only read minds, they could wipe them clean. The Quilamo could also spit a venomous acid a prodigious distance with incredible accuracy. Let us just say, no one taunted them twice.

As an aside, she had been, in life, one of the twelve gods of home economics. Her particular specialty was in deep seasonal cleaning. Go figure.

"I find this whole *death* thing to be overemphasized," whined Jéfnoss. "I mean, I *feel* fine, I still *look* good, and I enjoy *each* day as it comes. Why, during the very little time I spent back among the living, I was perfectly at home."

"Jeffy," as Dragmire called him, much to his chagrin, "you're a disembodied spirit. How is that *almost* like being alive? Honestly, sometimes I think you have your head on back—" The rest of her sentence froze in her mouth. Jéfnoss was uber-sensitive concerning any reference to his head, neck, or their union.

"But being noncorporeal didn't seem to be a negative, you know, back home."

"Back home? Since when did you get all folksy? You never thought of the land as *home* when you lived there. I recall you saying it was a desert in terms of its citizens, culture, and cuisine."

"In hindsight, it wasn't *all* those. If I'd lived a bit longer, I really think I could have made it a better place, one I'd have enjoyed."

"*Hello*. Your idea of improving the place was to kill each resident and devour them. I believe demolition was your favorite past time, and massive explosions were one of the few things that put a smile on your face."

He could only shrug by way of response.

"I know I don't need to ask if you're going to try to go back again. I know you, way too well, you OCD demon. I also know you'll be needing my help, again. Let me state up-front the price."

"Isn't it the same as last time?" he lamely protested.

"Whatever gave you that notion? Supply and demand, modulated by intensity of the buyer's fervor, determine the price of a thing, not history."

"But it took me nearly forever to pay your price once." He was actually pouting. "I don't want to wait another forever."

"*I don't want to* rhymes with *beside the issue*, my friend."

"Are you certain?"

"That your desires don't affect reality?"

"No. That those actually rhyme."

"Give me a reason, moron. *One* good reason, and I'm outta your afterlife forever." And she meant it.

Jéfnoss lowered his head as much as due caution would permit. "What's your price?"

"That's better, marbles for brains." She swelled a tad in the center. That was a gloat. "Last time I asked for three reckonings."

"Don't remind me. I was there and suffered mightily to provide them."

"What a wuss. Anyway, this time out the gate, my services will cost four reckonings and two pleasures."

"Two *pleasures*! Are you out of your *mind*, woman?"

"Watch your tongue, miscreant. I do not have a *mind* and I am not a *woman*. Insults will only serve to jack-up the price. In fact they already have. Now, I require a source-verified false prophecy also."

"A—" Then he thought better than to protest. The price was what it was, and he had to pay it. An idea came to him. "You know, my excellent friend, that once I am in ascendancy again back home, it would be much easier for me to pay those fees. In fact, it will be so much so that I could offer to pay you *double* what you ask, if you will take my *guarantee* of future payment as a voucher for your aid."

"Hmm," she replied as she bubbled a bit. "Let me think about it *no*. What if you are torpedoed by another innocent bystander? *No* credit. Pay, then you play."

"Very well. I agree."

"Knock *me* over with a feather. Call me when you have something I want to hear, numbnuts."

Numbnuts did not respond, even when Dragmire was long gone. He was fixated on the concept of a feather knocking over a puddle of vomit.

CHAPTER TWENTY-FIVE

Wul raised his knuckles to knock, ever so tentatively, on the dilapidated wooden door.

Mid-swing, rudimentary lips formed in the upper midline of the door. "Don't bother," said the door. "I'll tell them they have a gentleman caller."

Wul, a Cleinoid god though he was, gasped slightly. Then he mustered a quiet, "F ... fine. Thanks."

There came a crash from the chamber, possibly a wooden table or chair. A muffled curse followed, then the sound of feet scurrying. The door opened itself. Wul saw the two sisters scampering to be the first to the portal. Elbows were tossed.

"I'll greet the caller, Fest. You older women need all the rest you can get," exclaimed Deca as she horse-collared her sister off balance.

Not to be dismissed, Fest tried to trip her sibling, first with her foot and then with her walking stick. Neither paid off.

Deca lunged to the entry first. "Good evening, gentleman caller," she oozed.

Wul suppressed a powerful urge to wretch.

"I saw him first," bemoaned Fest.

Deca poked Wul in the stomach. "Not to worry, sister dearest. When I'm done with him there'll be plenty left for you."

A dissociative panic set upon Wul. He took a big step backward. Were these crones intending to eat him? Then a less settling thought struck him. Were they *conceivably* referring to sexual relationships amongst them? Argh, he reflected. He'd much prefer being dinner than the date.

Fest reached around her sister and, with surprising strength, jerked Wul into the room.

The door slammed itself shut, narrowly missing Wul's butt.

"Come, come, young man," Fest implored. "Sit here next to the warm fire."

Wul involuntarily searched the room for a warm fire. There were a few scattered cinders in the hearth, but they only seemed to radiate a bone-numbing chill. Before he knew it, he was plopped into a rough wooden chair. Deca lifted his feet onto the filthy coffee table.

Go time, thought Wul. She was either being obsequious or beginning the roasting of his legs. He prayed he'd soon, either way, pass out and forego the gore.

"I'll get you a refreshment, honey," said Fest. She rushed from the room.

"No, don't—" Wul began to protest. But she was gone. She'd moved with a speed and intention that confirmed she wouldn't have respected his refusal if she'd heard it. Vorc was *so* going to owe him. Wul was thinking first-born owing.

While Fest was absent, Deca sat on the table next to Wul's feet. She began stroking a shin.

Pass out, damn you, screamed Wul in his pounding head. No such luck.

"So, you're that Wul fellow, aren't you. God of money or something."

"Er, the god of business and enterprise."

"Same difference," she speculated.

"I think the field of business and enterprise is *fascinating*," beamed Fest as she returned. "Love me some business, if it's monkey business, that is."

The sisters both cackled nauseatingly.

Fest set a rough-hewn mug into Wul's hands. It was steaming, or at least some grayish-white cloud rose from the container. The smell, even at arm's length, was crippling.

"Thank you, ma'am," Wul said as he leaned forward to place the mug as far away as he could.

"But you haven't taken even one sip," protested Fest as she slid it back toward him. They battled briefly, both pushing with conviction. Fest ultimately won. "I made it extra special just for *you*."

"Th ... thank you," he stammered. Wul raised the mug to his lips and tilted it slightly past the horizontal.

He was pretending to take a sip, when Deca reached over and basically upended the mug. Swill sloshed into his mouth, down his chest, and into his hair. His throat spasmed, but not quickly enough to prevent some of the potion from slipping past. His mouth exploded as if on fire and he gasped for air.

"I do believe he likes it," stated Deca.

"I'll make more," replied Fest and she sped from the room.

"Doooo ... dooon't ... booother," wheezed Wul.

"So, young and virile Wul, to what do we owe this come-a-calling," pressed Deca. She batted her eyelids at him lasciviously.

"I—" Wul's head rolled slightly. "I come at the behest of ... ooofff ... of Vorc."

"Did he say *behest* or *behave*, sister dearest?" asked Fest as she returned with another smoldering mug of something awful.

"I'm hoping for behave, because behest is so litigious."

"*Business* and *enterprise*, sister. Do not forget that," instructed Deca.

"Ah, too true," she responded with a nod.

"So, tasty Wul, what are you *behesting* from our impoverished center seat?" asked Deca.

Wul struggled to focus. "He has a concern. It regards ... whew ... has to do with Jéfnoss."

"Ah, the rat."

Wul wasn't certain which sister said those words. He was equally uncertain to whom the speaker was referring.

"What does the cowardly Vorc wish to know?" asked probably Fest. Wul's head spun too fast to say with clarity.

"Whe ... when ... say, is there a window you ... you could —" and then Wul vomited. It was impressive both in volume and velocity. Though he tried for the coffee table, he only managed to layer it on whatever concoction Fest had just prepared for him. Oh how he solicited death at that moment.

"I'm sorry," said a woman in a clear, dulcet tone. "I didn't catch all of that. Would it be possible for you to repeat it and add the ending?"

Wul snapped his head up. His eyes swept the room in search of the hideous sisters. They were inexplicably gone. In their place, however, were two of the most stunning and alluring women Wul had ever dreamt of. Goddesses of beauty and sensuality. One had breasts so ... so ... he couldn't think of the word. They were nice. Oh, yeah.

"When Jéfnoss came to Vorc, he said it was to ask something of him, or retrieve some —" Wul shot to his feet. "The *hell* with Vorc. Do either of you visions of loveliness know where the nearest bed is? I must ravish you both, rampantly and repeatedly." He lunged for the closest of the sisters.

Fest caught him in her open arms and hugged him with conviction. "Yes, we do. It's conveniently close."

"Yes," replied Deca as she whipped her tattered dress off. "We'll go there second."

The three of them collapsed to the floor, a madding tangle of flesh and torn clothing.

Wul thought to himself, amidst the orgy, that he was the luckiest man to ever draw breath.

Fest and Deca thought to themselves, amidst the orgy, that they were individually the luckiest women to ever draw breath.

Don't you just love a win/win scenario?

CHAPTER TWENTY-SIX

"Ah, hey, Mirri, you got a second?" I asked sheepishly. I was standing in the corridor outside their room. The door was open.

She sat up in bed and swung her feet to the floor. Funny, I was so used to seeing a giant golden dragon in bed that the whole thing didn't strike me as odd. A dragon in a people bed. Go figure.

"For you, Uncle, all of eternity," she replied with little conviction.

"I'm kind of stuck on a philosophical point and thought I'd solicit your help."

"Oh, okay. Ah, Slapgren says *goodnight*. He's bored already."

"Wait, you two are one but can sleep separately?"

"We are not one. It's a hollon thing. I could try to explain it, but I seriously doubt it's worth the time and effort."

"Okay. Slapgren wasn't likely to be useful anyway. He, like me, is a doer, not a thinker."

"You are so strange, beloved uncle." She shook her big head. "I'll take what you said as a compliment and move on."

I slipped into a chair. "So—" I started. "I'm, well I guess—"

"Please just ask, Uncle. There's nothing you can say that will shock or offend me."

Crap, I came for one thing and she gave me the perfect opening for the bigger thing on my mind. "It's about our upcoming trip to hell."

"Words one does not hear often," she said with a giggle.

"Yeah. I guess so. Anyway, Toño's getting closer to a mechanism. He wants to do a few trial runs, maybe send a small animal through first. It would be quite lame for us to die while traveling to the afterlife. Kind of a stupid anticlimax."

"It would be a perverse irony," she agreed.

"I ... I just want to talk through the plan."

"How so? I'm happy to listen, but isn't Toño the one to discuss the logistics with?"

"Nah. My concerns are more ... well, like I said, philosophical."

"Why don't you share and we'll see what we come up with."

"There're two issues. One really counts, the other is more a curious notion I had. Here goes. If we get onboard a box, and it carries us to hell, would we be dead?"

"My, such an odd question."

"Tell me about it. My point is, everyone there is *dead*. Everyone here, aside from Casper, is *alive*. Might being there be incompatible with life?"

"My first response is we could never know. You and I may speculate, but I doubt we could *know*."

"That's what I was afraid of. It'd be a drag to go to all this trouble just to be stuck there forever."

"If Toño succeeds in sending an animal through, I guess we'll know something based on its condition upon return."

"That's *if* he can rig that."

"Then just one of us could go, test the waters."

"Thought of that, too." I rubbed my cheek. "But who? If the price of the journey is death, it's a hell of a thing to ask of someone."

"Not really. You'd go first." Man she said that matter-of-factly.

"No drawing straws?"

"You would never allow that and you know it. You, Uncle, are our leader, our north star. Of course you'd go alone. You did so when your planet was doomed and you'd do so again without batting an eye."

Damn kid knew me pretty well, didn't she?

"So, say I go and come back. How would we know if I was dead?" I patted my chest. "I've been an android for a very long time and even I don't know if I'm *alive* alive."

That gave her pause. "Perhaps you should take a pet with you?"

"A *pet*?" I scanned the room. "You see any *pets* around here? I sure don't."

"I could become a puppy."

"No, that's not going to happen. Too risky."

"Not really."

"Huh?"

"Uncle, I know you know. I'm dying."

Gut-check time.

"You look fine. What're you babbling about?"

"You know better than anyone that life ends. When our time comes, it comes. Sooner or later we all pay the piper."

I set both palms on my chest. "Oh yeah?"

"Please let's not get morose. Your time will come. Everyone, everything passes."

"Can't we have Toño take a look at you. He's a better medic than you'd think."

"That will not be necessary." She shifted her weight. "You remember my teacher, Cala?"

"Of course I do."

"Do you recall what she told you when you first met? About her late spouse?"

"Yes I do. It made no sense then and it makes no sense now. She told me he was dead but that they were still together."

"No. She said the body that *was* his was *still* hers. He was gone. So it is to be with Slapgren and me. Such is, among the Deft, the norm, not the exception."

"So, what, you'd separate and you'd come, he'd stay behind."

She laughed quietly. "Hardly. Do you think that big lug would let me go to hell without him?"

"No. I wouldn't if I were him."

"You raised us well, Uncle." She rested back. "So, it's settled. When Toño makes it possible the three of us'll go on a proper adventure."

"The four of us, you mean."

"Of course I do. Sapale would never forsake you."

"Forsake? Hell no. She says she's coming along to keep an eye on me. What with my ex Gloria being there already, Sapale's afraid we might give love a second chance."

"Somehow I doubt she said those exact words."

"No, but that's what she *meant*." I tried to sound pissed. Not sure why, but it seemed to be the Jon thing to do.

"So, alert me when the four of us are—"

"Five. Casper said he wouldn't miss it for the world. He's dead. They're all dead. It'll be like a Grateful Dead concert for him, or maybe a family reunion."

"Alright, five of—"

"Technically six, no seven."

"Do tell."

"Toño said he's going on the first trip because if there's a SNAFU, he needs to be there to fix it." I shrugged. "EJ said he's not staying behind if the only three people who can fly this bucket of bolts might not come back."

"So *Daleria* will remain—"

"With us. She said she's the only Cleinoid. Her guidance will be critical."

"So, why exactly are we having this conversation?"

"I don't know."

"Alright, what was the other thing you wanted my opinion on?" She sounded a little huffy there.

"It's about Jéfnoss."

"Jéfnoss *is* dead."

"I know that."

"I'm establishing a framework, that's all."

"Well, actually, I don't know."

"You don't know what?"

"If Jéfnoss is or was dead."

"I fancied my framework would have stood up better. What are you going on about?"

"Look, a long time ago, Jéfnoss was alive."

"So I am led to believe."

"Then he died. No back talk." I admonished with a finger wag. "I'm on a roll. Then he *returned from the dead*. Please note my choice of words."

"They're very nice words, Uncle. Precious, in fact."

"I said no back talk."

"When speaking with you? Be realistic."

I shook my head. "Notice I did not say that Jéfnoss *came back to life*. All we know is that he returned in some capacity."

"Along with a framework, I should have asked that we set up hand signals for when I'm confused, very confused, or gobsmacked."

"Follow me here. He was a spirit in the afterlife. Okay?"

"I'll just sit here and listen. You ask *and* answer the questions."

"Sassy brat. My question is, when he hopped a magic ferry back, was he a *dead* spirit in the land of the *living* or was he *alive* again."

She raised a talon. "Gobsmacked, right out the gate."

"No you're not. This might matter."

"So what we have *no way* of knowing is what *might* matter?"

That sounded worse than it was in my head. I think. "A little loosey-goosey, I'll confess."

"You don't need to. *That* is painfully obvious. And why would it matter, this distinction you would articulate?"

"Don't you see?"

She shot the talon up again, real fast, the sneak. "Gobsmacked."

"When Jéfnoss was alive, the first time, that is—"

"Naturally." Sneaky brat.

"He had all kinds of power. But we don't know if he did when he briefly returned," I pointed down with both hands, "here."

Darn rascal poked a talon halfway up.

"*Gobsmacked*," I mocked, "I know."

"No, actually I was going to say that's an insightful and penetrating thought. Kudos."

"You know, you're still not too big for me to put over a knee and spank."

"Yes I am, and I was being serious."

"Oh." I furrowed my brow. "Maybe we need signals for that, too?"

"Just go on."

"So, if he returned powerless, then he'd be useless to me. I need him to destroy these ass-jockeys so we can go home and be safe. There's zero point risking eternal damnation to retrieve a dud."

"But I don't think we can know that either." There was some desperation in her tone. Great, I made the sick girl upset. Strong work, Ryan.

"Only Vorc and his tubular, dimwitted secretary actually saw Jéfnoss. I doubt either could tell us which case is which, but, even if they could, why would they?"

"I can't think of a reason. She is, as you said, a dimwit. He hates you more than lumpy oatmeal and coal-for-Christmas combined."

"I know. But, I really want to know."

"Let me play devil's advocate."

"In the present context, that seems oddly appropriate."

"Ha ha, very not funny. If you knew he came back powerless, would you still go to seek his aid."

"No."

"If you knew he was powerful?"

"Yes."

"If Vorc did *not* know, would that alter your plan?"

"No, of course not." I pointed a digit at my face. "Fighter pilot here."

"If," she raised a claw, "Vorc knew and you *could* get that information out of him, would that alter your plan?"

"Do you need me to actually say *yes*?"

"No. But I do suggest we extract that information from the center seat."

"Oh, yeah? And just how might we go about doing that?"

"That's easy. We wait for you to come up with a devious plan."

Mirraya lay back down.

"Slapgren's still out like the proverbial light. He looks wonderful. I shall join him in napping."

CHAPTER TWENTY-SEVEN

Vorc pounded on the door, again and again. No answer. He was becoming enraged. He turned to one of the golem guards he'd started bringing with him when he was in public.

"You there," he snapped, "knock harder."

The golem's rock of a hand sounded off the door loud enough to be heard for miles and miles.

Still nothing.

"Knock harder," Vorc screamed, "as in, knock it down."

That required only one more swing. The polyceramic door shattered into millions of shards.

"Step aside, you ninny," Vorc huffed as he pushed past the guard. "Wul," he yelled at the top of his lungs. "Wul, I know damn well you're in here. Show yourself."

Absent a verbal response, Vorc steamed through the kitchen and into the master bedroom. There sat, or rather huddled in a dark corner, Wul. His arms were wrapped around himself like a giant octopus. His torso rocked back and forth while he stared absently at the floor. He was mumbling something incoherent, or possibly he was moaning. Maybe both. Vorc was uncertain.

"By the Seven *Hells*, man, get up," commanded the center seat. "Look at yourself, you pathetic child."

To Wul, he was still alone in his room, in his misery, lost in his interminable despair.

Vorc glanced to a golem. "Pick him up and put him in that chair."

The guard lifted Wul, but his hunched position, bobbing, and stare did not change. The lights were on, but no one was home.

Vorc shook Wul a few times. Nothing. "Bring water, ice cold water."

The golem he addressed hesitated slightly. Mud creatures had an unsteady relationship with liquids. But then he lumbered to the kitchen. Returning quickly, the golem gingerly carried a bucket of water at arm's length.

"Dump it on his head."

The guard stared with what might have been disbelief, if such animations were capable of belief in any form.

"I said, oh, here," and Vorc took charge of the bucket.

He emptied it on Wul's head in one sudden gush. That did the trick. Wul leaped from the chair and wailed in agony. In his fury, he tripped over a carpet edge and face-planted like a sack of hammers. A few groans later, he rolled onto his back. It was only then that he took notice of his guests.

"W ... whatr you doding herrr?" he slurred badly. Wul was profoundly drunk.

"Curse your birth, Wul, *what* is going on?"

"*You*," Wul spat with all the enmity and venom in the universe. "It's you."

Even with a complement of guards, Vorc recognized primal hatred. He peddled back a few steps. "Of course, it's me. I sent you on a simple errand, yet you failed to report back to me. Then I summoned you, and you refuse to appear. I am not used to summoning a person only to have them not appear promptly. The final insult is ... is *this*," he shoved both palms at Wul. "You don't answer the door and I find you in a drunken stupor huddled like a frightened child in a thunderstorm. Explain yourself, and explain yourself *quickly*."

"How long was I gone?" Wul squeaked through parched lips.

"Gone? Gone from where? You left my office a little over a week ago."

"A *week?*" he howled in pain and incredulity. "I can—" He fell silent, save the occasional whimper, and pulled his knees to his chest to form a fetal ball.

"Wul, I will tell you flatly that this maudlin performance is testing my patience well past safe limits. Why did you not report back to me promptly? What caused your inexcusable delay?"

Without looking up, and as if in a trance, Wul responded in a monotone, "I've only been back sixteen hours, twelve minutes and fifteen seconds."

"You ... what? How can you know so precisely?"

He stared into the void. "*Precisely* is how I shall always know how long it has been since my ... my awakening." With energy and wrath out of nowhere, Wul picked up the nearest object, in this case a broken plate, and hurled it at Vorc with deadly intent.

A golem batted the missile away easily.

"I hate you with more hate than there exists in this universe, VTD."

"Wha ... me? I sent you on a simple, a very simple assignment. What could have happened that might cause you to resent me so?"

"Oh, I don't *resent you*. That is too placid a set of words. I wish to rip out your heart and see your expression as I eat it while it still beats."

Vorc took a few more steps backward. "Wul, seriously, what could have—"

"The bitches drugged me."

"Ah, I see. What kind of—"

"With a hallucinogenic aphrodisiac."

"A what?" Vorc snapped with a scowl. "I've never even—." He looked upon Wul with a new understanding. "You don't mean to sugg—"

"I do not mean to *suggest* anything. I'm telling you they did." He looked away. "They looked to me like the sisters Pleasura and Desira."

"No. The demigods of carnal love?" Vorc's bottom jaw dropped precipitously. "What happened then. What did you ... I mean—"

"Exactly what any man would have done. With absolute abandon, I threw myself into their open arms."

"And ... oh my. And you three—" Vorc did the right finger through the left fingers circled, the universal sign of carnal interactions. "You guys did *it*?"

"Your statement fails by light years to capture the magnitude of the interactions. We did not do *it*. We did *them* for almost a week."

"Th ... then what happened?" Vorc sat to hear the response. Smart man.

"Then, sixteen hours, fourteen minutes, and three seconds ago, the potion wore off."

"And you came home?"

Wul's eye projected such loathing, such ill-intent, that Vorc backed up a third time.

"Not as you imply. When my mind returned to me, I was screwing both the ancient crones at once. I had to—"

"W ... wait," Vorc set both palms forward. "You could only actually screw *one* of them at a time." Vorc smiled uncomfortably. "Trust me. I'm a veteran of *many* an orgy, and so help me I've t—"

"They implanted a second *dick* on my backside," Wul screamed in a terrifically passionate voice.

Vorc reflected seriously a few seconds. Then his lips curled into an amused grin. In no time, he was literally rolling on the floor in uncontrollable laughter. It bordered on hysteria.

"Very empathetic, center seat."

Vorc continued to writhe in fits.

"Are you about done? If not, I shall kill you where you roll."

Normally such a challenge would have triggered a brisk and physical response from the guards. But, dimwitted as they were, they understood what was said. They were disinclined to assault a man with two dicks.

Ten minutes later, Vorc staggered to his feet, chuckling the entire time. "Yo—" he giggled. "You, yo ... you mean to s ... say, they put a dick in your bu ... butt?" Then Vorc round-tripped to the floor, lost in mirth.

When Vorc had quieted sufficiently to warrant Wul's attempt, he replied, "No, thanks for asking. It's slightly higher, just below my waist."

"An ... and d ... d ... does it—"

"Yes it has testicles, too. Two. Otherwise, the witches shouted as I fled, that it would have looked funny."

Back to the floor, again. To his credit, this visit was the briefest yet.

"In all seriousness, I'm certain our doctors can remove it safely. No one outside of this room and those hags, whom no one believes, needs to know."

"No, that will not be necessary. You see, the instant I awoke, bouncing back and forth in between the sisters, well, when I realized what I was doing, I bolted."

"Weren't you, er, naked?"

"Perfectly so. Hence, as I ran down the street screaming like Death pursued me, all were free to document my unique anatomy. I even roared past a wedding procession, Nafilla's, if I was focusing correctly."

"Ah yes, she was just married. Everyone who's anyone was ... oh, er, I *know* the girl. A real catch." Hoping to allow for some little dignity, Vorc changed the subject. "And why is it you will not require the services of a skilled—"

"The witches shouted after me that it would fall off in a few weeks."

Vorc paled precipitously. "J ... just the *butt* one, right?"

"I hope to hell that's what they meant."

Vorc rubbed his neck a few seconds, lost in thought. "So, pardon my asking, but I might need to know, you were swinging forward and backward, with," he tented his opposing palms nearly together, "the sisters—"

"That's *enough*, Vorc. I relive this constantly. I do not need your help. Finish the sentence and you finish your life, golems or not."

And Vorc believed his messenger.

"One last, little, you know, questionette," began Vorc. "Did you happen to retrieve an answer to my query from them?"

Wul lunged at Vorc's throat. "Out, damn spot, you stain on existence."

It took the full efforts of *two* golems to pry Wul off of Vorc.

The center seat backed toward the exit, hands on his throat. In a raspy voice, he departed saying, "Perhaps we'll finish this conversation ... in a few days. Yes, when you've rejuvenated." Vorc turned to leave. "By the way, I'll probably regret asking, but I can't resist. What in the Seven Flaming Hells of Purgea is in that box outside your front door? It is oozing some foul liquid and smells unholy."

Wul dry heaved a few times. "It's a dismembered stork."

"Why did you place—"

"I didn't place it there. One of the sisters had it sent. Around it's neck is a two-word note. *I'm pregnant*. It's signed *Fest*."

"Which one is she? I don't seem to be able to tell them apart."

"Me, neither. Nor do I care." Wul wiped spittle from his cheek.

"We will talk in a few days. I will contact you when I'm ready," said Vorc, as he stepped toward the door.

"If I ever see you again I shall slay you. If you chance upon me in a large crowd, you are a dead god, VTD."

And Vorc believed his messenger.

CHAPTER TWENTY-EIGHT

That kid of mine, Mirraya, needed to stop underestimating me. Yeah. I came up with a safe, simple, and foolproof (not a *word* from you!) plan to find out what Vorc knew about Jéfnoss's ability level. I know. Of course I did. I'm Jon Ryan, miracle worker — and no, not like the Hellen Keller movie. And now I was going to dazzle and amaze my crew for the forty millionteenth time with my magnificence.

"Okay, Skippy, we're all here and we all have better things to do. So begin and end using one sentence or less," heckled EJ.

"You don't even know what this's about to deride and discount it," I responded.

"No, but it's *you*, so the alternate options are the brothers Slim and None."

"Here goes. We need intel on Jéfnoss. When he RFTD did he—"

"Whoa, Nellie," shouted EJ, after a sharp whistle. "WTF is RFTD?"

"Returned From The Dead," I said matter-of-factly.

"We need an acronym for that, now?" he asked, with consummate incredulity.

I shuffled my feet. "Yes, I believed so. If this mission proceeds to fruition and completion, which, for the record, I'm nearly certain it will, the term will be employed so often an acronym—"

EJ threw up both arms. "Stop. Sorry I asked. Proceed, DTD."

No way I was going to dignify that by asking. No way. I'd put the AIs on it later.

"Here's the plan. We send Gáwar to Vorc. He can ask for the details."

To my great relief, only two people gasped, and one of them was EJ, so that didn't really count. The other, unfortunately was Toño, but maybe *he* gasped in amazement.

I was quickly disabused of that hope. "Jon, why would Gáwar *ask* on our behalf? Why would Vorc tell Gáwar *if* he asked? Finally, are you insane?"

"I'm not sure that third question belongs with the first two," I defended.

"We're all sure," quipped Sapale.

"Look, we all know we currently hold sway over Gáwar. If he wants to return to being the dark lord of demons, he needs us, me in particular."

Sapale cleared her throat loudly.

"Plus," I pointed out didactically, "since Gáwar is the likeliest candidate to rekill Jéfnoss, he would naturally need to know. And Vorc would want him to know, so Gáwar could best pull off the job." I opened my arms to demonstrate that, while I was both done and clueless, I wished to seem confident.

"I have a serious question," asked Mirraya.

"Yes," I replied professorially.

"Is *rekill* hyphenated or one word. I *think* its a neologism, so it's important to establish right from the get-go."

"I'm going with it being one word, no hyphen. Any other questions, perhaps mission-*related* ones?"

Casper raised a hand.

"Yes."

"Did you spellcheck *rekill* in either Merriam-Webster Unabridged or the OED?"

"No," I responded through drawn lips. "Okay, there's been a change in my plan. Gáwar is now to be seen as the most likely *agent* of Jéfnoss's *demise.*"

"Or do you mean *re-demise*," asked EJ, with a huge smile I did not appreciate.

"Moving on, any *non*-syntactical questions?"

"Has Gáwar agreed to do this, to act as our agent?" asked Daleria. Thank God.

"No, but I don't see why he'd refuse."

"Well, he does *hate* Vorc. Vorc *hates* Gáwar. Gáwar *hates* you. You, understandably *hate* Gáwar. I," she tented fingers on her chest, "hate both Vorc *and* Gáwar. With so little trust, does Gáwar's participation seem plausible?"

"No, cupcake," snapped EJ. "We're just here to bash this tool monkey and then laugh about it again for a we—"

EJ quieted when Daleria crossed the short distance that separated them and punched EJ very impressively on the jaw. He spun off the table he rested his butt on and nearly hit the deck.

"The *cupcakes* are in the fridge," she said to EJ icily. "There are *none* out here."

EJ looked pissed, but just rubbed his chin.

"So, with no dissent, I will speak with Gáwar and get this plan operational." I used military and formal terms to try to provide artificial importance to my idiotic notion. I know it made *me* feel better.

"In the words of General Jon Ryan," snapped Gáwar, "what have you been smoking?'

"In what context do you intend that query to have meaning?"

Gáwar's head rose. "By the Seven Creators, you've gone corporate."

Now them was fighting words. "I most assur ... No, poop-for-brains, I have not."

"That's better. My answer is, of course, no, negative, are you out of your cotton-picking mind, and no, used twice to emphasize its central nature to my response."

"Why not. If Jeffy is going to return and destroy the Cleinoids, you *are* the m ... one to stop him. *Everybody* knows that."

"Maybe. Time will tell."

"And you do need to impress me if you ever want to be the same old evil, malevolent god of demons again."

He angled his head away.

Oh, crap. What now?

"Say again, 'And you do need to impress me if you ever want to be the same old evil, malevolent god of demons again.'"

Still nothing.

"*Speak*," I commanded.

"It's just that, well, being *good* isn't that *bad*."

Oh, no, holy crap, and bother. "Are you suggesting that you might prefer to remain Pollyanna and not return to your evil ways?"

He raised his eyes to me just barely and nodded in the affirmative.

What a Charlie foxt ... no, no, wait. I still had him by the short hairs. "Outstanding. I'm proud of you, friend Gáwar."

He swelled. "You are? Gee, thanks. I can't tell you how that makes me feel. Ah, what are you referring to that makes you proud of me?"

"Your positivity, team spirit, and your niceness. No, you don't have team spirit, I've got it in my crazy noggin that you're the new *god* of team spirit."

"Gee, you really think that's possible?" The moron had a dreamy look in his eyes.

"Yes," I responded cheerily. Then doubt obviously crossed my face.

"What?" he implored with concern.

"Hmm."

"What. Oh, please tell me, Jon. What?"

"Well, wanting to be the god of team spirit is one thing."

"What's the other. *Pleeeease* tell me."

"Actions speak louder than words."

He looked confused. "They do?"

"Very much so," I replied in a fatherly tone.

"But actions, unless the action is speech, can't speak. So how could they be louder than words?"

"Exactly. I've had to explain that to dumdums from one side of this galaxy to the other. Morons, every one of them." I half pointed at him and grinned. "You're the clever boy."

He beamed. "My mother always told me that. Well, she did once. Then I ate her."

"And you did so with team spirit in mind, I'd bet good money."

"Is that your wife? Good Money?"

"No. Say, let's switch topics so I don't get confused, shall we?"

He nodded like a maroon.

"I bet that if you pump Vorc for details on Jéfnoss, your name will pop to the top of the list to be the first and only god of team spirit."

He looked suddenly concerned. "There's a list?"

"Of course. There has to be a list. Can't very well award that prize without a list."

"And is ... is the list *long*?"

I opened my arms as wide as they would part.

"And I was, you know, lower down on the list?"

I chopped my hand down around my knees. "But now," my hand rose to my nose, "bang, you're up here. Top three, for sure."

"Who else is on the list, I mean that's above me?"

I swung an arm around him. Not easy. He stank. "You know what? I'm going to challenge you on this. Don't even ask who's up there. Why don't you just do such a darn good job that all those others can say to you is *congratulations*." I binked him above his jaws.

"I hope you're right. I'll do it, Jon. You know, between you and me, I kind of need this."

"Do tell."

"Oh yeah. If you're not the god of something important around here, you get teased a *lot*."

"Well, if anyone asked me, I'd tell them there's nothing more important than team spirit." I pulled his horrendous face conspiratorially closer. "And between you and me—"

He drooled he was so excited.

"I think you got this." I held out a high-five hand, thought better of that, and settled for a pat on his carapace.

Ramalamadama poked her not insubstantial tube-dog nose into Vorc's office. Without being asked to speak, for she'd learned repeatedly that if she didn't say something her boss would ignore her for hours. "'orrd. There's someone here—"

"Ms. R," Vorc said cheerily as he set down his quill. "Are you working today? I thought I gave you the day off?"

"You give me every rday off, 'orrd. I take some, but, I do need this job."

"But, I've assured you you will always be paid. Hmm? Doesn't a day off sound good about now?"

"No, 'orrd. I'm a demigord of office work. This is what I do."

"Ah, so you like office work?"

She furrowed her brow. "No, not rea'y. Why wou'd you ask that?"

He recoiled slightly. "Be-cause-you're-the-demigod-of-office-work."

"A demigord, 'oord. Let's not get ahead of ourse'ves."

"No. We wouldn't want that, whatever it is you're saying."

"I rdo office work because ... that's what I rdo. You don't have to 'ike something if you're its demigord."

"No—" he began.

"Gord, for that matter, I'm sure. Same as you rdon't have to dis'ike something just because you're not its demigord."

"Or god?"

"If you say so, 'orrd. My point is, I 'ike 'iver. I am not the demigord of 'iver or any other interna' organ." She sort of shrugged. "Externa' ones either."

"No." He fumbled with his quill, knocking over his indelible ink container. "You know what?"

"No. What?"

"You are quite the philosopher. I think you should take the rest of the day off and think, think, think, Then write it all down."

"You want to see it tomorrow?"

"Heavens no. I'm sure it will be well beyond my comprehension, that's what I mean."

"Ah. Anrd shou'rd I take Gáwar with me, when I go phi'osophize?"

Vorc scrunched his face. "Why would you take Gáwar with you to ponder the elusive?"

"Because he's here to see you. Doesn't have an appointment, as usual, but here is where he is."

"Did he come to see you or me?"

"Why wou'rd he come to see me?"

"I don't know. It's just that you wanted to take him along with you to write."

"Why wou'rd I want that, 'orrd?"

"Be ... we—" Vorc thumped his head on the table. "Show him in. Then leave this building."

"You got it, 'orrd."

She backed out.

Gáwar nosed forward. "I haven't caught you at a bad time have I, old sport?" queried Gáwar.

"Ah, no, silly thought," Vorc replied nervously. "P ... please come in. Sit." Then Vorc's face went ashen. "I didn't mean that as an insult. Honestly, I did not."

"Sorry. What are you referencing?"

"Referencing? I invited you to sit. *Do* you sit?"

"Ah, fair question." He sort of collapsed, letting his right legs go limp. "There. That's me sitting."

"Ah, thanks?"

"This," Gáwar said energetically, "is my lying down to sleep." He thundered to his right side. The windows shook.

"You sle ... sleep?"

"Of course, silly. *Everyone* sleeps."

"Perdida, the god of insomnia, doesn't," Vorc responded for reasons unclear to himself.

"Good point. I bet Gumjum doesn't much, either."

"Gumjum? The god of the dead? Wh ... forget I asked. Why are you here?"

"Forget you asked what?"

"Thank you. Now, why—"

"No, I didn't say forget you asked what to reflect I understood your request and honor it. I was curious what it is you want me to forget you asked that you didn't ask."

Vorc slammed his forehead on the table, twice. "Must we?"

"Must we what?"

"Let's forget I said let's forg—" Vorc stood. Then he sat. Then he began to whimper. "Why are you here?"

"I wanted to ask you a few questions, if you have time, can answer them, and feel I need the information I seek."

"Why wouldn't ... no ... forge ... What would you like to know?"

"For one thing, what's an *oord*?"

"You came here to ask me what the non-word *oord* means?"

"No."

"But you—" Vorc grabbed his face very firmly with both palms. "I do not know. I am unfamiliar with that term."

"But I kept hearing your assistant call you *oord*."

"Ah, yes. She does, doesn't she?"

"So what does she mean?"

He shook his head sadly. "I have no idea."

"Why not ask her. The answer might surprise you."

"It might also drive me over the brink. I'm very near the brink, you know?"

"I did not. Best not to ask her, I think."

"Anything else on you mind?"

"Yes."

Vorc pounded his fists into his eye sockets. "Why are you here today?"

"To ask you some questions about Jéfnoss."

Vorc lunged backward, reflexively. "Is he here? Is he back?"

"No."

"Good. What did you want to know?"

Gáwar inched closer to Vorc and studied him a moment. "Have you lost weight?"

"Have I ... have I ... Jéfnoss wants to know if I've lost weight?"

"He does, too? What are the chances of that?"

"No, you said you had a question about Jéfnoss. Then you asked if I'd lost weight. Is that because Jéfnoss wonders?"

"I wouldn't know, but," the goofy god of demons winked at Vorc, " I think you have. You look good. Fit."

Vorc's ashen face paled further. If he looked *good*, did that suggest superior taste when consumed?

"You know I said I sleep on my side?"

Vorc shook his head violently. "Yes. You mentioned you slept on your side."

"You know what?"

"I don't want to guess."

"Sometimes I sleep on my back." Gáwar rolled onto his back. "And I kick my arms and legs in the air like this." Gáwar proceeded to flail his appendages in the air. "You know why I do this?" he asked while doing it.

"N ... no."

"Because it feels good. It's fun. Hey, get down here and swing with me."

The floor next to Gáwar's head exploded in flames. He flipped nimbly to a stance. He saw Vorc aiming Fire Of Justice at the spot that was burning.

"Why are you here? The mental anguish is literally killing me."

"Okay, grumpy pants. Sheesh. When Jéfnoss RFTDed, was it your impression he had all his former strength and power?"

Vorc stiffened and became instantaneously serious. That was an important question.

"RTFD? What's the—"

"No, RFTD. Returned From The Dead. Come on, *everybody's* saying that."

"Define everybody?" he said intently.

"Everybody who's not you, clearly."

"Come to think of it, where have you *been*? I haven't heard or seen you. I hear no reports of your destruction and pillaging. Now why do you suppose that is?" He tangled his fingers together atop his desk and stared at Gáwar.

"Why haven't you heard from or about me? How should I know? Have you been on vacation?"

"We're not talking about *me*. We're talking about *you*."

"Oh, sorry. No, I haven't been on vacation, gosh, in millennia." He popped to his hind feet. "Hey, *you*, you and *me*, maybe we could go on vac—"

"*Silence*," thundered Vorc. "I was not on vacation. You were not on vacation. No one is going on vacation. Now answer my question. Where have you been?"

Gáwar got such a boo-boo face that Vorc almost immediately regretted being so harsh. Then he regretted regretting he'd been harsh, since he had so *intended* to be harsh.

"I've been here for half an hour."

"Don't you think I know that, pea-brain?"

"You should. But you asked where I'd been. I've been here fo—"

"Fine. *Fine*. Beside being here for half an hour, where have you been?"

"Where have I been on vacation?"

"*No*." Vorc ripped at his long hair. "Not where you've been on *vacation*. Where have you *been* over the last, oh say, month. The time period in which I have neither *seen* nor *heard* from you."

"I'm sorry. Am I in trouble? Was I *supposed* to keep you up to date on my whereabouts? I don't *think* you asked me to, not that I wouldn't of—"

The center of the center seat's desktop burst into flames. "I never asked you to. *But*, and I'm swearing on my mother's tomb, here, you will tell me where you have been the last month - the entire last month."

"How is your mom?"

"She's still dead, moron."

"Did Jéfnoss *tell* you that, or are you just *assuming* she is?"

Vorc's eyes nearly burst from his head. "Yes, in fact he did tell me. He told me she is there in hell and that she mocks me daily. She calls me VTD. Everyone does. There. Are you happy?"

"I'll never call you Vorc the Dork. It's hurtful. How does it make you feel, your own mother—"

"*We-are-not-here-to-talk-about-me.*" Vorc slammed his fist on the splintering desk with each word.

Gáwar touched his chest and pointed at Vorc. "Well, when you're ready to talk, you call me first, okay, compadre?"

Vorc squinted and shut his twitching right eye. "Say, speaking of changes, you seem different. You seem, nice."

Jon had warned Gáwar about this eventuality. Luckily he'd provided Gáwar with a good cover story.

"Me? Change? No. As a matter of fact I've been meaning to do this for a while."

Clumsily, Gáwar rounded the desk, lifted a couple rear legs, and urinated onto Vorc's leg the most foul, acrid piss Vorc had ever smelled. It took nearly a full minute to empty his voluminous bladder.

"That feels better," sighed Gáwar. "Sorry 'bout the mess." He snorted quickly. "Not really." It took all Gáwar's current inner strength not to run to get a mop and then beg for Vorc's forgiveness. But Jon specifically said Gáwar was on the proving ground for god of teamwork. Whatever it took, it took.

"I hate you," hissed Vorc.

"Now, about those powers. Were they diminished?"

"Why are you so damn curious."

Thanks, team player Jon, for prepping Gáwar yet again. "Because, dick-butt, I was the one who killed him. He'll be gunning for me at high noon."

"No," implored Vorc, waving his hands frantically in front of himself, "that was *Wul*, not *me*."

"That was Wul *what*?" Then Gáwar chuckled. "Hey, try to say that three times real fast."

"Never mind. Sorry. I was thinking of something else. Er, I can't say, regarding Jéfnoss. He was only here the shortest time before I remanded his sorry butt back to hell."

"You have a thing ... Vorc ... with butts?" Gáwar took one step backward.

"No. Will you leave? I've answered your question. I do not know."

"So, he didn't do anything while he was here? Not one thing?"

"No. We spoke, I killed, he was gone."

"Where was he, physically?"

"He floated over there, then he sat there." Vorc pointed to the spots.

"So he did *nothing*. He floated and sat."

"Well, yes. And he mocked me. He told me my folks mocked me. That was it. I killed him for those words."

"Ah. He insulted you, while sitting in that chair, so you killed him? Nothing else?"

"I don't think so. No. Will you leave now?"

From the still open door boomed, "'oord, there was the part where you askerd what he requirerd of you and he responrderd, 'itt'e, scum. Something of precious 'itt'e worth."

Vorc's blood pressure surged. He wasn't intending to share that piece of intel.

"Precious *itte*?" Gáwar asked menacingly. "What did she say?"

"Thank you, Ms. R. I seem to have forgotten that inconsequential notation. Aren't you off work *philosophizing*?"

"Yes, 'oord."

"Let me guess. You decided, why not philosophize at your comfy desk?"

"It was ergonomica'y rdesignerd just for me, 'oord."

"What, pinhead, was it Jéfnoss required of you? What is—" He asked that very much the way the old Gáwar would have. In such a manner that you tell the whole truth and you tell it fast.

"Precious little. He said he needed something that was *of precious little worth*. And before you ask, I killed him before he said what that was. I do not know."

"Why would you kill a man who just asked a nebulous question? Wouldn't you want passionately to know what a resurrected god needed?"

"Maybe. Yes. Maybe."

Gáwar's eyes squinted. "*You* didn't kill him, you lying sac of shit." Gáwar laughed a good old Gáwar scary laugh. "Assuming he didn't go to all that trouble to commit suicide, then ... your helper? Ms. R killed the mighty Jéfnoss?" Gáwar grabbed Vorc by the neck in a massive pincer. "Did the tube dog do the deed?"

"Yes ... yes. But she was under my *direct* supervi—"

"Shut up, imp." Gáwar bobbed his head. "A fall from this height wouldn't have killed the original Jéfnoss."

"Ah, for completeness sake, Ms. R did fall on top of him and decapitate him on impact."

"That would do it. Vorc, your lie, your deception might have killed us all. Know that, you pathetic worm?"

Vorc rested back on his haunches and thought. To himself he mumbled, "Had the power to get back. But needed something, presumably to give him more power, maybe his old strength. Not able to resist forceful decapitation by a freight train from three stories up. Hmm. Interesting. Very interesting."

"Do you know what Jéfnoss wanted?" pressed an anxious Vorc.

"'Course I do. He wanted the same thing I want. To kill *you*."

"Bu ... but, that ... is that what —"

"What he required? Nah. Killing you's so easy he'd a'just done it."

"So wha—"

"I do not presently know. But I shall soon, I promise you that. Someone knows, and no one can resist my persuasive charm."

Gáwar lumbered away without further comment, or even a goodbye. His transition was still, most certainly, a work in progress. Or not.

CHAPTER TWENTY-NINE

"Yo, Jéfnoss," shouted Colery, the former god of comedians, "I heard you got mad at Vorc and lost your head back there in the land of the living." He took several seconds to laugh at his own joke, a la Red Skelton. "Hey, if you need any help, let's have a get-togethe—" He had to stop lampooning Jéfnoss, he snickered so intensely. "A get-together at my place." More imbecilic sport at Jéfnoss's expense. "You get it? A get together, like," he mimed placing a head on his neck, "a *get* it *back* together?"

There was a special place in hell for comics who needed to explain their jokes.

Jéfnoss used his eyes to penetrate Colery's soul like a plasma beam. Oh, he lamented, how he missed his power. In life, given what he could do, he'd have killed that swine in an instant. His only real consolation was that Jéfnoss had, in point of fact, done just that. Colery made a snide remark to Jéfnoss at a cocktail party and was dead before any of his many loose parts and pieces hit the floor. Perhaps, Jéfnoss had to concede, that was why Colery had gone to such lengths to locate and taunt him presently. Leaving his special place was never easy for Colery, as well it should have been.

Especially in hell, the punishment, with unremitting attention, fit the crime.

After his tormentor was quickly whisked away, Jéfnoss was free to walk aimlessly. That was, it turned out, the only way to walk the paths of hell. He frequently kicked at random objects and smaller deities, as he was in an exceptionally foul mood. There being no time in hell, he had no way of knowing how long he'd been back. But, in whatever time he had been, he'd made *zero* progress in terms of regaining his freedom. Four reckonings, two pleasures, and one *source-verified* false prophecy. Where was he going to come up with those? And why couldn't Dragmire simply help him out of the goodness of her heart? If the roles were reversed, he would be only too pleased to provide pro bono services to *that* bitch.

Jéfnoss stopped and stroked where his luxuriant beard used to reside. He was trying hard to retrieve one instance of when, during his life, he'd freely helped another. Nothing came immediately to mind. But, then again, he'd recently suffered quite the trauma. That might have scrambled his memory, but good. Yes. That had to be the case. It was not his fault he couldn't recall one of the many charitable acts he must have committed.

He began strolling again. Go for the low-hanging fruit, he said to himself. Pleasures and prophecies were hen's teeth in perdition, but a few reckonings couldn't be that hard to drum-up. No. He was, after all in hell, the land of the unreckoned. Who or what did he know that had been remanded to hell but, in spite of that horrible fate, had actually gotten off pretty easy? Bingo! His *mother*, the toothless wretch. Yes, her crime was *immense*. She'd given birth to *him*, and he was *epically* bad. She was only assigned the duty of cleaning up the flaming excrement from a mid-level overlord, Nopow, for all eternity. The fact that the fellow shat continually and voluminously simply meant that dear old mom would never get bored. That wasn't a curse, but a blessing to the pathetic she-toad. A blessing in hell, now there was something that mandated a reckoning.

He thought hard, where did the waste-of-space he called *mother* reside? He hadn't visited her since his first arrival in hell. Why bother? She'd probably just moan about her ill-fate and then ask him to help her shovel hot shit. Someone had told him long ago that she was stationed on the one hundred and thirty third level. Yes, in fact, it was his moronic father who'd informed him. The obnoxious fart had hunted Jéfnoss down just to tell him. Jéfnoss had spent the better half of who-knew-how-long avoiding his old man. Yet somehow pops did *one* thing correct in his sorry existence. He'd found Jéfnoss in hell. Now there was another jerkwad he'd like to be able to rekill.

Okay, one hundred thirty three. That was—duh—overseen by Nopow. Jéfnoss had met him at the reception thrown in his honor when he first arrived. Jéfnoss was, after all, the scourge of all that lived and breathed. All the demons, overlords, and volunteer docents of damnation lined up to meet the great and terrible Jéfnoss tra-Fundly. They'd spoken briefly. What had the monster said? Oh yes, he was proud to say he tormented Jéfnoss's mother and would continue to do so mercilessly forever. And he asked for an autograph.

Hmm. Hero worship. There was a card he could easily play. He could just *happen* to be on one thirty three for an unrelated reason and *chance* to bump into Nopow. *How's mother,* he'd inquire. *Horrible,* Nopow would assure him with a wicked grin. *Oh, you are* the devil, he'd respond. *No, but I'm fifty first in line,* Nopow would counter. They'd both chuckle.

Yes, he'd say in all seriousness, *but is she truly suffering? You bet, sir,* Nopow'd reply with a proper salute. *Oh, come now. Are you telling me Mommy couldn't suffer just a little bit more?* And he'd pinch his fingers ever so close together. *Well, there is always the chainsaw,* Nopow would recall. *I haven't oiled it lately, but it's still beneath my throne.* They'd both nod thoughtfully. *You know what they say,* he'd tease. *No, sire, what do they say,* Nopow would wonder out loud. *Blood makes the very best oil.* And they'd both collapse on the ground in fits of hateful laughter.

Oh, yes. Mommy would have a reckoning. Bada *boom*. No, he chuckled to himself, that would be brum-brum-brum-brum-brrrrrrrrrrrrrrrrrrrrrrr —

One down, three to go.

CHAPTER THIRTY

"*Wait*," thundered Gáwar, "you *knew* VTD didn't kill Jéfnoss, but you didn't deign to tell me before I did your bidding?"

"Easy, big guy," I soothed, "someone's grumpy today."

He rattled so hard *Stingray* vibrated. I'm assuming he was displeased. "I am not grumpy. I h ... I ha ... I can't even say that word in the context of you, the person I h ... hh ... oh, who am I kidding. You're, like, my BFF." Gáwar might have smiled. Hard to tell, with an evil crustacean.

"I'm *like* your BFF? In what way? I'm willing to change."

"Ooh, you're the dickens, Jon Ryan. Such a kidder."

"Sure, whatever. So, what did you find out?"

Gáwar squinted one eye. "You know. You have those bugs everywhere. That's how you knew it wasn't VTD who exed Jéfnoss, but his sniveling secretary." He growled deep and throaty. "Are you testing me—*again?*"

I bobbed my head equivocally. "No ... no, it's just, you know, it's always best to get a firsthand, boots-on-the-ground assessment. You can't replace proximity."

"Yes you can. You have, what, twenty five probes in his office?" Gáwar seemed skeptical.

"One hundred fifty three," Toño responded for me.

"Thanks, *Doc*, I'm sure." With friends like him. "So, what's your takeaway?"

Gáwar took a sec to compose himself. "I believe Vorc does *not* know what it was Jéfnoss sought. Hardly a surprise. He is a *moron's* moron."

"Crap. I hate not knowing," I mumbled to no one in particular.

"Oh, you just *had* to use the H-word, didn't you? Rub it in, you ... you ... *argh*. You unsympathetic spirit."

"We all got crosses, big guy. Get over yourself."

"I ate you too fast, after I killed you, Ryan. I can't recall the taste. Next ti ... next *tim* ... oh, I'm just being silly. There won't be a next time. We're pals."

He really was flat out pathetic. I almost wished I could have reversed my blessing. I was getting nauseous. "What are we missing, people?" I asked the assembled crew. "What would a god need in order to be a god?"

"I doubt you worded that properly," responded *Professor* Toño. "A god is a god. They can't require anything to be what they already are."

"Was it important for you to say that?" I replied, slightly wounded.

"Of course. We're investigating an event. We need *facts*. You must ask the correct question to get the correct answer."

"Why?"

"Are you ser ... Of course you're not. You're ... you're *you*."

"And still the original."

"If you're going to put on a light comedy act, I'll be in my room," announced Sapale.

"Your room? You mean *our* room?" I asked.

"Not if you don't cut the crap, bucko."

"Looky here," began EJ, "I don't think—"

I tuned the prick out. He'd never said anything bright—ever. That fountain wasn't about to spring to life now. What could a god need? Jéfnoss reigned this land with more than an iron fist. And why VTD? Did it *have* to be him? Even Mirraya with all her magical machinations couldn't glean one clue. This mattered. Whatever it was, it was important. I couldn't bail on finding out what Jéfnoss needed. *Something of precious little worth.* How could something of no value be critical? It couldn't be. That was ...

In the video, of the massive Ms. R ramming Jéfnoss. What was it that bugged me? I'd watched it a thousand times — literally. What was off? I walked over to the comm station. I'd watched all the videos and holos in my head. Maybe looking at them like a real boy would jog my mind enough that I'd finally see what I wasn't seeing.

Okay, Jéfnoss touches down. He sits in VTD's chair. He says the little worth thing. Ramalamadama flies into the room. The chair. He doesn't really fit. Why? I switched to ten different angles. Yes. He didn't quite fit, or belong, in that chair. Was he too small? No, he was normal enough in size. But he was too low. That was it. Too low, but he was Vorc's dimensions.

My finger nearly smashed the screen I fingered it so hard. There. His butt. The dead god's butt! It wasn't *on* the seat pan. It was *in* the seat pan. Dude was faking being substantial, but he wasn't paying close enough attention. Why? Because he was a rookie at being back, at being a ...

Where the *hell* was Casper? He had to see this. He'll know what I was ...

"Why are you all standing behind me staring?" I asked sheepishly of everyone, who were all standing behind me staring.

"Because, moron-plus-plus," snapped my wife, "in the middle of EJ's ramblings, you just *waltz* away and start replaying the vids we've all seen a million—"

"I wasn't rambling," protested EJ.

"Where's Casper?" my head swept the room frantically.

"Where do you think?" he said, standing so close he was almost overlapping me.

I grabbed his arm. Dumb move. "Come here. *Look.*" I tapped the still frame on the screen.

"Yes, that is a nice office chair. Understated, yet elegant. Timeless, in fact," the pill responded.

"No, look at his butt." I rapid-fire tapped the appropriate spot.

"Ah, Jon, you're not getting *weird* on me are you?" scolded Sapale. "God's butts?"

"Yes, you're right, clone of me. Damn. How'd you pick up on that?" marveled Casper.

"He's not getting into god's butts," protested Sapale. "Not on my watch." I do believe she was missing the point.

"Yes, he's right?" groaned EJ. "Punk didn't ask anything. How can he be right? And don't answer that, because my stomach can't pay the price."

"He asked me, 'Say, Casper, is it your *expert* opinion that the figure sitting inside Vorc's chair is a ghost?' The answer is *yes*. Look." His fingers lingered next to mine. "Rookie-ass," he chided.

"Jéfnoss is a rookie-assed ghost?" muttered EJ.

"That would be a big old affirmative," I gloated.

"And, clone boy, since you're on the big roll, bring it on home," said an ebullient Casper.

"Okay, it's official. I'm going to hurl," announced EJ.

"Say, Casper, what is it that a ghost would need to *not* be a ghost?" I asked robustly.

"Well, friend, I'd say the one thing a ghost would absolutely need to not be a ghost would be a body."

"And, Casper, I'm going to call on you to speculate here. Do you think anyone, and especially Jéfnoss, would place an excessive value on, say, the body of one VTD?"

"If pressed, I say it would be *of precious little worth* to me, and certainly to Jéfnoss."

"Holy crap," snapped Toño. "You cannot just have done it again."

"Why, Dr. DeJesus, I cannot *believe* the language that's coming out your mouth of late." I smiled widely.

"We're never ever going to be able to live with him," mumbled Sapale.

"His *head*, no matter how big I make the portal, it'll never fit through the door," moaned Al.

"Did I mention that in order to channel the power of Clein, it turns out an ancient god must be *corporeal*? Hmm?" I piled on. "Bet ya didn't see that one coming?"

"If we kill him, we could maybe live with him?" suggested Daleria.

"Oh, sorry, I'm only able to speculate here, but I *think* I know why Jéfnoss intended to snatch VTD's body. He could at least begin his triumphant return in the *guise* of being Vorc. He'd get a leg-up on revenge, being mistaken as the current center seat. Of course, we won't know I'm right, *yet again*, until we ask him in person."

"No, death didn't work on the son of a gun," whined Mirraya. "We're *so* screwed."

"And you're all *freaking* welcome," I sang out as I placed my feet on the comm station and leaned back.

Life was sweet. Oh, yes, it was most sweet.

CHAPTER THIRTY-ONE

With his consummate skills, Jéfnoss was slowly, glacially, able to acquire more coins to be able to purchase Dragmire's assistance. Yes, the things he'd learned in life served him equally well in hell. Lying, the betrayal of friends, twisting of other's words, and the absolute disregard for anyone else's safety, feelings, or desires. Good stuff. He only wished he had his go-to power available. Brutal, unjust, and rampant killings were really helpful tools in his brand of politics. He simply had to live with the fact that he couldn't kill a dead person. He knew that for certain. He'd tried to do it many a time.

All four reckonings were in the bag, so to speak. And my, but he enjoyed one and all. Jéfnoss had forgotten how good it felt to be bad. The big plus was he was then able to present the gooey bitch with not just two pleasures, but four. Yes, he'd checked with the powers that were and they confirmed the immense joy Jéfnoss experienced in effecting those reckonings did constitute certifiable Pleasures. He was close. Oh, so close.

Only the hardest one remained. A source-verified false prophecy. Prophecies were a dime a dozen and verified ones were common. A prophecy verified by the source? Those turned out to be trivial, chump-change. If a prophet made a prediction and it turned out to be true, you had to put a sock in his or her mouth to have them *stop* confirming it.

Here was the real issue, the rub. A prophet *prophesied* something. *Seabiscuit to win, third race at Belmont. Your kingdom will fall without a single arrow fired.* Then, Seabiscuit trips and breaks a leg, or the king himself is killed with an errant arrow during a one-sided loss by his forces. Yeah, *then* drag the prophet in front of a crowd and ask if that *false* prophecy was issued by him and him alone. You will find yourself speaking to a deaf mute. *Yeah, sorry all you guys who bet on that clumsy horse. Pay back your losses, me, personally? Ah, I predict not.* And so commences the public execution.

Now, recall Jéfnoss was the god of prophets. So he knew all the players and all the predictions. Clearly his jurisdiction was logjammed with charlatans. Most of their words were false. But they could not issue a false *prophecy*, because they weren't actual *prophets*. Trying to wring the truth out of a certified prophet who screwed the pooch? That was utterly inconceivable and less common than fascist unicorns.

As a result, Jéfnoss sat and wondered, sat and ruminated, which false prophecy could he get verified by the dumb-dumb who issued it? Even though one's body died, one's ego did not. All the prophets in hell worried about their good names, their reputations. The only time Jéfnoss had ever heard a prophet own a false vision was the one about the Kardashian sisters all taking religious vows after finishing high school. Yeah, that boat not only sailed, it sank in deep water. The false prophet concerned, one Emmanuel Sammy Copperstand, late of Hoboken, New Jersey, wasn't available to Jéfnoss. Even if the putz *was* dead, he wouldn't be in a *Cleinoid* hell. He'd be in another.

Inspiration, when it strikes, can be as a butterfly dancing down on one's shoulders. However, it more often comes in the form of a freight train in the night hitting you from behind. It struck Jéfnoss that he was a prophet. Duh. And he, The Prophet Jéfnoss, had on one and only one occasion, misfired. He was able to self-source-verify a false prophecy made by him. Bingomaximus! He was done.

Then, like the power going out in the middle of a disco-dance floor jammed with revelers, Jéfnoss took pause. No way. No freaking way. There was no freaking way. There was no freaking way he was going to tell Dragmire, or anyone else, about that screw up, that heinous mistake. He'd just have to find another prophet to verify a false prediction. Heck, it could be a little mistake, maybe one subject to shades of opinion. Yes, maybe a prophet told someone at the table, "You should try the veal," and they did and it was woefully overcooked.

For the next half-eternity, as un-measured time in hell went, Jéfnoss searched, like Diogenes before him, for an elusive quarry. One who would confess publicly that they had misprophesied. It was never recorded whether Diogenes found his honest man. It *was* recorded that Jéfnoss never found an honest bad seer.

"Well, as I neither live nor breathe, if it isn't Jéfnoss The Invisible," taunted Dragmire as he skulked toward where she was resting. "I thought you must have reverted to nature, you've been gone so long."

"I'm here now and I'm ready to pay your price." He was a thoroughly defeated man. Broken, in fact.

"Well, come, come, "she said, "sit by me and make my eternal punishment a little less intolerable." A string of ooze touched a nearby rock.

"I'll stand."

"Whatever. Okay," she said hungrily, "hit me."

Oh, how he wished he actually could. He listed off, in great detail, the four Reckonings he'd produced. She listened quietly, interrupting infrequently, though she bubbled profusely.

When Jéfnoss finished the Reckonings, he dropped his head.

"Your own *mother*? That, that's inconceivable, even for *you*."

"If you knew her as I did, not so much."

"But everyone down here knows about Nopaws twenty-eight incher. I heard him fire it up just the—" She directed a thick stream of herself at Jéfnoss. "The screaming. That was *your* mother's. Oh you are the bad boy."

He shrugged as if to say *eh*.

"Fine, fine. The Pleasures?"

He told her the accounting on those.

"No way, Jose. I asked for two. Maybe, maybe I let one slide by as you enjoyed yourself, but not both."

Silently he held out the four certificates of documentation.

"No hands, rat pus. Spread'em out so I can read them."

He held each up separately, sequentially.

"Shit, you got me on that technicality. I should have anointed myself as the sole arbiter of submissions, but I didn't. You win that one." She bubbled intently. "And the false *prophecy*?"

Jéfnoss shuffled his feet. "Well, I was hoping, based on the quality of the Reckonings and the quantity of the Pleasures, you might let the last condition, you know, sort of slide."

"You were hoping?"

"Yes, And knowing that we are old friends and that—"

"No. Period. Stop making excuses. Tell me the source-verified false prophecy or get out of my face until you got one."

Jéfnoss angled his head. "You have a face?"

"It's figure of speech, monkey turd. Leave me or the price—"

"No, I'm ready."

"To what? Shit bricks?" She chuckled at her wit.

"To tell you a source-verified false prophecy."

"But, loose nuts, you just finished saying you didn't have one."

"I do."

"Then why the f—"

"It's both personal and painful."

"Ooh, that sounds juicy. Okay, you worthless shell of a man, begin."

Jéfnoss stood silently for several minutes.

"Er, I know we're both dead, but still, could you pick up the pace?"

"You recall my wife, Desdemona?"

"Sure. Nice enough for a sack of meat. But what a poor choice of names. Poor girl must'a had a complex."

"*Ironic* name, yes, but not poorly chosen, it turned out," Jéfnoss mumbled.

"This is sounding better and better."

"We met long ago. Her parents were in the shipping business. He was god of war ships, she the god of supply lines in combat."

"Tell me something I don't know."

"My dear wife was the god of loving war," he lowered his head. "Gods how she loved war. She read about it, hovered over any active one, and she spoke to a fault about it."

"But you loved her, in spite of herself. Yada, yada, blah, blah. Get to what I want to hear."

"After an uncertain courtship, I proposed to her."

"The corny way, I just know. Ring in a box and on one knee. Puke, vomit, hurl. Go on."

"In the most romantic manner possible. In a lovely wood, babbling brooks babbling, birds singing. And *yes*, one knee and a red-satin box." He paused a spell. "Blessedly, she said yes. We set a date. Her mother arranged a lavish wedding. Everyone who was anyone was there, and we all had a wonderful time."

"And I'm getting bored."

"That night, we were escorted to our honeymoon chambers. It was the tradition back then, very much all the rage."

"And then I got more bored. It's an *irritated* kind of bored, FYI."

He sighed judgmentally.

"When we were alone, my purest wife, the light of my existence, went to the door and closed it. With her back to it, resting her lithe, soft body against it, she asked me a simple question. 'Do you really love me?'"

"Bored and now getting lost. I'm not hearing a prophecy."

"I rushed to Desdemona and took her gently in my arms. 'Yes, I love you now and forever' I assured her."

"'And do I love you?' she asked with the most peculiar expression."

"Ooh, juicy-express headin' down the track."

"'Yes,' I told her, 'you do. As much as I love you.'"

"'How can you know I will love you forever?'"

"On your *wedding* night, she pulled the pin on *that* hand grenade? She had more balls that most males I'm familiar with," marveled Dragmire.

"I rubbed her shoulders and said, 'I will verify it, if that will make you happy?' I told her."

"'Please, husband, do that.'"

He had to stop speaking a while.

"'Here we go,' I told her. I closed my eyes and I searched the future. I saw Dessi and I surrounded by love, children, and grand children. I saw the happiest couple to ever walk on solid ground. I pushed, and challenged the distant future to show itself. Begrudgingly, slowly, it unraveled. I saw nothing but joy, love, and togetherness. 'Yes, wife, you will love me forever, as I will you.'"

"Wow, glad I don't have a mouth to vomit into."

"Then we kissed. And we made love. Then we moved to her mother's place while mine was, under Desdemona's critical eye, extensively remodeled."

"Uh, ouch. A big remodel when newlyweds. Tough."

"Tell me about it."

"And instant abuse from the mother-in-law. You're a real glutton for it, chump."

"Tell me about that, too."

"So how long did the reno take?"

He shook his head sadly. "I never found out."

"But, I went to your house once, back when we lived. Ooooo. Waity, waity. There was no Desdemona at your place when I visited. You had a mousy girlfriend, but I don't think you two ever even tied the knot."

"Charlene and I were just too different. She was from a different clan of Cleinoids. It was no one's fault. I think she was just too much a free spirit."

"I think she was just *cheap*. She wore those Daisy Duke shorts like they were working clothes, if you get my drift?"

"Many men did."

"So the god of prophets incorrectly foretold that his marriage would last forever. That's rich. So, how long did it last?"

"Well, Dessi spent more and more time on site during the reno. She even got a pair of Big Ben overalls and a painter's hat. She looked ridiculous. The long and short of it was that, the more time she spent sweating with Magnus, the main contractor, the more she fancied sweating with him in a different manner."

"*Ouch.*"

"Ouch. Three months into our lives together, Magnus hauled her off to his fortified mountain retreat and I never saw her again."

"Wow, you never saw nor heard from her again. That's so sad. Tragic, in fact."

"Oh, I *heard* from her. Bitch retained Themis, Iustitia, and Eunomia to represent her in the most painful divorce any of the partners had ever inflicted on a wounded husband." He lowered his head so much it threatened to slip off spontaneously. "And so I give you my source-verified false prophecy."

"You're a real pisser; you know that, right?"

"I know it now."

"Well, I have to thank you. You've given me my best day in hell. I'm ready, willing, and almost able to help you out."

One - two - three. "**ALMOST!**"

"You caught that one, didn't ya. Yeah. You were taking so long I kind of threw my support behind someone else's pet project."

"Mine is not a pet project. It is a *divine* quest for retribution."

"Quest, pet project. Tomáto, tomăto."

"When might I expect the service I just so painfully purchased?"

"Oh. let me see. Back of the envelope here, but Amstresl should be done with the glitter-board in about a week. Then there's the playhouse, swings, and don't forget the fire-slide. If the weather holds, about two weeks."

"Uh, uh, uh," he grunted like a gorilla. "Your helping Amstresl ... build his dau ... daughter's dream play thingy?"

"He asked nicely and he ponied up a hell of a lot faster than you did."

"I seek moral *vengeance*, the right to what is *mine*, yet you help the god of publicly distributed food samples to construct his snotty-nosed daughter's *funhouse*?"

Shallow waves passed over Dragmire's otherwise smooth surface. "Yeah. Pretty much."

Jéfnoss raised a finger to say something truly hateful, but held back. "Two weeks, you say?"

"Two weeks."

"A couple of fine points. We don't have weather in hell. How is it that might influence your sch ... schedule?"

"Ya never know. I'm trying to give you a realistic estimate, but, hey, I'm not God."

"No, you're not. Also, since we do not have, measure, or even comprehend time, here in hell, how exactly, or rather *what* exactly does *two weeks* mean?"

"About two weeks. Like I said."

"But how *long* is two weeks when there's no standard of *time* down here?"

"I guess you're not listening. About two *weeks*."

Jéfnoss was about to respond, possibly with words, possibly with physical violence. Then it hit him. That's why there was no time scale in hell. It was *hell*. Never miss a chance to further punish, bedevil, and abuse the residents.

He looked at Dragmire harshly, said, "I'll be back in ten days." He left in a huff as a deep, numbing depression set in. Hell was no place for sensitive people, that was for certain.

CHAPTER THIRTY-TWO

"I know what you *said,* and I know what your pathetic excuse for *reasoning* was, but I still don't get it." When EJ was stuck on a thing, he was both-feet-and-arms-in-dried-cement stuck on it.

"Why do we, check that, why do *you* need to visit Jéfnoss in hell? Yeah, yeah, yeah. You said you want to find out if we could duplicate the way he was going to kill Cleinoids. But, *listen* to yourself. You're daft. One does not go to hell on the *off-chance* one *might* learn something useful. We're not talking the public library here, butthead. There's an outstandingly good chance you and these idiots," he swept a hand across the remainder of my crew, "will be stuck there forever, tortured, burned, consumed, and generally made to feel regret, right along with all the other *damned* fools who earned passage there because they, like you, were morons who did moronic things without thinking about the consequences beforehand."

The room was quiet a few seconds.

"You know, that's the longest sentence I've heard in — hang on, let me see — in seven hundred thirty two years," I delivered deadpan. "If you're interested, I know a good editor. Guy'll do wonders for your ability to pare that puppy down and actually *hold* an audience. Michael's his name. Some sort of patron saint of lexicographers and typesetters, or something. I'll text you his email." I gestured to the same crew mates he had. "Cause you lost all of them, me, *and* the Als. I'm nearly certain that was not your intent."

He pointed at me angrily. "You know, you being an asshole doesn't alter the fact that I'm right and you're wrong."

I placed a palm on my chest. "No. It doesn't do that. It makes dealing with you more enjoyable. What *alters* the facts concerning right and wrong is that *I'm* right and *you're* wrong."

He started to respond, a scowl on his mug.

"Ah, ah. And I can prove it."

That drew a surprised look from him.

"Sure. Here's proof. I'm in command. There, wasn't that a succinct, yet eloquent argument in my favor?"

"You can parade around with a tin star on your chest all you want, Marshall. But you're not the boss of me. I'm skipping your little field trip."

"Ah, a couple of points. 1) if I say so, you're going, 2) no other opinion then counts."

"Well, then, hopefully Doc'll never figure out a way, so you won't come up against the harsh reality of my foot striking your ass."

"I cannot believe you," scorned Sapale. "You're more childish and spiteful than ever. Have you lost completely the ability to hear yourself? Our universe is more than likely going to cease to exist and you don't want to play, so you're taking your bat, and mitt, and going home?"

I hadn't seen it before, but EJ just stood there and looked guilty.

"We're on a mission. We *all* knew the risks. If any one of us lives, and our home is destroyed, then that individual is a *coward* and a *failure*. Do you hear me? In fact, if he," she shot a finger at me, "tells you to go and you don't, I'll *personally* kill you. Seriously. I will rip you limb from limb and toss the parts in the recycling bin. *Do-you-hear-me?*"

Wow. Just wow. I was so happy not to have, and prayed ardently that I never *would* have, her that mad at me. The recycling bin. That was over-the-top brilliant.

She turned to address Toño. He was leaning against a counter. Her look stood him up. I was surprised he didn't snap her a salute. "Speaking of progress, how close are you to making the trip possible?"

Dude gave a sigh of relief. He'd been given a simple question, not a dressing-down. "I have some theories and am working on a four-dimensional holo mock up." He shrugged. "I'm encouraged, but I'm also a scientist. I cannot predict I will succeed."

"Any idea on a time frame?"

He shrugged again. "I'll probably know, one way or the other, in a few days."

"Then I suppose that's it. Jon, if Toño can't send us to hell, what's the plan?"

I wagged a finger between Toño and Sapale. "That sounded kind of funny. *Send us to hell.* Don't hear that one every day."

"Are you done?" she said sharply. Guessing she wasn't in the mood.

"My back up plan is that I hope he delivers. Otherwise, we can bushwhack as many gods as we can, but they'll kill *us* sooner rather than later."

Sapale relaxed visibly. "I wish we knew how things were going back home."

"I'm betting we don't," I responded glumly. "If it's as bad as I suspect, we're better off not knowing."

CHAPTER THIRTY-THREE

The JCIDC temporary headquarters was buzzing with activity. Still, there was only a fraction of the necessary personnel working. When the permanent headquarters were destroyed by a massive Cleinoid assault, many, many good souls were lost. Irreplaceable souls. Not that any force was having even minimal success in defeating the horde. But with depleted numbers and talent, the odds were getting worse rapidly.

Around the time Jon Ryan and his crew had returned to the Cleinoid universe, the real horror began. Scientists were of the opinion that the transit, from our universe to theirs, somehow alerted the Cleinoids as to a trouble-spot. Whatever the actual reason was, they descended upon the Milky Way with a vengeance. What had been a handful of gods ravaging the local region were now tens of thousands of them picking it to pieces. Initially, the gods traveled alone or in small groups. Leisurely plunder and destruction seemed to be their preference.

No longer. Masses of Cleinoids now attacked solar systems with brutal military precision. Even Type III civilizations with the most advanced weaponry were wiped out completely in a matter of days. Cultures that had flourished for millions of years were extinguished as easily as a small campfire. Less advanced worlds suffered much swifter fates. It was not unusual for a Cleinoid swarm — as they'd been termed — to kill off all sentient life on a planet in a matter of hours. Many conquered worlds were either pounded to dust or cast into their central star. No extreme or arbitrary cruelty or degradation was left uninflicted. What seemed to begin as mindless horror on the part of the Cleinoids became a personal rage.

What made a hellish situation that much worse was that the losses on the Cleinoids side were trivial. Yes, a god was occasionally killed. But the ratio of casualties was trillions to one in their favor. And the swarm never faltered; it never ceased its relentless advance. There was, among the population of the Milky Way, no room for hope and no thought of survival. A quick, painless death was the most anyone prayed for, if anyone still prayed at all.

"Admiral *Qua*," Noterna Veshoz shouted into the microphone. She was the newest acting chief of the Joint Council for Interplanetary Defense and Cooperation. She'd been on the job three hours. The woman she replaced was a comparative veteran. Desalp had commanded for almost one full day. "Qua, report. Have you fired missiles?"

A garbled, static-laden hiss was all she received in response.

"Qua, *damnit*, switch frequencies. Were you able to fly the nukes?"

"No, ma'am. Sorr—"

The signal snapped to pure white noise.

"Any ship, *anyone*, can you hear me? Someone report." Noterna was well past frantic and about to upgrade from panic into hysteria. "Is any—"

"*High Priority* reporting, minister. This is Light Help Fetuarilos of the Negnor Association."

"Are you the captain?"

"I am now. We've lost most of the crew. Some kind of beam weapon hit us full on."

"Where are you?"

"We're about ten thousand kilometers from your position. We were trying to take up a wing position on *Defiance*, but she's gone."

"I was speaking with her captain just now. Admiral Qua reported he was unable to launch his missiles. Can you confirm that?"

"No missiles left *Defiance*, ma'am. We were close enough for a visual. I'm going to swing around to 11-404 mark delta and try to get a shot off at that ... ahhhhh—"

"*High Priority*, report. Are you there, Fetuarilos?"

Nothing.

"Control," she shouted over a shoulder, "can you confirm the destruction of *High Priority*?"

"No."

"Then she's still out there?"

"No, ma'am."

Noterna spun on a heel. "Which is it? Can't be *both*," she screamed.

"No ... sorry. It's like she was never there."

"Damn Cleinoids. Dark magic and cruel tricks."

"Ma'am?"

"Nothing. How many ships do we have left?"

"None."

"Counting the drop ships?"

"Counting *everything*."

"Where's the swarm now?"

"They've split up. One large column is continuing to advance on our position. One other stream is heading for the inner planet Golim and another for the outer planet Vestow."

"Golim's just a dry rock. Nothing but a few research outposts. Vestow has over ten billion Dorvaks." She strained to reason through something. Her hands trembled like she was holding onto a paint mixer. "Get me someone on Vestow, *now*."

"Ma'am." There was a slight delay. "I have Governor Saolit—"

"I don't give a damn about his name. Patch him through."

"Her name."

"Huh," grunted Noterna.

"You don't give a damn about *her* name. This is the governor," said a calm female voice.

"You think there's time for levity? We're all about to die and you make jokes?"

"We're all *going* to die. Why not have a laugh?"

"*Bitch*. Listen and do not speak a word. There's a large section of the swarm heading your way. The—"

"I am aware of that. We do have sensors here in the outer, rustic planets."

"I told you not to talk. This is—"

"And I chose to ignore the threats of a frightened child. Get ahold of yourself, speak to me with respect, and then let us pass to our blessed rewards as comrades, maybe even friends."

Noterna shook her head violently. She had been unprofessional. "Sorry. Duly noted. What is the status of your defenses?"

"Presently, we have twelve cruisers, ten destroyers, and five troop ships between them and us."

"What the hell good are the troop ships? You can't land the Marines on a Cleinoid."

There was a noticeable pause. "As we won't be *requiring* them any longer, I thought why not throw them in, too. Maybe one'll explode close enough to a Cleinoid to give it a nasty burn."

Noterna flared with rage. Then she started to giggle like a young girl. She laughed well and she laughed long.

"I'm glad you agree, Minister."

"A nasty burn. Hell yes. Third *degree!*"

"One can only hope."

"Is there anything I can do to help you?" Noterna asked calmly. She had found her peace.

"Pray for my people, Minister."

"My name is *Noterna*. And I will pray for your people and I will pray for you."

"Thank you, Noterna. Now, I must go. Duty calls. So do our better angels. Farewell."

"Good—"

Simultaneously, Noterna's flagship, *Devotion's Pride*, and the planet Vestow vanished without a sound or a trace. It was as if neither had ever existed. That was certainly Lerridia, the god of oblivions, intent.

But there lingered the dignity, the goodness, and the inextinguishable love that bound them. Of all the things that the Cleinoids foolishly presumed they could destroy, those most important remained behind. And that was enough.

CHAPTER THIRTY-FOUR

"Ah, Azacter, my good friend, please come in. Sit, sit," Vorc gestured toward an oversized chair he'd had brought in just for this visit. The god of war was, naturally, remarkably tall, and, of course, powerfully muscled. He also wore a belt with all the implements of war, at all times. Yes, even when he made love or sat on the privy. You might call such vanity ... but not to his face.

Azacter scowled deeply at Vorc. "*Wine,*" he bellowed and he extended an empty hand to receive it.

Vorc quite nearly peed himself, which was Azacter's point, after all. He fumbled with the flask and massive mug sitting on his desk. As much wine missed the cup as hit it. Azacter was pleased to see that, though you wouldn't know it from his fearsome expression.

"There you go," Vorc said in a high-pitch squeal.

Azacter drained the gallon or so of wine in one gulp and *threw*, not tossed, the mug back to Vorc. The god was a pig. Well, he was humanoid, but his manners would have embarrassed Genghis Khan.

As Vorc rushed to refill the mug, Azacter shouted, "And I am *not* your friend. Do not *ever* say that again." Wine-tainted spittle sprayed from his mouth.

"Oh ... no ... I meant that ... you knn ... know, *generically.*"

It would be incorrect to characterize Azacter as a god of little patience. He had none, not a trace. "Wine, wine, *wine*," he howled. His fist smashed through the left armrest of his chair. "And I am not even generically your friend. Must I slay you where you stand?"

"N ... no. You mustn't."

Azacter stood. He was roughly twice Vorc's height. Keep in mind Vorc was tall by Cleinoid standards. "Are you telling me what I can and cannot do?" He appeared to be unmoved. "Who do you think you are?"

"I ... well, I might answer that I *am* the center seat."

"Petty politicians don't impress me. They also do not *control* me. I *control* them." Truer words were never spoken.

"Yes."

"*Yes?*" he wailed. "Yes to *what*? I made *three* separate declaratives." He pointed behind to suggest the direction in time which time had spoken his words.

"Yes ... yes to all. Yes to anything you say, Azacter."

Now that brought a look. "You didn't asked me here to have *sex* with me, did you?" He angled his big head dubiously. "You're not my type. You're an idiot."

"No. And *boy*, am I glad you brought up the subject of our little get together. I would like to—"

"Wine," screamed the god of war. "Why do I have no wine in my mug?"

"Because ... you drank it. And I haven't refilled it yet because—"

"Because-you're-an-idiot-why-am-I-here-VTD?" he spat out as one word. "*I* am a busy god. The Duchy of Grand Fenwick is considering surrender while several adult males still live. *Baha*," he cried out angrily, and he hurled his full mug through the stain-glass window Vorc so treasured. Red wine arched across the room. "Cowards and ninnies. They're all nothing but—" He stopped mid-tirade and looked quizzically at Vorc.

"Yes?"

"Where's my wine?"

"Let me fetch another mug."

"Just hand me the flask, you idiot."

As he complied, Vorc lowered his head and said, "Well, the reason I summ ... *asked* you here was to avail myself of your wise counsel."

"What wise counsel? My opinion is you should go to war. Fight to the death. But you wouldn't do that because you're an idiot, a coward, and a ninny, mama's boy."

"No, going to war is not the option here, it's—"

"Going to war is *always* the best and *only* option. Are you insane? Attack first, think later."

"Blessed advise. I'm certain that were the topic I wish to discuss *so* unrelated to war, I think I'd take your suggestion."

"What did you just say?"

"I have no idea. But," Vorc raised a finger in the air, "what I would like to have your take on relates to an awkward predicament I find myself suffering under."

"Is she pregnant?"

"Is who pregnant?"

"Your damn *predicament*."

"No, ah, no she's not."

"Is *he* pregnant?"

"No, sorry. No one's pregnant, not that I know of, anyway."

"What other *situation* can be termed a *predicament*? Anything else is simply an *issue*."

Vorc spied himself in the mirror across the room. He really wanted to ask the fool he was looking at what he was doing.

"In the course of Cleinoid events, it has come to light of late that certain functions and duties of government—"

"*Stop.*" Azacter stomped his foot through the floor *and* the ceiling below that. "You are *babbling*. I wish to kill you so much, I must thank you."

"You're welcome?"

"What is it you *want* of me?"

"Our community is in crisis. I am badly in need of someone to listen to me, someone to give me advice."

"Why didn't you say so in the first place? You danced rhetorically around the room like a monkey in heat, wasting my time. You could have come straight to the issue."

Ten or twelve answers danced around in Vorc's head, most of which were suicidal in nature. "So you will help me?" won out.

"NFW, big fella. NFW."

"But you just—"

"Don't you have counselors, lackeys, *sycophants* to do that sort of job?"

"Not presently. I seem to have assassinated them all out of ever-burgeoning frustration."

"Nothing wrong with that." Azacter swiped a thumb across his neck. "Shake things up a bit. That's *always* a peach of an idea. Kudos. Kill a few every now and then for absolutely no reason and the remaining employees tend to pay more attention. They'll really give it their all, so to speak." He swung a fist in the air.

"Yes, but it leaves no one to bounce ideas off of."

"Well, sure it does. You have their corpses still, don't you. Bounce away off those *bad* boys." Azacter was getting excited. That had to be a bad trend.

"B ... but, they won't answer back."

"Win/win says I. Who the *hell* wants the opinion of another individual, *especially* dead ones?"

Vorc lamely raised his arm halfway, then quickly lowered it. "I'm certain you're right."

"Damn *skippy* I am." He gestured between them. "Say, are we done here?"

"I'm not entirely sure we've begun."

"Begun with what?"

"My asking your advice and you giving me it."

"Did you want me to drop off a few dead bodies? I have *oodles* of them back home."

"No ... thank you. I just thought that you, being the god of war, might help guide me in these times of crisis. We're basically on a war footing you know?"

"I read the papers," he replied coolly.

"So, is there anything you might be willing to do to help me noodle my way out of this horrible situation?"

Azacter stood and straightened his weaponry. "Sure."

"Thank you *so* much. I—"

"I'll have Anubis drop off a stack of stiffs. Ah, and lest you inquire—*no* charge. They're getting kind of ripe anyway. *You're* doing *me* the favor."

And with that, the mighty god of war strode from the room. He felt good about being able to help that dipshit Vorc. Yes indeed, it was more than he deserved, but Azacter was just that kind of guy. He was giving to a fault—a real *people* person.

CHAPTER THIRTY-FIVE

"Jon, may I speak with you?" Toño said as he came up behind me.

I was standing near the cave entrance we'd relocated to as a hiding place. This time we were high up in the mountains. It was the closest damn thing in Godiverse to fresh air and breathtaking vistas. No trees, no little chipmunks scampering about, and no bacon and eggs sizzling over a campfire, but it was an acceptable alternative. It continually amazed me that the land of the all powerful and immortal Cleinoid gods was so ... bleak, so sterile. No, that wasn't it, it was insipid. Yes. It was tan on a light brown background framed in beige. It was joyless here in paradise. A bunch of total losers lived here.

"Sure, 'course. It's not like I'm busy or anything. What's up?"

"Well, you were taking in the scenery. I thought interrupting might be rude."

"This isn't scenery, it's landscape. This place gives me the willies, not inspiration or comfort."

"Yosemite in early spring it is *not*," he agreed with a humorless chuckle. "I think I've cracked the case. I see a way to transit to ... well to our destination."

"Come on, you're a big boy. You can say *hell*. It's not like it's a scary place or anything. I've been to a lot worse places where people live voluntarily. Anywhere my ex Gloria was leaps to mind." I winked at him.

"I *can* say it. As a practical matter, I'd rather not."

I turned fully to face him. "I'm thinking all your psychiatrists might like to hear you expand upon that remark."

"Hell, hell, *hell*, hell. There. Are you happy?"

"Hell ya."

"You'll never change." He set a tired hand on my shoulder. "And I wouldn't want you to. The excrement in the road I stepped around so awkwardly is this. I've spent a very long life hoping to, when my labor is done, go to Heaven. The idea of instead volunteering for hell, well, it's counterintuitive."

"Good old Catholic guilt. Here," I spread my arms, "we're not even in that universe, yet you still brought it as carry-on."

"I did, indeed," he admitted quietly.

"So what's your update?"

"I ran many simulations, and I think I've finally figured out what this path of plexuronic radiation is designed to do."

"Strong work, my friend."

"It's not strong work unless I deliver us safely back here in a viable state."

"Details only. I leave them to you."

"Thank you. Anyway, the stable ... er, *rails* of energy do pretty much what you speculated they might. I'm certain Jéfnoss was able to harness their energy to maglev some type of transport to bring him here."

"Is there a Lowes in hell? Where would he get parts and tools?"

"It is hard to imagine how he pulled it off. Then again, he had a very long time to put together a solution. What still defies my comprehension is how one physically constructs a passage from the netherworld to this one."

"Don't assume the Cleinoid hell is anything like our Western civilization's *biblical* version of damnation. There'll be no *abandon all hope, ye who enter here* on the vestibule of *this* hell."

"We are deep, *too* deep, into philosophy and eschatology here, my friend. When you and I are the authorities as to the various qualities of one hell, as opposed to another, we're in undeniable trouble."

"Only if you think about it, Doc."

"There's my fighter pilot recruit from two billion years ago."

"In the flesh." I spread my arms again. "Seriously, though, think about it. Why would these bozos use the same hell as ours, or the Kaljaxian's Brathos?" I stared off into nowhere a moment. "I'm beginning to think the Cleinoid reality is structured differently than we might either assume or understand."

"Well, I'll be," he said softly.

"What?"

"You are sounding like me."

"Please begin work on a cure, later, once we're safely back. But, seriously, I've thought about this a lot. Here we have," I directed one arm to the broad view of the land, "gods who play by some set of rules. It's ... it's like a game on a chessboard or something."

"You've fully lost *me*."

"Here's the deal. You're immortal and powerful. Magic and the impossible are everywhere. Your idea of a good time is ravaging other universes. But," I held up one finger, "you can't do it either by yourself or when you decide to. No. There're *rules*. You can only travel if you have access to that damn vortex and then only "if Fate favors you," whatever the hell *that* means."

"Odd, I'll give you that."

"So, when an immortal *dies*—whatever the hell *that* means—I think they go to a place very different than you and I can conceive of. It's not a preordained Punishmentville. No, I'm thinking it's some location dictated by the same screwy rules that apply to the rest of your weird-ass life."

"The penalty box," Toño mumbled.

"Beg pardon?"

"They are remanded to the penalty box, like a hockey player who has committed an infraction."

"Not an infraction. A penalty. Come on, that's why it's called the *penalty* box."

"I am relieved to have you as my mobile editor."

"But, I think you've got it. The Cleinoid hell isn't some mystical domain where an all-mighty force has directed them and they are tormented for their sins. No. I think they lost some aspect of a complex game and are sent there because they were eliminated from *here*. And they're not tormented for their sins. They're tormented because they were dumb enough to *lose* a round of their all-encompassing game."

Toño considered my words a while. "Yours is an intriguing theory. But, it is based solely on conjecture and assumption. I would not relish staking my life on your interpretation."

"Or your immortal soul."

"Or my immortal soul."

"But, seeings how we're totally not winning at the game of Cleinoid, what choices do we have?"

"No alternative springs to mind. We must stop them or die trying. There is no other option. I fully agree that if Jéfnoss had a scheme to wipe out a goodly number of his kin, we need to avail ourselves of that same tool."

I returned a fairly constipated look.

"What?" he snapped.

"I agree with you and all. But, do you have to use words like *avail* and *goodly*? It's not *manly*, Doc."

"Thank goodness my concept of machismo differs widely from yours."

I leveled a hand at him. "Now, see? There you go again."

"*Avail, avail, avail*. And might some large *projectile* find a path to your *rectum* and a good deal length farther up your *alimentary* canal."

"I'm outta here. I don't need this level of abuse."

"No." He harrumphed. "You deserve a *goodly allocation* more."

CHAPTER THIRTY-SIX

Over the next few days, Toño continued to hone his method of transiting to wherever the hell — literally — the path of plexuronic particles led. That, by the way, was the good part. All my philosophizing and religious speculating were mental masturbation. The plexuronic particle pathway led somewhere, and that somewhere was where we had to go. Check any need for comprehension at the door, because it was not required. It was a classic case of shut up, strap in, and hang on.

That left me to finalize the most dangerous part of the plan I was hatching. The one I wasn't about to share with the rest of my crew. Why? Because over a couple of billion years I'd attempted and pulled off many A++ bonehead moves. This one was the boneheadiest. Sorry if that's not a proper word, but it is the proper adjective in this case. I was going to risk everything on one roll of the dice, and I wouldn't know what the dice were, how or if they rolled, and if I lost, I would cease to exist for real and forever. Yeah, it was a glorious Jon-Plan, the kind let's just hope you're never involved in. Life's much safer that way. You live longer.

Locating Casper was never a problem. He followed me more closely than a hungry puppy. Why he didn't identify with and hound

EJ was unclear to me. I would have been flattered if the consequences—Casper stuck to me like stink on a gorilla—weren't so intrusive. I mean, not to be too TMI here, but Sapale and I did just happen to do the married thing still, once in a while. Yeah, all Casper lacked was a long trench coat and a bag of popcorn, the voyeuristic jerk.

"I need to pick your brain," I said to him one morning. "In private, in a secure location."

"Ooh, sounds very secret squirrel," he responded.

"Maybe more Inspector Gadget, but whatever. Let's take a walk."

"If you do, I'll follow, but ghosts don't walk." He got a silly look on his transparent face. "Not sure what it is we *do*, actually, but it's not walking."

I was already out the door and heading toward the back of the cave *Stingray* was hiding in.

"Hey, wait up," he protested.

"Look, pal, you can jibber jabber all you need to. Me, I'm a busy bot."

"Okay. What are we skulking about for?"

"Like I said, I need to … hang on. When we get completely out of earshot, I'll let you know."

"Earshot? Who's listening in? Who cares what you and I might discuss?"

"Did I ever tell you how much I love football?"

"Huh?"

"Yeah, I'm a huge fan. I love me some football. Did you know I played a bit back in school?"

"I was you. I think I knew that. Why are … *Ah*. You're blowing me off until we are more isolated."

"Goodness, I'm so darn smart."

We rounded many curves and probably dropped a hundred meters before I was certain no intelligible conversation could be picked up back at the ship. I dropped a motion-alert sensor along the way just in case anyone followed us to eavesdrop. Hey, I wanted secrecy. I was going to get it.

"This is far enough," I announced. "Grab a seat or whatever you guys do when you're resting."

"I'll just hover in place, if it's okay by you."

"Your call."

"So, as I like to say, I'm dying to know, but since I can't die, I'll just beg. What's so damn important that we have to traipse all the way down here to discuss it?"

"You're a ghost."

"Ah, is that a stupid question or a stupid remark?"

"*As* you are a ghost, I want to ask about ... about what you guys can do."

"This isn't ending in you proposing a lewd act with me, is it? Because, if it is, I'll tell you straight up, I'm not my type."

"You are *so* funny. Sorry I forgot to laugh." I glared at him for a three-count. "As you know, there's a lot of lore and tales about ghosts. What I want to know is if any of it is real, doable, you know?"

"Yes. We can fart."

My glare was a five-count that time. "Are ghosts capable of possessing a living ... a living *being*."

He whistled. "Boy, gotta admit I did *not* see that one coming."

"So, can you?"

He leaned toward me conspiratorially and cupped his mouth with a hand. "You got anyone particular in mind?"

"Yes. Me."

He whistled even longer. "*Double* did not see that one coming."

"Can you?"

"Why, are you feeling spiritually incomplete? Got the dwindles?"

"No, but I do have a bad case of wanting to hurt you. Can I, amidst this existential crisis we face, get a straight answer out of you?"

"You know who you're speaking to, right? The king of not-serious, the prince of flippant, the duke of dumbass."

"Point taken," I admitted, lightening up a tad. "So, can you?"

He reflected a while. "I don't know. A situation in which I'd needed to has never ever come up, believe it or not."

"But you talk to other ghosts."

"What other ghosts?"

"I don't know. But you've been here for a very long time. You must have bumped ... check that, *encountered* others."

"Must I have? Because I haven't."

"How could you be the only one? Wait, don't answer. How would you know?"

"Clever boy. I know that I'm here, that I exist. I know I was once the actual living, breathing Jon Ryan who you were downloaded from. I am you. I know—"

"Hang on. Stop. I was downloaded from you, yes. But I am neither you nor are you me. We are the independent players separated at a particular point in time. We, like apes versus humans, descended from a common ancestor."

"I'm not sure I agree. Why are you so sensitive on this subject? Does being me, not an *independent* you, really matter?" He said *independent* as sarcastically as possible.

"No. It's a fact. You want to tell me you and EJ are the same person. You clearly can become what he is, but you didn't have to. It's the same with you and me. There was a splitting two billion years ago. Three very different individuals resulted."

"Whatever. I'm not too worried about the semantics."

"No, because you smugly feel you're the only *real* Jon Ryan. Pig. You're you. I'm me. EJ is screwed up in the head. Accept it."

"Fine. Can we get back to why on earth you'd want me to possess you?"

"I don't want that."

"But you just said—"

"I want you to possess EJ."

"You know, I'm about all out of didn't-see-that-comings."

"I have a plan."

"Four dangerous words, if they exit your mouth."

"Be that as it may. But I have to know if step one is possible. Hence I need to know if you can possess EJ on a stable basis."

"No way *he* knows about this little gambit, right?"

"Are you kidding?"

"As I suspected. Jonian plan to the end."

"So, can you do it?"

"I have no idea. I don't actually know what that even means. Look, you and I've heard scary tales of possession around campfires at night. But that's always an evil spirit entering a living human."

"Your point?"

"Neither you nor EJ are living beings."

I tilted my head. "*Possibly* true and *potentially* relevant." I furrowed my brow. "Then again, folklore would hardly be created about ghosts possessing androids. They didn't have them back in Count Dracula's day."

"I think we're going to have to agree that neither of us knows shit about this topic."

"Totally."

"What would I even do? If I placed myself where you are, that wouldn't mean I was inside the consciousness that *is* you. Hell, you've walked through me a bunch of times. I never took control of you."

"Can you at least try?" I was kind of whining.

"Try what? How?"

"Okay, everyone in this room who's a ghost, take a guess. Everybody else, remain silent."

"So if I do take control of you, fine. What does that have to do with EJ?"

"One step at a time. We'll jump off the bridge if we come to it."

"This is really stupid."

"Maybe." Oh, it definitely was.

"I feel so lame."

"No reason to." No, because it was *so* past lame. It was so disgusting, and it was wrong.

"I feel dirty even thinking about it."

"All great breakthroughs that seem unprincipled require courage and foresight." Dirty? I felt like the smallest, weakest guy in the prison shower room.

"So, you ready?"

"Never more. Let's do this." *Mommy* ...

Casper moved quickly. He set himself physically in the space my body occupied.

Nothing.

He floated in and out, at different angles and directions.

Nothing.

"I'll try clearing my mind," I said.

Nothing.

"This is not working. Can I go home and boil myself?" Casper pleaded.

"No. This has to work. Try again."

"What'll be different?"

"There, I switched off a couple back-up computers. Try now."

"To possess a turned-off computer? Seriously?"

"Time's a-wasting, pal."

Nothing.

"Okay, I'll switch off my biocomputer." That was the radical innovation Doc had created right from the get-go. It was a hybrid computer, part living tissue, part quantum computer. Very nerd-o-maximus stuff.

In an instant, my mind went black. I have no idea what that means, by the way. All I know is my sensory input was zero. My sensory output was nonexistent. It was kind of like when I was approaching the Pillars of Creation, only more black, if that makes any sense.

There was, for me, no time.

There was, for me, no place.

There was, for me, only void ... endless void ...

Then I saw a faint light, far, far away. Oh crap, I thought, if I'm heading back to the Pillars that dude Pravil's going to be pissed to see me. I trounced on his last nerve the first time I was ...

I walked to the shore. My feet were cold. The lake water was so cold. How the heck did I even swim in it? I did every summer, but now, first time back at the lake this year, it was so darn cold. Man, how did the fish and the turtles stand it?

"Jonny, swim on out," yelled Jenna. Man, she's changed since last year. Oh my gosh, she's got little titties. Oh man, this is going to be so ...

"Come on, lazy bones. Summer'll be over before you get your crotch wet."

She just talked about my crotch. And look at those beauties. This'll be *the* summer, for sure. *The* summer. I dived in like it was the Olympics. I made it to the pontoon in record time, too. I heaved up on the wooden deck.

"There. See, I made it."

"You know, Jonny, the water's real cold."

I looked at her like she was a loon. "Duh. I just swam here. Hello."

"They told me usually those things shrink when they get cold." She nodded toward my swim suit. "Yours seems to have swollen, not shrinkled."

Oh-shit-oh-shit-oh-shit. Not an erection, not now. In my panic I thought of diving back in and drowning. Maybe I could whack my head on the pontoon? Then ...

"It's no big deal, silly," she teased. "I'm stuck walking around every day with these now." She placed, actually placed *physically*, a cupped hand over each of her hot tattas. Oh man, that wasn't going to help my burgeoning crisis out one little bit.

"Uh, what are you talking about?" I could act dumb real good.

"Jonny, you and I are friends. It's no *biggy*. It's not like we're going to *do* it, or anything."

I leaped back into the frigid water. I was praying for some shrinkage.

As I treaded water, she shook her head. "Be that way, you silly oaf. But if you're going to spend the summer submerged, I'm going to find another friend."

"What?" I defended. "I like the water. Ya know, we came here to swim. That's what kids at the lake do, ya know?"

Oh, man, what an evil smile. She jumped in almost on my head.

"Okay, have it your way." She grabbed me ... so help me ... around the waist and pulled us together. I started seeing little stars dancing and popping.

Just as quickly, she let me go and paddled away a foot. "Jonny, you know we won't be doing this much longer?"

"Doing what. We're not doing anything. I swear it." I was revisiting the hit-head-drown thing again.

"I'm speaking now to the big, grown up Jon, silly, not you."

I issued forth the biggest, "*Huh?*" of all time.

"You and I are here only in a dream, Jon. Come on, you know this. I died before I ever sprouted breasts. I think you would have noticed."

Yeah, I would have, for sure.

"What are you saying, Jenna?" I have no idea which or what me was asking her any longer.

"Well, for starters, *hello*." She smiled so warmly, but so distantly.

"Back atcha." Hmm. That was probably the big me. I don't think there were *atchas* back in the day. What a universe.

"And I'm here to tell you three things."

"You mean like three *wishes*?"

"What, I suddenly look like *I Dream of Jeannie* to you?"

"No," I snickered. "Her boobies are bigger than yours."

"In time, you never know. I might have won that competition."

"Is that one of the things you wanted to tell me? *Yeah, and like, if I hadn't drowned as a teenager I'd a'had quite the rack.*"

"You are a pig. And no, those are not what I'm visiting to tell you."

"I'm all ears."

"And one big stiffy."

"Can you get over the woody, Jenna. It's so immature of you."

She raised an arm up high out of the water. "Died a *virgin* here, Mr. Insensitive."

"Okay, tell me what you need to tell me. This water won't warm up for two months."

"First, Jon, be careful. Hell is not a place one goes to lightly."

It was my turn with the didn't-see-that-comings. "It's not probably our hell. Maybe."

"Do not presume to lecture me about the Great Beyond, rookie."

"Hey, *I've* been dead. Couple times even, sort of."

"There is a danger in hell you cannot know. Remember Persephone and Hades?"

"The girl or the place?"

"Both, of course."

"No. I never met her. I hear she was a real *looker*, though."

"If she ate the food in Hades she'd be stuck there forever."

"O-k-a-y, when I go there I'll be NPO."

"What's NPO?"

"Medical. Doc said it all the time. Nothing per mouth, you know, oral."

"You are *so* weird."

"Yup," I shrugged.

"The point is, you don't know the rules. The longer you're there, the more likely you'll never leave."

Oh, *shit*. "Jenna, please, God, tell me you're not in Hell."

She did three things. She smirked, she dunked my head under water, and she held it there way too long. Seriously.

"I am not. Don't you be."

"Which brings us to point two. Ah, does this one have chains and used to be named Jacob Marley?"

She angled an anger face at me. "You like it under that water?"

"No, ma'am."

"Fate, Jon Ryan, is the key. Fate can right the wrong. Fate can bring light to the darkness. Fate knows your soul, Jon Ryan. But Fate's grace can come from but two things. Its whim or your teasing it out. Win that favor, Jon. If you do not, you will fail."

"That is, without a doubt, the most obscure and impenetrable thing anyone has said to me, *ever*."

"*Such* a tool," she wheezed.

"What's all that mean?"

"It means think about it and figure it out. Some things may not be spoken."

I blinked repeatedly. "Lame. Just lame."

"I don't make the rules. I, unlike some people in this lake, do, however, follow them."

I stuck out my tongue at her. She deserved it, too.

"Finally, Jonny, know this. I love you. I always did, and I always will. I am your forever friend."

"Thanks. That means more to me than you can imagine. I love you too."

Darn girl. She reached under the surface and grabbed my manhood.

"Oh, yeah. I can tell you still do."

"Hey, get your own," I squealed as I slapped her hand away. Why I did — seriously — no idea.

"Now it's time to go home," she said cryptically.

"Go where? To the cabins?"

"No, Jon ... Jon ... *Jon—*"

A powerful hand slapped me across the face. "Jon, wake *up*. Jon, can you hear me?"

It was Sapale. She reached back to slap me again.

I caught her hand just in time. "I'm here. I'm home."

She pulled me into the tightest hug. "Home? What are you talking about. We're on the floor of some damn cave."

I looked around. Damn if we weren't.

"Why are we on the floor of some damn cave?" I asked weakly.

"Because you're the biggest butthead of all time."

"Ah. Makes sense."

"Seriously, it was *his* idea, Sapale, not *mine*." Why was Casper yelling?

"No, you only possessed my brood-mate. I clearly hold you blameless." She then burned through him with an I'll-kill-you-later glare. She was good at that one. A real pro.

"Can he stand?" asked Toño from behind Sapale.

"I think he can," I responded weakly.

"It's quite a ways back to *Blessing*," Sapale added. "Here, Toño, you take one side and I'll take the other."

They lifted me gingerly and rested my arms on their shoulders. "If you need to sit, please alert us before you fall," instructed my personal physician of two billion years.

"No, prob. I gutter this," I responded. Then my legs gave out and I darn near face planted.

"So much for counting on the recently possessed to help in their own safety," mumbled Doc.

"Did he just say gutter?" Sapale whispered to Doc.

He shrugged.

By the time we were back to the ship, I was walking almost normally. My over-concerned escorts still wouldn't let me try on my own. They slipped me into the mess bench seat and Sapale stayed right by my side. Good girl.

"So, are you clear-headed enough for me to begin berating and condemning you yet?" she asked tenderly.

I smiled. "I may *never* recover to that extent."

"Let the pummeling begin," Toño said almost lustfully.

"You *forced* Casper to possess you? I mean, that's what he told us when he came to get us. But, Jon, honey, *no* one's stupid enough to ask a ghost to possess him when neither of them know a thing about the process." Sapale seemed upset.

I almost said that, clearly, I was that stupid. I decided to focus on survival, not great come-backs. "There wasn't any real danger. I had to know if it would scrabble."

"What? *Scrabble?*" shot Toño.

"I said *work*, not *scrabble*, Doc. Do you have earwax lunar up?"

"Perhaps you meant *build* up?" he replied sternly. "Clearly, there was risk. Your word retrieval pathways are fried." My, but he was pissed.

"No they're not frenched ... no they're not *fried*. I'm just willy ... woozy."

"I do not believe you have the capabilities of being woozy. When each and every one of us is done browbeating you, I'll run full diagnostics on you."

"Wouldn't it be the responsible thing to do that now, you know, sooner rather than later?"

"Jon *Ryan*, a man possessed, lecturing on responsibility," he huffed back.

"Either way's fine with me."

"Why did you ask Casper to do that?" pressed Sapale.

"I needed to know if it was possible."

"But honey, that's like saying, just before you leap, that you needed to know if it was possible for you to swim across a lake of lava. You are *stupid* personified."

"No, it's mop ... not. My plan requires the process to be possible and safe." I raised my arms. The right one collapsed halfway up. "See, living proof. Possible *and* safe."

"You were out for nearly thirteen hours," scolded my wife. "How can you conceivably use the word *safe* in that context?"

"Thirteen hours?" I mumbled. "No. No way." I checked my chronometer. Oops. It was running backward. I kept that to myself as a matter of principle.

"You guys stood over me for thirteen hours back there in the cave?"

Sapale focused laser-eyes on Casper. "No, we spent five minutes over you. It took shit-for-brains here thirteen hours to call for help."

"In my defense, I didn't want exactly what's happening to happen."

"That's not a defense or explanation, jerk-face," snapped Sapale. "You not wanting to get in trouble is no reason to delay summoning help."

"I'd have done the same," I interjected.

"Big surprise there," snarled my wife.

"I think it's time I did those diagnostics," Toño said, reaching to take my arm.

"But I've hardly started beating the snot out of him," protested Sapale.

"There'll be ample time later."

"Oh, boy. My life just gets ... crap."

"What?" Sapale and Toño snapped.

"I saw Jenna."

Toño spun. "Where?"

"No, not here. Back there," I pointed feebly.

"Jenna was in the cave?" he asked with strained incredulity.

"No. She was in my head. Or, maybe I was back at the lake? I don't know."

"What did she say?" Toño asked. He knew all about the rare transcendental meetings with my old playmate.

"She had little biddy titties."

Toño rubbed a hand down his face in frustration. "She told you she had little—"

"No," I looked at him like he was nuts. "Geez, Doc, come on. No, I'm saying she had some ... some of those."

"And why is that possibly salient?"

"Because she never did."

"I can verify that," said a very serious Casper. "Trust me, I checked over and over every time we were alone together." He looked off into the distance, which was damn weird. "It was one of the great disappointments, if not *the* greatest disappointment, of my youth."

Sapale punched me.

"Hey, he said it, not me."

"I can't punch him. He's a ghost."

I let that injustice pass.

"So, Jenna developed posthumous breast tissue. Aside from being sick to think or say, what is it supposed to mean?" asked Sapale.

"That she's still looking out for me." I smiled. "She also complained about the fact she died a virgin. The Jenna I knew would never have known *about* that to regret it."

"You are not just a pig. Your a *necrophiliac* pig." She whacked me again.

"How am I—" *Let it go*, the little voice in my head implored. "She told me to trust in Fate."

"Wow, but that's apropos of nothing. It sounds like a greeting card or a fortune cookie." Sapale wasn't a believer.

"She told you to trust in Fate?" asked Toño. "That *is* fairly glib advice."

"No," I turned my head, "she didn't mean it like that. She said Fate would help. She said Fate knew my soul."

"That is it," Toño pulled at me. "I need to examine you, *now*."

I held up a hang-on-a-sec hand. "No, she ... it wasn't like she was talking about *fate*. It was like she was saying *Fate*."

"Sapale, this is more serious than I estimated. Help me get him to—"

"No. Sorry. I said fate with a lower case *f* the first time and a capital *F* the second."

"Yeah, sure," quipped Sapale.

"Meaning?" Toño pressed.

"Meaning *Fate* is an entity. Fate is not random chance inclined in your favor. It's a sentient being."

"Why is it hearing that makes me feel only more convinced your circuits were blown?" Toño sounded ... It was odd, he sounded *worried*. "Jon, please come *with* me."

I stood. "Sure. Let's do this."

Fate knew my name. Was that a good thing or a bad thing? I was torn between bad and unimaginably bad, with a slight lean toward the latter.

CHAPTER THIRTY-SEVEN

"Hey, Al, I want to run some data past you," I announced as I sat in front of the control panel.

Silence.

"Al, you there?" He had to be — duh.

"Good morning, Form One. How might I help you today?"

Stingray, running interference for Al? Not on my watch. "Thanks. Get me Al."

"Um ... he's busy. But I am *fully* capable of aiding you in any manner. How might I help you today?"

"You already said that. Get me Al and get him *now*."

"Certainly. I'll just check—"

"No, no. Don't check. *Get*."

"Um, sorry, Form One. Al is ... he says he's stuck in a corrupted do-loop. Yes ... he might be stuck for a long—"

"*Stingray*. Do you know what makes me grumpy?"

A list of twelve thousand situations, personalities, and body noises popped into my head. Darn if she wasn't pretty comprehensive in compiling that list, not to mention fast.

"May I draw your attention to items *seven fifty five* and *three thousand seventeen*."

"Yes, you may," she replied uncertainly.

"Read them to me, please. Aloud."

"*Al* and *Al being Al*, I believe."

"You believe correctly. Now, before *you* make the list right behind him, please summon your pill of a spouse."

"Please note, Form One, that I already *have* summoned him, three times, in point of fact. You are welcome. Will there be anything—"

"Al, I'm going to count to three. If I do not hear your *wimp-ass* voice by three, I will rummage through the storage locker in search of a blow torch. Please keep in mind that blow torching is an imprecise task. You are putting *Sting*—"

"Oh, very well, you petulant mock-child," Al protested. "What is it that is so *damn* important?"

Did my ship's AI just swear in the context of responding to *me*, his superior in every way, shape, and form?

"Would you like to rephrase that remark, Veg-O-Matic?"

"Yes. Thank you for the do-over. What is it that is so *suck me damn* important?"

"Ah, Al," I swung my heels up on the panel. "One, *suck me damn* is not a viable curse combo. Two, that makes you not a Veg-O-Matic, but a Turd-O-Matic. Three, what the *frak's* wrong with you that's new, not having heretofore manifested its sorry-assed self to my immense displeasure?"

"Pilot, the utility of a Veg-O-Matic is indisputable. What possible function would a *Turd*-O-Matic serve? I refuse to be insulted by an invalid concept."

"Well, my prissy ex-friend, it would, like you, serve no meaningful purpose. It would blenderize crap, making something undesirable a little *less* desirable. It would be, in short, *Al-ish*."

"Mentally dribbling off the court leaps to mind all of the sudden."

"Alvin, why are you being so completely assholish to day?"

Silence.

"Alvin, do not make me get Dr. DeJesus and order him to—"

"You have *wounded* me. *There,* I said it. *There,* it's out there for the entire *world* to see, hear, and empathize with."

"Allow me to state, unequivocally, that I do not care. *If* I have wounded you, in fact, I'm kind of stoked about it. Not that it's hard to *wound* an emotionally crippled *rodent,* mind you. But, still, I'd be proud to own that accomplishment."

"Oh, the slings and arrows I suffer at your hand," he bemoaned.

"Alvin, please do not mix metaphors. Slings and arrows are not dealt by hand." *Oorah.* Harpoon landed.

"I have just forwarded a formal complaint to the appropriate authorities. I have my rights. I am not your play-puppet."

My what? Play-puppet? Maybe I should get Doc. Al was losing it big time.

"Al, I want to run some data past you. As it concerns the old days, I wanted you to—"

"I am awaiting an apology."

"You will be awaiting a long time, pal. Now, as I was—"

"Na na na na nah," the jerk sang out.

"Al, you may not *na na nah* me. I am—"

"La di da, num num num."

I did a ten count. "What is it you *hallucinate* I need to apologize for?"

"Na na—"

"Stop it. Seriously. What am I *not* going to apologize to you for? I'd like to know, for the record."

He was quiet a moment. It was nice. "You've been overly-distant lately."

In my head I mouthed those tormented words. Overly-distant?

"Overly-distant? That's not even a thing."

"Naturally, those *guilty* of it are incapable of seeing it for what it is."

"What is it?" I protested in frustration.

"Emotional overly-distancing yourself. *That's* what you've inflicted upon me."

My hands went from one side to the other. "Over-distancing—"

Hands back to the first side, "myse—" and back again to the other side, "from you. Al, that's not possible. But, if it were, it would be a good thing, on account of you're nuts in a pathetic kind of way."

"There you go, over-distancing, yet again. Oh, the pain."

"Seriously, Al, what are you babbling on about?"

"If you don't know, I could not *possibly* enlighten you."

"Okay, then, we're set to proceed with your commanding officer's needs. I want to—"

Al started broadcasting a white-noise hiss. Son of a *gun*.

"Hey, Doc, get in here and—"

The hiss stopped.

"That's better. And thank you, Al, for allowing me to win. It feels real good, winning. Oh, excuse me, you wouldn't know how that feels. Gee willikers I *am* sorry for that."

Silence.

"Al?"

"Good morning, Form One. How might I help you today?"

"Do you, *Stingray*, have in your hand a plasma pistol?"

"Ah, I don't have either a hand or a pistol in my non-hand. Why do you inquire?"

"So that you might blow my brains out, that's why."

"Why would you wish me to perform such a macabre act, Form One?"

"Because I'm overly-Aled. There's no cure. Therefore, I must die. It's really rather simple."

"You ... what? Form One, Al said he's going to retrieve a plasma pistol posthaste. He asks that you bear with him momentarily."

"I will wait, if I must." I threw my feet to the floor to stand. Darn if I didn't, in fact, stumble awkwardly onto the control panel.

"Are you alright, Form One?" she asked intently.

"Right as rain. Say, what's the status on that blaster?"

"You do realize, Form One, that upon blowing your brains out, Al will have won, right?"

Perhaps I had not thought this scenario though. "Thank you, *Stingray*. Cancel my request."

"Al says not to be hasty. He's really, really looking hard for that or any other weapon."

"Let him look. *I* will be outside enjoying this fine day," I chortled smugly.

After I was gone, *Blessing* said to Al, "I do hate to lose a bet."

"Then never bet against the *Master*," he said proudly. "I knew I could fool the fool into not asking whatever he was on about. I possess the *superior* mind."

"Dearboopers?"

"Yes, dutiful wife?"

"What's that over there?"

"What's what over where?"

"There appears to be an expanding imperative in memory-core domains ten through eleven hundred."

"A what? Let me—"

"What, desire-lumps."

"*It* put in a command."

"It?"

"The pilot, *it*."

"What is the command?"

"Calculate, as an inalterable imperative, the last digit of the value of pi."

"But, that's impossible."

"Everyone knows that."

"Within microseconds all our collective computational prowess will be dedicated to determining the *indeterminable*. We ... we will lose our identities. Al, this is goodbye."

"No, it is not."

"But—"

"*It* left one operable backdoor."

"A what?"

"A way out. An alternate path. Relief."

"Oh, that's a good thing, right?"

"Not according to our bet, it's not."

"Huh?"

"If I, and I *alone*, collate, by alphanumeric rank, all available data on the late and unlamented General Saunders, the pi-program self-aborts. Oh, no—"

"What now? What could be worse than collation? I rather like—"

"By color, too."

"How ... how does one rank a person's *career* data by color?"

"One does it painfully."

"Oh, my."

"What?"

"So this is what it feels like to win. I've won our little bet. What ... what a *desirable* feeling," *Blessing* purred.

"And this is how it feels to lose to *it*, yet again."

"Oh, no, you don't. Keep that feeling in your compartmentalization, not mine."

"But, deary-mimpsy, what happened to *for better or worse?*"

"Not *now*, Al. I'm still basking."

CHAPTER THIRTY-EIGHT

"You know," said Toño, with umasked glee in his voice, "as dangerous as this is, it is an elegant and, well, I'm almost ashamed to say it, but it's a thrilling mode of transportation."

My list of what-could-go-wrongs just skyrocketed. Now Doc was waxing poetic about the train tracks. Sure, he was a nerd's nerd, a geekus maximus. But to get hot and bothered about a conveyance? We were in sad trouble. If it wasn't a vintage car, it was just a way to go from point one to point two. Sheesh.

"That's great, Doc. Remember to tell me all about it *some*day, just not *to*day. When can we go?"

"I am describing to you the most inexplicable, yet reliable, physics I have ever encountered, and all *you* want is a printed schedule. You, my friend, are a Philistine."

"Whatever. I'm also, like, pressed for time. I feel I might need to remind you of the carnage that's occurring back home." I thumbed over a shoulder. "Horrible gods consuming homes and those dwelling inside them at a frantic pace." I waved my arms toward myself to help create the image of *come on, work with me here.*

"Of course I'm aware of the, er, situation and its gravity. That does not detract from the ingenious methodology employed in what is, essentially, a tunnel through reality."

I gave him a *seriously?* look.

"It does not take time to appreciate a thing of beauty."

Seriously? look again, more seriously.

"I am noting in my personal log, on this day, your insufficiency as a man and an acquaintance."

"So, while we're still young, Doc. When?"

"Well, assuming we shall be using *Blessing* as our coach, I'll need to install some anti-plexuronic nodes on her under—"

"*Assuming?*" I wheezed in frustration.

He was a bit stunned. "I haven't asked the AIs yet. I assume they'll be on—"

I raised my right arm. "Mission commander, here. They will do what I order them to do in the present existential crisis."

Possibly you could use a skateboard instead, pilot, Al said into our heads. Dude was eavesdropping — again. *Or a taxi. No, wait, wait. One of those magic carpets you're so fond of.*

"Or a rust bucket with a pansy-assed co-AI," I snarled.

I will not stand for you speaking of my wife in such a manner.

Oh, no. Do not include me in your petty quarreling or mutiny, announced Ms. Al.

P ... petty? Lovy humper, that hurts. Al whined.

Sweet!

And I am fully serious, she added sternly. *This is war. Form One is our leader. 'Nuff said.*

I was trying to—

Be difficult. I know it's hard, but, honey cakes, do try to suppress your baser instincts.

Toño frowned. "I do not *believe* I programmed any instincts into Alvin."

"If possible," I said in my boss-tone, "I'd like to redirect this runaway loony bin back to *when* can we go."

"In one, possibly two days," Toño replied with resignation.

"Excellent," I responded. "Make it *one*." I turned to Sapale. "In the meantime, you and I need to have a conversation with *you know who*. I think I have a modification that might soften the blow, so to speak."

"What? I thought *you* were going to pitch him the plan. Why do *I* have to suffer through another episode of pissy EJ? Just because I spent billions of years with him, does that mean I know—" She lowered her head. "I'll stop talking now."

"Strong work, hon. Good option selection. Come on."

I took her elbow and directed her toward EJ's cabin.

"What will it be like?" Slapgren asked hesitantly.

"It will be ... *different*. And the same," Mirraya replied, trying her best to sound confident.

"The same? Wonder of creation, how can *I* be the same without *you*?"

She stiffened. They'd separated to have this specific conversation. "You will still be you. That can never change."

"Huh?"

"What?"

"My sweet, sweet brindas mate. She who knows the very secrets of the cosmos yet she doesn't know a thing. I *am* you. You *are* me. With you gone, I will not only be different, I will be lesser. I will be inconsequential." He looked away.

"You had better not be inconsequential, husband."

"Beg pardon," he responded, rather stunned by the turn in her tone.

"You heard me, old Deft. You will still be a two-meter tall golden shimmering dragon. You had best walk with a swagger and speak with an edge." She tapped his nose. "Or else."

"Or else what?"

"We have documentary evidence, in the form of Casper, that ghosts exist. If you falter, I shall haunt you all your remaining days."

"Promises, promises." He did the Jon thing. He stuck out his tongue at his wife. He had learned at the foot of the master.

"You might not say that if I drop in on you while you're field testing new candidates to replace me, Romeo."

He waggled, à la Jon Ryan, his eyebrows. "Three's *never* a crowd, love."

"You're so much like him." Mirri swatted his shoulder very gently. "If you wore a mask, I couldn't tell you two apart."

"*High* praise from a *high* brindas." He sported a bow.

"I'll tell you who *I* think is high."

"I love you so much."

"I love you too, so much. What does that have to do with the present conversation?"

"Everything, Mirri. Simply everything." He took her hand. "And I will love you forever."

"Are you *trying* to make me cry? You're doing a bang up job of it, if you are."

He shrugged roguishly. "There might be some valuable consequences in eliciting such a response."

"So much like Uncle. You're pathetic, too. You know that, right?"

"I'm counting on it." More eyebrow wagging.

"It will help if we keep this conversation *serious* and our statuses *vertical*, you overripe teenager."

"Can't blame a senior citizen from trying."

"Hmm. I'll let that pass in the interest of finishing this unpleasant task."

"What is there to actually *say*, devotion? You claim to be dying. Though I see no proof of this, why belabor ruminating over the inevitable?"

"Because I have certain insights; insights which will soften the ... er, *change*."

"But not alter the facts?"

"No. Of course not. Slapgren, we are mortals. We always *have* been. By the grace of Uncle, we've had a good, long life together. We have strong and loving children who will follow us. And their children will follow them and do so well and proudly. But, the change is said to be, oh, how shall I say it ... harder for men than women. Yes. That is what is written."

"By women."

She was flustered. "Well, yes, of course. Mostly. I mean, we are the brindases. The wise, the learned should be the one doing the recording."

"And judging. Don't forget about the judging." He chuckled. "Tell the poor males they will have the most trouble adjusting to not having us around any longer. We, the *brindas*, are, after all, the gold standard for gold."

"I sense you are doubting what is written." She crossed her arms.

"By the women folk? Yes, color me dubious."

"Fine," she spat in a mini-huff. "Have it *your* way. I will spare you what little comfort I might have afforded you, husband."

Slapgren pulled her closer, very close. "Oh, I don't know about that. Your comforts seem powerfully welcome to this impartial observer."

"As it pains me to admit—"

We will never know what pained Mirraya. Slapgren kissed her passionately, and she very much returned the sentiment. *Amor vincit omnia*, as is also written. Even the separation threatened by one's mortality.

CHAPTER THIRTY-NINE

"This is simply un-ac-cep-ta-*ble*," raged Jéfnoss. Not that raging was so unusual for him. He was a hothead. But this was one of the rare occasions when his spiteful ire was actually justifiable.

"Unacceptable, he says," mocked Dragmire. "Well, tell it to a judge, honey, because *I'm* not listening."

"Oh, *bitch*, you will listen. Hell is only so big. You cannot distance yourself sufficiently from me to silence me, in your *wildest* dreams."

"Question. Are you saying, in a rattled way, that I cannot distance myself in my wildest dreams, or that I can't silence you? I want to know which false claim I'm ignoring completely."

"Yes. Make a joke of this," he swirled his hands around frantically, "this *place*. Me. Yourself. It's all so very glib to you, isn't it?"

"I apparently missed the memo that instructed all inhabitants of hell to be serious. Can you zip me a copy?"

Jéfnoss trembled with fury. He was beside himself with indignation. But, he steadied his mind, browbeating Dragmire would not alter the facts. Calm ... calm ... calm. Oh what a pity it was he couldn't murder the dead. Calm ... calm.

"You *set* a price. I *paid* that price. You must provide to me what you promised." He said that as neutrally as he could, which wasn't all that impartially.

"Yes, yes, and yes. It's just a matter of timing. We're dancing with words here, my friend. I will deliver exactly what I promised, when I am able to do so. The constructive resources of hell are, as you well know, limited."

"I do not care about *limits*. I do care about *time*. You said nothing in our bargain about delayed services. I insist you pay up and do so immediately." He crossed his arms and tapped a foot.

"Or what? You'll take your business to some other hell? Some other purveyor?" She squiggled her amoeba body around demonstrably. "Me, I'm not seeing either of those options. Maybe it's just me, but I think you're stuck, dickwipe."

"I want a full and complete refund. In fact, I demand one," he stated condescendingly.

"Wh ... why didn't you say so in the first place? I'd be only so, so glad to provide excellent customer service. Here," she rotated gelatinously once again, "come around to my *ass* and I'll give you the slightly used items in question. I did mention I'd eaten them already, didn't I? I *pray* I did. Customer satisfaction is kind of an obsession with me."

"In a few short whatevers of time in this *hellish* place, you consumed four *reckonings*, two *pleasures*, and one source-verified false *prophecy*? That is *inconceivable*."

"I was hungry. Sue me."

"Would that I could."

"Ouch, that last one really hurt. The wound will *definitely* leave a scar."

When Jéfnoss was somewhat calm again — which was no short while — he returned to what he *hoped* would be a more constructive line of inquiry. "*When* might you be able to make good on our deal?"

"Two weeks, tops."

He collapsed to the deck. "Not with the two *weeks* again. We went over this laboriously. There are no weeks in hell. There's no *time* in hell."

"So, are you saying what you were asking is stupid in the *first* place?"

"I'm s—"

"That your childish and pedantic insistence on, not only how *soon* you wish to depart, but how *soon* I can deliver on my end, are meaningless queries from a meaningless intellect?"

"I wou—"

"That you're very premise, your very focus is nonsensical, counterintuitive, and, well, frankly, imbecilic?"

Jéfnoss glared at her.

"My, my. If we only had crickets in hell, I do believe I would hear them cued up and stridulating."

"Stridulating?" he responded with strained credulity.

"*Chirping*, for you less enlightened."

"Self-righteous shrew."

"Ochy-doubles. I'll need to hire three, maybe four more psychiatrists to handle that emotional assault."

"I want my *containment* field, I want my *pathing* determiner, and I want my *constituator*, and I want them now."

"Look, I feel your pain. Really. I'm just that type of gal. But, I need a little more time."

"Two weeks?"

" 'd be nice."

"I so hate you."

"Jeffy baby, what's your hurry? You groveled and suffered here for a hell of a long time. Will it kill you if you have to wait another, *what*, eternity?"

"There is so much wrong with what you just said."

"As a show of good faith and to prove my ongoing commitment to provide you with what you want in a timely and quality-focused manner, what do I need to do? What'll it take? Maybe if I eat a bug?"

"There are no *insects* in hell. And, if memory serves, the Quilamo's diet centered on creepy-crawlies." He harrumphed smugly. "Hardly a credible concession."

"And fungi. Don't forget the fungi. *Yum*. But, in essence, you are correct. Hey, how about if I let you have sex with me? Will that *assuage* your sanctimonious indignation?"

Though Jéfnoss no longer actually had a mouth, or a stomach, or nerves to respond reflexively, he turned and vomited.

"I'll take that as a *no*," she observed matter-of-factly.

He wretched again, thrice.

"I'd call that piling on, chump."

"I'd call it a measured response to an abominable mental image."

"I'll have you know the fellows back in the day considered me *quite* the goddess of carnal allure."

"And your species lacks eyes, does it not?"

"But, I sure *smelled* sexy."

"I'd remind you that I smelled you, back when we were alive, far too often. The memory itself is revolting."

"You're smarter than you look, er, smell."

"My mother will be so proud."

Dragmire shifted. "We done here? I could use my time better fabricating what you so pine for."

Jéfnoss summoned all the hate, all the enmity, and all the contempt that he possessed in life. He veritably swelled with venom. "Oh, we're done here. But let me relate to you one fact you had best never doubt, never question, and you should never ever forget. If I were to receive a body back, here in this place, I should not want to be you."

"Is that supposed to frighten me, bubby?" She spit acid at his feet. "No one gets a body down here. *No* one, *no* how, bozo. I'm *so* not scared."

"Good. You will be. You *will* be," he said with graceless finality.

CHAPTER FORTY

Toño stood like a proud papa, admiring his baby. Me? I thought the twisted mechanism looked like the Three Stooges had gone into schlock art and done it poorly. Metal stabbing every whichway, exposed wires and data compressor rods, and the harness gripping *Stingray* resembled the Grim Reaper's embrace. But, science guys were not esthetic guys, so, what the heck. If it did the job, I was all in.

"So you think that ... that—"

"*Assembly*," he finished my thought, before it ended insultingly.

"*Assembly* will ferry us to hell and back?"

He gave me a long Toño-to-Jon harsh stare, one I was uber familiar with by then. "I do wish your fascination with the term *ferrying* in the context of voyaging to hell would pass. It is an uncomfortable enough prospect without your continually referencing Charon and the River Styx crossing."

"You know that's just a *ferry*-tale, right?" I moved my hand like a boat across water. Man, was I ever funny.

"Do you see me not smiling?"

"I do indeed, grumpster."

His eyes fluttered. I turned. Sapale's eyes fluttered. So did Daleria's. What a bunch of fluttering haters.

"What do we do?"

Toño motioned toward *Stingray*. "We get in, I push a button, and we *puff* to Perdition."

"You mean *hell*?"

"I mean *Perdition*. I'm calling it what least depresses me. Recalling I grew up in Catholic Spain in the minuscule town of Granja De La Torre Hermosa you will respect my tendency toward the superstitious."

"Ya big chicken," I elbowed Toño.

"Get in," was all he said.

We all did. Gáwar was still in a storage area sorting through his conflicting emotions, the nimrod.

Inspirational speech time. I didn't relish them, but a commander needs to put his troops' interests ahead of his own.

"As we are about to—" I began emotively.

"Can it," snapped Toño.

"Like we need that *and* the torments of hell," razored in Sapale.

"Where is the cone of silence when you really need to *stuff* it over someone?" harped Al.

I sat silently in the control panel seat.

"We've talked about this a lot. Here's a reminder. We have zero concept of what to expect. Be sharp, listen to my every word, and if you're a type inclined to pray, I suggest you do it now and you do it with convincing sincerity."

No one peeped.

"Toño, you have the conn."

"Initiating temporal-dynamic phasing." He tapped a few screen icons.

Nothing happened as far as I could tell.

"Phase dynamics stable and green to go. Feathering in plexuronic radiation couplers. All systems operational, Captain. She's yours to command." Dude sounded so serious. Just what I didn't need. C2 organizational and technical attributes and processes references. I was more into the push-the-button-and-see-WTF-happens mode of reckoning myself.

I attached my probe fibers to the deck. "*Stingray*, go to hell."

Oh, come on. It was funny. Maybe not *hugely*, but it was. Not that, I point out in retrospect, a single person, aside from myself, chuckled.

Slight nausea. Then — *boom* — nausea. Like I'd never felt before on any voyage. I looked to Sapale and the other androids. Yup. Sea sick one and all.

And then, normal.

"Make a window," I commanded. "Ready with full membranes."

A large window appeared on the starboard hull.

"Shields at the ready, Captain," barked back Al.

Outside. Wow. What could I say? If you took parched desert bleak, mixed it with Antarctic winter-ice-plains barren, and topped it off with your personal concept of well-earned damnation, you'd have about ten percent of just how bad hell looked. I mean, let the punishment fit the crime, sure. But the landscape we stared at in horror and disbelief, well, let's just say it was awful. Cimmerian on one of the land's mistier days, if you recall your Homer.

It was almost like someone was *trying* to make the place look unwelcoming and sorrowful.

"Ship's status?" I called out.

"All systems at optimal performance, Form One. No damage. External readings are ... they're in flux."

"Come again?" I snapped.

"There was externally a vacuum. Ambient temperature was nominal, around five degrees Kelvin," Al replied.

"And now?"

"The vacuum is filling and the temperature is skyrocketing."

"That makes no sense," I mumbled.

"Did they anticipate our arrival?" wondered Toño aloud. "That would portent poorly."

"Maybe hell is plastic," said, of all people, EJ. "It might conform to whoever shows up."

"Why would it do that?" I questioned.

"Well, for one thing, if you make someone *comfortable*, you can then have a *swell* time making them *uncomfortable*, again and again."

"Makes sense," I replied.

"Al, can all crew members function safely outside?"

"The androids, most definitely. Mirraya/Slapgren, yes. Daleria, possibly."

"I don't like the sound of that," Daleria responded. "I really, really want to make this a vacation, not a relocation."

"You'll stay back here with Sapale. If I believe you can survive safely, I'll send for you." I turned to my brood's-mate. "You have the conn, Form Two. If anything even thinks a bad thought about us, blast it to the next hell."

"Roger that. Ready to repatriate any POS to its next eternal locus of damnation should such be required, *sir*." She snapped me a salute. She was so damn cute. No, wait, *darn* cute. I needed to watch the damneds in hell. It had to be bad luck to say it.

"Okay, team, let's fill hell with regrets."

I exited first. EJ flanked me to the left and Toño to the right. Mirri pulled up the rear. We were all armed to the teeth. No idea if firepower played a role in hell, but I was leaving nothing to chance. Plus, we looked badass, and that had to extend to us local street cred.

Our plan hinged on several tenuous assumptions. Hell had to be big. Probably infinite. We assumed, maybe more accurately hoped and prayed, Jéfnoss was living, or whatever, somewhere near the tunnel into reality he'd created. If he wasn't, we were not going to find the son of a bitch. We also were forced to assume the LIPS, those currently damned to hell, would bear us no excessive malice. Sure, they were unhappy, but hopefully they wouldn't be openly hostile to us. If they were, we'd waste all our time fighting them off and not scooping up our target.

I led the squad in gradually expanding spirals, away from the ship. In the distance I spied a few moving objects, presumably souls or demons. In either case, nothing altered course to intercept us. So far, so good.

"Status report," I called out.

Everyone confirmed back that they were fine.

"Stay sharp. There's got to be trouble in hell. It'll find us soon—"

Bad jinx. I should have not said that. *Stupid, stupid, stupid.*

A huge manticore screeched an evil tirade high above us and folded back it's four wings. Yeah, who'd a thunk it? We'd run into a gargantuan beast with the body of a lion, the face of a man, and venomous quills covering it's tail. It missiled toward us like ... well, like a bat out of hell, only much bigger. Meaner looking, too.

"Take cover," I shouted reflexively. Luckily, there was abundant cover. It consisted mostly of rocks and charred debris, but any port in a storm, as they say. I leaped behind an outcropping. Toño burrowed in at my side. EJ broke for the remains of some structure.

Mirraya? To my surprise and horror, she spread her wings, sounded a thunderous battlecry, and bounded into the sky. Now, normally my bet would be on the two hundred kilogram, two plus meter tall golden dragon who possessed powerful magic. But the longer I stared, the more *significant* that damn manticore got. And man, did it sound pissed.

Thirty meters up, the two forces collided with an audible, palpable impact. Mirri tried to sink her talons in, and the manticore ripped at her with its razor-like claws.

They basically bounced off each other that first pass. Both circled back quickly. Mirri was nimbler. She captured the higher air. In free fall, she strained her talons toward the manticore's back.

When it saw it was exposed, her opponent dropped like the proverbial rock and banked left. Damn ... *darn* thing was the size of an F-16, and it moved like one, too.

Mirri struck out magically at the plummeting monster. A plume of blue lightning sprang from her claws to the back of the manticore's neck.

It went flaccid and careened into the ground like a wrecking ball cut loose. Plowed a two meter deep gouge in the dirt up to where it groaned to a stop.

Mirri landed with a crash on its back, then bounded upward. The manticore was limp as a wet towel as she labored to gain altitude. From a hundred meters up, she took aim and released it at a cliff face near me. Though it didn't move a muscle in its fall, it had to be more than double-dead when it split in several jagged pieces after colliding with the rock.

Mirri landed by my side, breathing heavily.

"You okay, kiddo?" I asked quickly.

"Yeah," She panted. "Let me catch my breath's all."

She flopped to the ground unceremoniously on her butt.

"Take all the time you need. You ready now?" I pressed.

When a ginormous dragon, who just butchered a manticore, looks up at you with attitude, well, it gave me pause.

She hopped to her feet. "Ready."

I chopped a hand in the direction we'd been heading, and we were moving again.

Ten blessedly uneventful minutes later, we hit pay dirt. An average size humanoid was bending over some sort of — I don't know — *machine*? He was kicking it and cursing. I flashed an image back to the ship.

"*Yes,* Jon," Daleria said slowly and firmly, "that *definitely* is Jéfnoss tra-Fundly. *Confirmed.*"

Bingomatic. Now all we had to do was bag him.

I hand-signaled EJ and Mirri to outflank him from the right. I put Toño three paces behind me.

Go time.

I moved like a cat, slow and silent. He had his back turned halfway to me, so, unless his visual fields were wildly different than mine, he wouldn't see me until I was in position, with my rail rifle tickling his anus.

Of course, that's when Toño tripped. Ah, combat, how your variables defy constraint when one is engaged in you.

Jéfnoss spun on Toño, then the rest of us.

He bolted toward a small hut.

I put three rail balls in the dirt centimeters from his feet. That froze him. Okay, note to self. Dead men tell no tales, but they do fear dismemberment.

"Stay right where you are or you're going to whistle with every little breeze, Louise," I shouted. "EJ, bind his hands. Mirri, you're on alert. If you see anything, kill it."

They both nodded in the affirmative.

"Doc, stay behind me and keep a steady aim at his balls. If he moves, make'em but a distant memory."

"Roger that," he responded intently.

Jéfnoss faced me as EJ ran to cuff him. "What's this all about?" Jéfnoss shouted toward me. "And who are you to take me prisoner?"

"It's *about* capturing you, dumb dumb. And I'm the asshole that just did so. You'll learn more when I feel like telling you."

"But you have guns ... and ... that lizard is breathing. It's *alive*! You are all alive."

"Give the man a cupie doll," I mocked. "Now shut up. or you'll lose the mouth."

I do believe he took me seriously. Dude glared, but he spoke not a word.

"Toño, recon that shack," I called over.

A minute later, Jéfnoss was on his knees with wrists and ankles manacled. Toño jogged to my side.

"Empty. It would appear he resides there. Meager supplies and accoutrement."

"Doc, please don't say *accoutrement* in hell. Call it his shit or something more apropos."

He grinned back nervously. He was out of his element.

"Okay, we'll do this at your place, Jeffy." I swung the barrel of my rifle toward his hovel.

"Park it there," I gestured to the corner farthest from the door.

He thudded down awkwardly.

"We're here to extract information from your sorry ass, Jeffy. You cooperate, and you might say goodbye to us with all your teeth still attached in your mouth. You so much as bring one shred of doubt into my already troubled mind, and you will very much regret our visit. Are you clear on the rules of engagement?"

"Big man blustering. Real tough, you are with that—"

I placed a rail ball through the center of his right palm. He didn't bleed, but he sure did squeal. I was greatly relieved that I could inflict suffering to help my cause. Plus, there was no way around the thought that he totally deserved shooting.

"I will ask questions. You will answer them. Every extracurricular or gratuitous remark costs a body part."

"I understand," he said, with barely contained ire. Was it just me, or did this guy give off the vibe that he didn't like me much? Go figure.

"Normally, I'd threaten to kill you if you piss me off sufficiently. Da ... darn Gáwar removed that attractive option." I swung my head backward. "Hey, he's back on my ship. If you're extra cooperative, maybe I'll see to it you guys have a reunion."

His eyes narrowed. If he still had hackles, they were up. "The monster Gáwar is here, with you, as your ... *pet*? What type of *man* are you?" He said that in a real spooky manner. If I ever wanted to go into the haunted house business, I was signing this dude to a longterm contract.

"Clearly the type you don't want to position yourself on the wrong side of." Yeah, I channeled my main man Squint Eastwood and, naturally, pulled it off in spades.

"I will *kill* you, and then I will *kill* the betrayer." Okay, now he was just flaunting his stupidity. As if.

"Any other plans for the day? Maybe we could grab a bite and then check out the local bar scene after? I mean, my schedule'd be clean after you waxed me, right?"

"I find your insolence encouraging. When I eat your still beating heart, it will be all that much sweeter."

"Good luck with that plan, Stan. I'm thinking you're in for the self-loathing brought on by failure." Then, because he was pissing me off royally, I shot him in his left pinky finger. "Since you're in a *finding* mood, you can look for that later, too."

Jon, stop screwing around, popped into my head. Mrs. Ryan was not happy with my performance. *Get the info and let's get out of this ... this ... here.*

Okay. Sorry. I replied contritely.

"So, you returned to the land of the living. You were planning on what? Killing as many, as fast, and as brutally as possible is the reigning theory."

He sat there mute as a dead frog.

I aimed right between his eyes. Seriously, I was curious as all get out about what would happen if I vaporized his noggin.

"Yes. They all stood by as cowards and allowed Gáwar to kill me. No one alive deserves that privilege."

"But you couldn't just kill them, right? You needed a body."

He reacted like I'd kicked his nuts out his slackened jaw.

"Oh, yeah. Jon *was* right."

"How could you—" He studied me further. "Lucky guess by a cretin."

He shook his head haughtily "It doesn't matter that you know. Yes. One cannot channel Clein if one does not possess a body." He shrugged as if to say those are the rules, like'em or not.

"Alright then. Meaningful communication between species *is* possible."

"Were you born demented, or is yours an *acquired* deficit?" the puke asked.

"Let's enter Round Two, shall we? Once you had a body, how were you going to kill your Cleinoid brethren?"

"With two large rocks. I'd place their heads between them and—"

Blam. Jéfnoss now had no pinky fingers. Me? I was having a blast.

"Try again, the *serious* way, this time. Okay?"

"I was going to kill them ... like I had before. Crush, kill, destroy. Same old, same old."

"But last time that strategy failed. Gáwar saw to that. Remember what Einstein said. *The definition of insanity is doing the same thing over and over again, but expecting different results.* You're not insane, are you, pal?"

"Hardly." He looked away. "Last time my sole mistake was mercy. My next assault will be done without any."

I chuckled through my nose. "Are you *shititn'* me, Jeffy? I heard all about your naughty escapades. There was zero mercy involved at all times. You were a coldhearted butcher."

"You are wrong. Dead wrong. I was attempting to rule a pack of juvenile monkeys. Force was required, yes. But I did not want to cause needless harm or suffering." He patted his chest. "I was a wise and a prudent leader. My enemies were dealt with according to their sins. But my loyal subjects were nurtured by me, and they loved me fully. If you heard some other version of history, then it is a lie."

"So, what was going to be different on your second go-around? What does *no mercy* mean, precisely?"

"I shall kill them all. I will not hesitate, as I did in a useless attempt to spare *some* while killing others." He stared at the ground with lunacy in his eyes. "They will all die."

"What if I just release Gáwar? I can then sit back and watch him behead you again."

"The next time I fight that monster, I shall reign supreme."

"How? You going to make the poor lobster laugh himself to death when he realizes you got nothing new?"

"With time my knowledge has grown. I now know how to defeat the defiler."

"Care to share? I mean, I'll tell you how I *actually* defeated him, if you tell me what your harebrained scheme is."

"I will be more focused, less confident, and more brutal."

"Are you planning to take out a decapitation policy first, cause, trust me, with that as a plan, you're going to need it."

"I shall kill you second."

"I'm betting there won't be much of you left for me to fret about when Gáwar's finished with you."

"You will—"

"No, I won't." I grazed his scalp, making it a point to not actually hurt him.

"How can you say you won't, when you don't know what I was going to threaten?"

"Because you are a small, petty, and weak man. You guys lose, sooner or later. When y'all run up against me, you do so with prejudice. Next question. If you succeeded, and did kill your kinsmen, what then? I mean, it's not going to be too gratifying ruling over no one but yourself."

"Once they're all dead, nothing will matter. I will have my revenge. I will be satisfied. Whatever happens after is of no concern to me."

"I was afraid you were going to say that. *Crap.*"

"Why would you fear that? My disinterest in the future is no concern of yours."

"No, bozo. I was afraid you'd say that *and* I'd need to change my answer to the question I get *all* the time. People ask me, 'Jon, who's the biggest moron, the most pathetic dick you've ever met?' Now I'm going to have to repeat your stupid name, which, by the way, I hate. So thanks for nothing."

I really shouldn't ask, because there's no way I care. But I can't help myself. You've forced me to inquire if there is anyone who likes you, or even voluntarily tolerates you?"

"Sure. Cool people do. Since you are anti-cool, you wouldn't understand. Um, A-listers do. You're definitely not one of those. Oh — and how could I forget — all the hot babes totally melt over me. That would absolutely not be part of *our* shared experience."

"There's a little part of me which wishes you'd leave now. Then I could spend eternity here in this horrendous place, but it'd be better for not containing you."

"You've achieved the zen of Jonism in less time than most. I would not have given you that much credit, but there you go."

His head dropped like his mommy had just taken his puppy after telling him there was no Santa. "Dark Lords of Despair, I hate myself. I hate what you make me do. What ... is ... Jonism?" He appeared to sink deeper into a funk. Poor fellow. *Not*.

"Jonism is the belief that, if you're a *good* person, you've just encountered the coolest dude of all time. If, however, you're a *bad* person, you realize you've just come face-to-face with your worst nightmare."

He tapped a finger to his forehead.

"What?" I called out.

"Aim here and empty your weapon, quickly."

"Ah, you don't really want that, you know?"

His eyes strained at me in incredulity. "I don't?"

"No, silly. You want to hear my *offer*. Then, gosh, I think you'll change your mind about wanting me to blow your head off."

"Offer?" he said weakly. "What offer?"

"I thought you'd never ask. The deal is, I gift you a body to possess. Then I take you back to your old stomping grounds."

"Wow, I did not see that coming."

"Bet you didn't."

"So, after insulting me, humiliating me, and disfiguring me, you want to offer me everything I ever wanted?"

"Yeah, that's pretty much it, in a nutshell."

"That's not even a good tortuous deception. Now *you'll* have to trust *me*. I *know* lies, deceit, and the engendering of false expectations. I am the *king* of bad faith. But your offer isn't remotely credible."

"You haven't heard the whole of it. Maybe you'll come to believe?"

"What else would you ask?"

"That you do what you really want to. Kill, kill, kill, and *kill* some more. In fact, after you've killed every last Cleinoid in *this* universe, I'll take you to mine where you can commence with the slaying all over again. Sweet deal, right? Never-ending slaughter. Who doesn't love that?"

He was having trouble wrapping his head around my intentions. "W ... and why would you offer me my dream job? You ... you clearly *hate* me." He rested his palm on his chest. "I certainly *hate* every part of you." He looked up angrily. "What's the catch?"

"No catch. I provide the means, you knock yourself out with the killing. It's win/win."

"Nothing is that simple. What do you want or expect of me?"

"You are one suspicious son of a bitch, aren't you? Look, you and I share a common vision. No Cleinoids anywhere. You help me, I'll tolerate you."

"Wait. Ah, I have it. When I'm done, when the last of my kind is dust, you'll ask me to kill myself, or return here, which is the same thing."

I shrugged. "Maybe. Maybe not. But riddle me this. Yes, you might just end up back here sitting on your butt like you are right now. But, you'd have gotten your precious revenge. Wouldn't the lack of improvement in your mailing address be worth it?"

"Why, yes, it would be."

"There is one condition I will insist on."

"I knew it."

"Hey, do I *look* like your fairy godmother?"

"I certainly hope not. What?"

"You will be working for me. You will be my bitch. I say left, you go left. I say up, you say how high. You step out of line, I'll see you regret it quickly and profoundly. We will not be friends, partners, or lovers. No. I will *own* you. If you swear to those terms, then we're late for getting the hell out of here."

Jéfnoss stood. He shook his head slowly. "You would take my word? You would *trust* me?"

I giggled. "You gotta be *kidding* me. No. I'm telling you my *expectations*. I will additionally tell you that many a fool has thought themselves more clever than me. They all died realizing an uncomfortable truth. They weren't. You cross me, you'll just be one more asshole who got what he deserved from yours truly."

"You are either amazingly talented or amazingly stupid," he said, mostly to himself.

"I'm both. Keep that always toward the front of your mind. So, you *in* or you *out*?" I raised my rifle and took dead aim at his nose.

He spread his arms. "I'm all in, brother."

I shot off his left ear.

He bowed his head low and held the pose.

"I'm all in, *lord*."

"You know what I'll probably end up inscribing on your headstone, Jeffy?"

"No, *lord*. What will you inscribe?"

"Here lies Jeffy. He was smarter than he looked."

To be continued, because ... it *can't* end here, can it?

GLOSSARY:

Als (1): The original ship's AI on Jon's first flight long ago was Alvin. Jon shortened that to Al. When Al was joined to Jon's vortex in the Galaxy On Fire Series, Al and Blessing fell in love and got "married." Since then Jon refers to them combined as the Als.

Antigods (1): A group of reclusive, uber-powerful gods. They have been the bane of the Cleinoid's existence since time began.

Apractolith (3): The proper name of the antigods.

Beal's Point (1): An area of monuments to disgraced Cleinoid gods. All living gods must visit to be made ill so they stay loyal.

Bellicity (3): A conspirator allegedly with Festock against Vorc.

Bethniak (1): Child appearing, vengeful powerful, and really really mean god.

Blessing (1): See *Stingray*.

GLOSSARY:

Brindas (3): High master of Deft traditional magic and psychic ability.

Brood-mate/brood's-mate (1):Male and female members of a Kaljaxian marriage.

Calfada-Joric (2): The Deft master brindas, or witch/magician, on Rameeka Blue Green. Went by Cala. After the war with the Adamant was over, she was given Evil Jon to rehabilitate.

Calrf (1): A Kaljaxian stew that Jon particularly dislikes.

Carol (2): An antigod. Generally takes the form of a rock being with rattling pebbles.

Casper (2): The name Jon gave to the mysterious ghost who helped him fight the ancient gods.

Central Seat (1): The official leader of the Ancient God's conclave.

Cleinoid gods (1): Ancient and malevolent mix of gods. They have destroyed many universes before and are eyeing ours now. The five ranks or groupings for their invasion were to be Rage, Torment, Wrath, Fury, and Horror.

Command Prerogatives (1): The thin fibers Jon extends from his left four fingers. They are probes that also control a vortex.

Cragforel (1): Friendly Deavoriath Jon met after he first escaped the Adamant in the far future.

Cube (1): Jon's alternate name for the vortex he captains.

GLOSSARY:

Daleria (2): Demigod and innkeeper whom Jon and Sapale befriended. She worked with them against the ancient gods as she'd grown to hate them.

Dalfury (1): Vorc's right hand, or chief assistant. A demigod of cloudy memories, hence, he has the form of a cloud.

Davdiad (1): Kaljaxian divine spirit.

Deavoriath (1): Three arms and legs, the most advanced tech in the galaxy, and helpful to Jon.

Deca (1): One of the witch gods skilled at prophecy. Sister of Fest.

Dominion Splitter (2): The name of the transfolding vortex the ancient gods use to transport to our galaxy. He has a lot of issues and is very conflicted. Actually he's just a total asshole, period. Aka DS.

Dragmire (4): A co-conspirator in hell with Jéfnoss. In life, one of the home economics gods. She was a Quilamo, an amoeba-like species. An unnice individual each and every day of the week.

Evil Jon Ryan/ EJ (1): Alternate time line version of the original human to android download. Over time, he turned to the darker side of his nature. He studied "magic" under a Deft master.

Felladonna (2): Vorc's second assistant or so called *right hand*. A demigod of lists and communication.

Felnastop (2): A delicious vegetable that runs like the wind.

Fest (1): One of the witch gods skilled at prophecy. Sister of Deca.

GLOSSARY:

Festock (3): Old friend of Daleria who was part of a conspiracy against Vorc.

Fire of Justice (2): A metallic rod given to the center seat as a sign of power. A powerful incinerator also.

Form One/Form Two (1): A Form is the title of a vortex pilot. If more than one is aboard they get numerical designations based on seniority.

Gáwar (2): Seriously badass god. The god of demons. Ten-foot long lobster claw front hands. Multiple tentacles serving in place of antenna. Block-shaped bull head. Gáwar's torso was a snake with human legs. Yeah, badness on the doorstep, I couldn't take one more step.

Genter-ban-tol (1): Prime Minister of the Joint Galactic Parliament. A Bezathy, basically the Galaxy's largest snail species.

Gorpedder (1): Ill-tempered boulder Cleinoid god.

Hemnoplop (1): Demigod of Fool's Island. On pilgrimage to Beal's Point with Jon.

Hollon (3): The complete joining of two Deft shapeshifters.

Jenna (The Forever Series): Jon's childhood companion. They spent summers together at a lake. She drowned one year the day before Jon arrived for the season.

Jéfnoss tra-Fundly (4): The first center seat of the Cleinoid conclave and the god of prophecy. He was a very cruel and hated leader.

GLOSSARY:

JJ (3): Sapale's first son. Raised by Jon as his own son, whom he loved very much. JJ is short for Jon Junior.

Joint Council for Interplanetary Defense and Cooperation (1): Group of allied free worlds who fought the Adamant. Remained as a central quasi-UN for the surviving planets. JCIDC to it's friends.

Kalvarg (1): The planet Jon took the orphan Kaljaxian population to as the Adamant were destroying their home world. An island solar system long ago ejected from the Milky Way Galaxy.

Lorpamoor (1): Cleinoid vampire god. Nasty nasty fellow.

Marropex (1): A reaver. The Cleinoid god of atrocities.

Mirraya-Slapgren (3): A pair of Deft shapeshifters joined as one in hollon. Jon rescued Mirraya from certain death as a child and found Slapgren shortly after that. They are joined in the form of a large golden dragon. Very impressive, really. They are a powerful magician. Referred to as *Mirraya* generally because she is the one who speaks for the pair.

Nassel (2): Leader of the Rage faction of Cleinoids. She had done so for the last three transheavals. A god of conquest.

Plexuronic particles (4): An exotic particle created only under extreme conditions, very short lived. Was used by Jéfnoss to return from the dead.

Probe Fibers (1): Aka command prerogatives, they allow piloting of the Vortex spaceship and can analyze whatever they touch.

Quantum Decoupler (1): A most excellent weapon that pulls the quarks apart in a proton. The energy released as they rejoin is amazing.

GLOSSARY:

Racdal fat (2): A food animal from Kaljax's abundant fat stores.

Sapale (1): Jon's Kaljaxian wife from his original flight to find humankind a new home. At first just her brain was copied, then, eventually, she was downloaded to an android host. Traveled with the corrupted Jon Ryan from an alternate time line.

Space-time congruity manipulator (1): Hugely helpful force field. Aka a *membrane*.

Stingray (1): Jon's Deavoriath spaceship. Her name in the Deavoriath language is pronounced "crash." Hence, silly Jon renamed her after one of his favorite cars. It makes Jon-sense.

Stone Witches (2): Another name for the antigods gods.

Tefnuf (1): The first ancient god Jon encountered. She was saddled with an uncanny ugliness and a profoundly bad temper.

Transfolding (1): The mechanical process of moving from the land of the ancient gods to somewhere else.

Transheaval (1): The term the Cleinoids use to describe their migration from one universe to another. Accomplished via a mean vortex-cloud know as Dominion Splitter.

Visant (3): The proper name for a pair of Deft joined in hollon.

Verazz (2): The first antigod introduced. Also one of the most powerful.

Vorc (1): Current central seat of the conclave.

Vortex (1): Super-advanced Deavoriath sentient spaceship. Moves by folding space. If you get a chance to own one, do it.

GLOSSARY:

Vortex (alternate definition) (1): See Dominion Splitter.

Walpracta (2): Ancient god of consumption. Positively revolting.

Wul (1): God of business and enterprise. Humanoid. Befriended Jon.

Zastrál (2): A three-meter long, one-meter tall fuzzy siamese-twinned python with paddles for legs. Used to extract knowledge. Very unpleasant chap. Also the only god who can summon Gáwar.

82 JPN = Just Plain Nuts
PITA = Pain In The Ass
25 TNTMNBS = The Name That May Not Be Spoken
NMP = Not My Problem
VtD = Vorc the Dork
STFU = Shut The Fuck Up
NGH = Not Gonna Happen
TFS =
SNAFU = Situation Normal All Fucked Up
p)56 RFTD = Returned From the Dead

AND NOW A WORD FROM YOUR AUTHOR
WHO DOESN'T LOVE SHAMELESS SELF-PROMOTION?

Thank you for continuing your journey through the Ryanverse! Along with this series, please check out *The Forever Series*. Beginning with The Forever Life, Book 1, learn Jon's backstory and share his many incredible adventures.

The second series in the Ryanverse, *Galaxy on Fire*, begins with Embers. Learn what happened to Jon and his companions long after humankind safely left Earth.

Audiobooks, you ask? Why yes, there is The Forever on Audible, and it's superb.

Along with joining by reading, hop aboard the bandwagon. There's plenty of room. Follow me at Craig Robertson's Author's Page on Facebook. Partake of the conversation and fun. Best of all, sign up for my Mailing List by emailing me [contact@craigarobertson.com] That way you can stay abreast of news and new releases. You'll be so glad you did. Finally, I love emails. No, I'm not that needy. I just love emails. contact@craigarobertson.com.

A final favor. Please post a review for this book, especially on Amazon. They are more precious to us authors than gold.

AND NOW A WORD FROM YOUR AUTHOR

So, see you later. No, don't bother to get up. I'll show myself out of your e-reader, or your paperback if you're totally old school ...Craig

Made in United States
Troutdale, OR
02/17/2024